Wrecked BY YOU

K

Edited by Bethany Pennypacker, Outthink Editing LLC
Proofreading by Katie Schmahl and Jacqueline Beard

Cover art by *CT Cover Creations*
Photographer: *Xramgrade*
Cover Model: *Roque*

Wrecked BY YOU

Will my broody, tormented billionaire boss wreck me—or save me?

Four weeks ago, I escaped from a monster in the dead of night, our five-year-old daughter asleep in my arms. Desperate and rapidly running out of cash, my luck finally turns when I land a bartending job at a swanky Los Angeles nightclub.

The owner is difficult and moody, and relentless in his crusade for perfection, but it's not hard work that scares me. It's the burgeoning swell of desire that consumes me every time our eyes meet across the crowded dance floor.

But if I'm damaged, he's wrecked. The truth is, we can't run from our pasts. The demons shadowing our steps always catch us in the end.

When mine comes knocking and the truth spills out, will he come to my rescue?
Or is he so broken by his own experiences that I'll have to face my nemesis alone?

A note from Tracie

Dear Reader,

Well, this was a different experience from Consumed By You. I knew before I wrote a single word that Johannes wouldn't give me an easy ride.

Boy was I right.

Usually, it's nice to be right, but not this time. I struggled, not because Johannes was reticent - to my surprise, he was talkative from the beginning - but more because he means so much to me, and I wanted to do justice to his journey.

Ultimately, you will be the judge of whether I achieved my aim. I hope I have. My trusty team who have read this before it goes out into the world absolutely adored this book, and I hope that you do, too.

Ella is the perfect woman for Johannes. She has her own troubles but once these two come together, it's a truly beautiful thing. They are a match made in heaven. Shame that Johannes takes a while to come to terms with that! I'm sure you're not in the least bit surprised. Neither was I.

Once again, especially for ROGUES fans, another of our beloved friends makes an appearance here. I hope you enjoy the cameo by Ryker. It's a lot of fun!

I do hope you enjoy sharing in Johannes and Ella's story. I'd love to hear what you thought once you've finished reading. Why not join my Facebook reader group Tracie's Racy Aces, and take part in the discussion over there.

In the meantime, turn the page and dive in to the third installment of the Kingcaid Billionaires. Enjoy every page.

Happy reading.

Love,
Tracie

Chapter 1

Johannes

Trust is a commodity I can no longer afford.

My exquisite woman, unashamedly braless, given the jaunty bounce of her breasts, twirled in the street, her skirts fanning out from her thighs as rain pelted the asphalt and soaked her from head to foot. She didn't care.

Nor did I.

Spellbound, I took shelter underneath the awning of a bakery long since closed for the night and watched as her nipples poked through her thin silk shirt.

"Join me," she cried, a joyous grin lifting her cheeks, her glee reflected in the sparkling green of her eyes.

I shook my head.

"Come on, Jo-Jo." She beckoned to me, the tendrils of my soul wrapping around her curling finger. "Don't be a spoilsport."

I smiled at the nickname, despite my distaste for it. Only

Sadie could get away with calling me that. But regardless of her plea, I refused her request for a second time.

"I have to go."

She stopped spinning, her lips downturned, disappointment at my declaration obvious in her expression and the curve to her shoulders.

"Not yet." She darted to where I stood, sheltering from the rain, and twisted her hair to wring out the water. "It's early."

I checked my watch, an exorbitant gift from my father, but one I treasured. He'd given it to me a year earlier, after I'd graduated from Cambridge University in England, his pride in my achievements apparent. I'd always wanted to study abroad, and while getting into such a prestigious school hadn't been easy, my excellent high school grades had secured my place in one of the best educational institutes in the world.

I guess having a billionaire for a father hadn't hurt my chances, either.

There were downsides to such wealth, but I preferred to focus on the positives. Being rich brought its challenges, but it also brought opportunities, ones I enjoyed wringing the hell out of. My family's riches had allowed me to spend more than a year after I'd graduated traveling through Europe and the Far East, finishing right back where I'd started, in England.

I shook my head again. "My flight leaves at nine in the morning, and I can't miss it."

Tomorrow, I'd fly back to America and join the family firm. I hadn't a clue what area of the company Dad expected me to assume responsibility for, but being a part of the Kingcaid organization had been written in my future at birth. Just like it had been for my older brother, Asher, whom Dad had already lined up to take over the hotel business one day, and my younger brother, Penn, who was in his second year at Harvard.

A perfect pout graced Sadie's plump lips, and she nudged me with the toe of her shoe. "All work and no play makes Jo-Jo a very dull boy."

She unfastened the top three buttons of her shirt, revealing pert tits and erect nipples that begged for my mouth.

I groaned. "Sadie, don't make this harder than it is."

She palmed my erection through my jeans. "Seems pretty hard to me."

I groaned again, slamming my lips against hers, stroking her tongue with mine. My hands dropped to her ass, her skirt dripping wet from the torrential downpour. I circled my hips, mashing our groins together.

"Come back to my place," I murmured. "Stay the night."

"Johannes." She sighed and stepped away, fastening her buttons. "You're leaving me, and I'm on the edge here. It's killing me that I have to say goodbye. To stay the night and have to tear myself away in the morning is only going to make it that much more difficult. And besides, you told me you still haven't packed yet."

"This isn't goodbye, Sadie. Not for us. Let me get settled back in Seattle, and then we'll work something out. I promise." I dipped my head to steal another kiss. "Come on. Let's make a run for it."

I gripped her hand, and, soaked through to the skin, we dashed to the set of steps leading down to the underground station. When it rained in England, it poured. At the bottom of the steps, I pulled Sadie toward me. Her train left from the opposite platform to mine.

"It's not goodbye," I reiterated.

"You say that now, but things happen."

Something in her eyes gave me pause. I searched her face. She appeared... scared? No, not scared. Apprehensive. On edge and unlike the confident woman I'd grown to love.

"Trust me." Kissing her again, I finally tore myself away. "I love you, Sadie."

The rain stopped as I alighted from the tube. I strolled along the riverbank toward my hotel, my mind and heart full of Sadie. I missed her already, but once I returned to America and had a chance to discuss my future with my father, I'd come for her. She belonged with me. It didn't matter that I'd only just turned twenty-three. The heart knew what it desired, and mine had chosen a funny, kind, amazing woman who wanted me for me, not for the riches I brought.

My room was bathed in a soft, golden light. Housekeeping had turned down my bed and set a chocolate on the pillow. I smiled as I picked it up and put it on the nightstand.

The blow to the back of my head caught me unawares. My legs gave way, my knees hitting the thick carpeting. I caught a kick to the kidneys, and I groaned. My arms flailed to stave off the assault, but the blows kept coming. Fists, boots. Multiple assailants. Thick blood filled my mouth. I tried to scream. Nothing came out. I felt myself weakening under the onslaught.

"Get the watch. Hurry."

"Please," I rasped. My chest felt tight, and I wheezed, sucking air into my lungs. It hurt to breathe. I coughed. A spray of red dots flew from my mouth. Blood.

"Shut the fuck up."

I took a fist to the face, another kick to the ribs. I curled into a ball as one of my attackers wrenched my graduation gift from my wrist.

"Grab his wallet, too. And his phone."

My vision turned red. I peered through the swollen lids. Shapes swam before me. Faceless men dressed in black hoodies and jeans.

"Hurry up."

A woman's voice. I squinted. A figure stood in the doorway. A familiar figure.

"Sadie." I reached out a hand. "Help me."

She moved toward me and dropped to a crouch. Her fingers brushed damp hair off my forehead. "I had to come," she murmured. "I had to see it through. I've invested too much to miss out on the fun part."

"Sadie, let's move."

She bent her head, pressing her soft lips to my forehead. "Goodbye, Johannes."

"No, Sadie." I tried to stand. Another vicious kick to the back sent me sprawling. I hit my head on the corner of the nightstand. White spots danced before my eyes.

"Let's go. I got what I came for." She straightened and walked away.

"Sadie," I croaked, my heart shattering into a thousand pieces, her betrayal a blade to the gut. "Why?"

She glanced over her shoulder, a wintry smile lifting her lips. "You had something I wanted." She swung my million-dollar watch back and forth. "You should have been more careful who you trusted with the truth."

Someone grabbed a fistful of my hair, yanking my head backward. A searing pain tore through my neck. I slumped on the floor, clasping at the gaping wound in my throat.

As my life slipped away, Sadie turned and blew me a kiss, her tinkling laugh the last sound I'd ever hear.

K

The car's engine emitted a thunderous growl, then fell silent as I cut the power. I parked in the spot reserved for the owner of Level Nine, the jewel in the crown of my growing nightclub empire, and entered the building through the staff entrance. Trekking through to the main area, I flicked the lights on, grabbed a bottle of water from behind the bar, and twisted off the cap, downing half as I took in the room. I normally enjoyed this time of day, before the staff arrived. Empty nightclubs had a strange vibe, an echo of the previous night when clubbers had crammed the dance floor and music had blasted from the DJ booth. The solitude often soothed me.

But not today.

The dream that had woken me lingered, souring my mood. Not that I was the sunniest of people most days, but on the days I dreamed about *her*, the flames of fury built within me. The desire to lash out, to make others hurt like I hurt besieged me, driving a wrecking ball through all that was good and replacing it with something rotten.

In the years after it happened, I often heard whispers behind my back, my family's anguished murmurings of how bitter I'd become, how angry and abrasive I was. Like I gave a fuck. They should try walking in my shoes before leveling any judgment my way. Eventually, they'd stopped and accepted me for the man I now was. Sort of.

I circled the perimeter of the main area of the club, my eyes catching sight of a glass tumbler amid the foliage screen that camouflaged the stairs to the upper level. Irritation pricked at my skin. I had exacting standards for a reason, and when they weren't met, I fucking hated it. I swiped up the glass and slammed it on the bar. That way, the dirty glass would be the first thing my head bartender, Stan would see when he arrived for work. It crossed my mind to leave a note along the lines of "What the fuck is this?" but often, passive aggressiveness accompanied by a hefty glower sent a clearer message.

I headed to my office and booted up my laptop, shoving one of several piles of paperwork to the side. It might have looked disorganized, but it worked for me. My office was my personal space, the place where I permitted a little chaos to reign, relished it, even. I checked my calendar for the day. Empty except for a liquor delivery that Stan would deal with... and a board meeting from five until six.

God-fucking-dammit.

When the hell had that snuck in?

And how many times had I told Dad not to hold the board meetings at that time of the day? It was right at the start of prep, and the obsessive in me liked to go over every minute detail to ensure we'd be ready for opening at ten o'clock.

Sighing heavily, I tapped my foot on the oak flooring and skimmed my emails. My gaze fell on one in particular with a subject line of "Resignation." I shifted my focus to the preview pane.

Fucking terrific.

My most proficient bartender had handed in his notice with immediate effect. Something about a family emergency, which had called him back home to Colorado.

I thumped the desk. Not tonight. For fuck's sake. The

timing couldn't be worse. The club was closed to regular patrons to make room for a VIP event for a Hollywood A-lister, and I needed a full complement of staff working behind the bar.

Reaching for my cell, I called Margie, the owner of the recruitment agency I used for non-managerial roles. She'd better send someone fucking good. I wasn't in the mood for mediocre.

My cranky mood worsened when Margie told me that they were struggling to find quality, appropriately experienced personnel. I could draft in someone temporarily from one of my other clubs, but that would leave them short-handed, too. Might not have a choice, though.

"I do have someone who might fit the bill," Margie said, interrupting my inner contingency planning.

"Experienced?"

She hesitated. Great. That meant no.

"She has a nice aura. Friendly, welcoming. I think the demanding clientele that frequents Level Nine will take to her."

Aura? What the fuck?

"I'm not running a fucking yoga retreat, Margie. I need someone who is proficient at tending bar, can work at the pace I demand, and knows how to deal with difficult customers without pissing them off."

She sighed. "Johannes, times are tough. There are too many vacancies and not enough people to fill them."

I was aware of the severe gaps in the labor market. Most of my clubs were down one or two staff members, but Level Nine was the venue I'd chosen to enter into a prestigious competition, and I couldn't afford for it to offer less than outstanding service. I had to win that competition. Dammit, I *would* win. The idea of coming in second didn't figure into my plans. No one remembered who the fuck came in second.

"I think you'll like her," she continued.

"I think you'll like the fat fee you get if I take her on," I countered.

"I won't deny that, but answer me this. When have I ever sent you a poor candidate?"

I cast my mind back. Ugh. "Fine, never."

"Never, and you know why?"

"Because I'd fire your ass."

"Exactly." She chuckled. "Look, Ella might not have a whole lot of experience, but she is keen and warm, and I think she'll fit in with the rest of the team very well. Just give her a try."

I took a steeling breath. I had two choices. Either interview the woman, and if she didn't come up to scratch, kick her—and Margie—to the curb. Or tell Stan we were shorthanded for the foreseeable future and deal with the fallout from a reduction in service to the kinds of high-rolling clientele that frequented my club.

Two choices, my ass.

The second one wasn't even worth a moment of consideration. Especially tonight.

"You'd better brief her that I have high expectations."

"Noted."

I checked my watch. "Get her here by midday, and I'll interview her."

"You won't regret it."

I hung up without responding. I regretted it already, and I hadn't even seen the damn woman yet.

Chapter 2

Ella

Maybe, just maybe this is my lucky day.

My tailpipe backfired as I pulled into the parking lot of the Level Nine nightclub, the sound reminiscent of a gunshot. Despite knowing what had made the noise, I ducked in my seat, my heart rate rocketing.

"Calm down. It's just your stupid car."

I sucked in a breath and held it, releasing it slowly. If I landed this job, then I *might* manage to save enough money to get my car fixed. I'd only been in Los Angeles for a few months, and one of the first things I'd learned was that public transport was patchy and unreliable. The entire city was addicted to their cars. If I was to show a prospective employer that I was a reliable employee, then I needed my car.

I also needed it in case we had to run again.

A shiver rocketed up my spine, the taste of fear sour in my mouth. I wiped my clammy hands on my smartest pair of jeans, unable to resist the urge to glance behind me.

Breathe. Nothing there. He doesn't know where you are.

For now.

He'd found us once already, not long after I'd escaped the compound in the dead of night carrying my sleeping child and dragging behind me a small suitcase crammed with as many of her clothes and toys as would fit inside. In my innocence—or rather ignorance—I'd kept my original cell phone, and he'd used his contacts to track me. I'd only gotten us out in the nick of time, my good fortune blind luck more than any kind of planning.

After driving halfway across the country rather than simply one state over from my former home in Oklahoma, I'd settled in California among the sprawling population of Los Angeles. How many people lived here? Four, five million? A place to hide among the masses.

And this time, I'd smartened up.

I slipped the burner phone from my purse, one I'd picked up at a refurbishment store in New Mexico for twenty bucks. My chest tightened at the picture on the screensaver. I ran a fingertip over Chloe's rosy apple cheeks, my daughter's beaming smile staring back at me, her dark locks a mass of curls around her angelic face.

"Love you, little bug. It's all for you."

When I'd turned eighteen, I'd married a much older man that I had thought I was in love with. I'd lived a life filled with all the comforts money could buy. But I'd been naïve and gullible, and my daughter had almost paid the price.

I'd rather live in poverty if it meant keeping us both out of his clutches. The fear, the suffering, the constant looking over my shoulder, the struggling to make ends meet. All of it was worth it to keep her safe.

The heat from the midday sun beat down on me as I made my way across the lot. As instructed, I went around the back of the building rather than use the main entrance to the club. I swiped at the sweat gathering along the back of my neck, my mouth dry as a desert. I hated interviews, even if those for bar work or waitressing were usually a tick box exercise. Most places were only interested in a pretty face and whether you knew the difference between a mojito and a cosmo.

Not this place, apparently. The lady at the recruitment agency I'd recently signed on with after my last temporary job came to an end had said this place was different, that the owner had high standards.

Hence my nerves were rioting, and my stomach had tied itself in knots.

Still there were positives. A year ago, I wouldn't have had a clue how to tend bar. Back then, I only knew how to drink cocktails, not make them.

Then I'd found out—the hard way—how my husband paid for our lifestyle. Drugs.

I tapped on the door, rocking back on my heels as I waited. When no one came, I knocked a little harder. Through a small glass panel, a man appeared, a scowl scoring his forehead, two deep lines that sent prickles racing over my skin. He yanked open the door.

"Yes?"

My tongue darted out to wet my lips. "Hi. I-I'm Ella

Reyes. The agency sent me. I was told to ask for a Mr. Kingcaid."

He towered over me by a good foot, and his attire of a black turtleneck sweater and matching black pants coupled with dark brown hair and pale skin gave him an intimidating air. His ice-blue eyes raked over me with disinterest and boredom.

"Follow me." He spun on his heel, throwing back over his shoulder, "Shut the door."

"'Please' wouldn't go amiss," I muttered, too low for him to hear. Sass wouldn't help me get a job I urgently needed. I'd lurched from casual job to casual job barely making ends meet, and I'd expected this would be the same, until the agency had assured me this was one of the top nightclubs in Los Angeles, with rich clientele who tipped well, and if I made a good impression, it could be the long-term opportunity I'd hoped for. A chance to squirrel a little aside for a rainy day I prayed would never come.

I followed the man into a messy office with papers strewn across every surface and a half-empty takeout coffee cup from a chain store. He invited me to sit by jabbing his finger at a chair opposite the desk. I perched on the edge and willed my legs not to bounce, which they often did when nerves got the better of me.

He stared at his laptop and then tipped up his chin, his glacial eyes boring into my face. I squirmed, the intensity of his gaze almost burning through several layers of skin.

"Your resume is scant. How old are you?"

I widened my eyes. Was he even allowed to ask a question like that? Yeah, I supposed he was considering his business served alcohol. I stammered an answer. "T-twenty-four."

He held out his hand. "ID?"

My hand trembled as I removed my ID from my purse. Diego, a forger who'd done work for my husband had sourced fake birth certificates and social security cards for me and Chloe. With those, I'd been able to get a fake driver's license, too. Diego had a soft spot for Chloe, and after what happened, he'd agreed to help me, at great personal cost to himself.

For my part, I'd promised never to reveal his part in my escape. And I never would.

Mr. Kingcaid scrutinized my ID, then handed it back to me. "College degree?"

"No. Do I need one to tend bar?"

He arched a perfectly shaped eyebrow, I guessed in reaction to the bite to my tone. I silently cursed, pasted a smile on my face—and lied through my teeth.

"I worked for my father's company for quite a while after I left high school, just helping out around the office, but I didn't put that on my resume, as, well"—I forced a chuckle—"it feels a little disingenuous. I didn't exactly interview for the role."

He grunted. I waited for a response. None came. I knitted my fingers together and placed them in my lap to stop the temptation to fiddle with the hem of my shirt.

"I'm a good bartender, Mr. Kingcaid."

If he was, in fact, the owner. For all I knew, he could be the janitor, and I, his entertainment for the day. I doubted it, though. He gave off an air of authority, and he hadn't corrected me when I'd used his name.

"I'm hardworking, I'm efficient, and the customers at my last place liked me. That counts for a lot in this business."

Another grunt. "You're not from around here. Why'd you choose LA?"

I swallowed. He'd obviously picked up on my Southern accent. "Why not?"

He arched that eyebrow again. I rushed on.

"It's the land of opportunity." I smiled. He didn't. I squeezed my hands tighter together and scrabbled around my mind for a reply he might believe. Then he spoke and saved me from adding additional reasoning.

"I see you worked at a place in New Mexico, but only for a month. Why'd you leave that job?"

Because my crazy estranged husband found me and our daughter, and I had no choice but to run.

"It was only ever supposed to be temporary."

He rubbed a hand over his jaw. "Temporary. Hmm. A lot about this," he drummed his fingers on the desk, "seems to be temporary. I'm looking for reliable staff, Miss..." He glanced at his screen. "Reyes. Not someone who'll leave me in the lurch because they're only interested in *temporary* employment."

I quelled my racing heart. *Stay calm.* "Not at all, sir. Since I came to LA, I've only managed to find temporary assignments, but I'm looking for permanent work, maybe even a career." Time to flatter him. "It would be an honor to work at Level Nine. I'm not planning to leave Los Angeles. This is my home, now."

Not planning to, no. But that didn't mean I wouldn't run

in a heartbeat, despite whatever lies I told to land this job. Chloe was all that mattered. I couldn't afford loyalty to anyone other than my daughter.

"Did you tell him or her the same when they gave you the New Mexico job?"

Heat rushed to my face. I had told him exactly that. God, why had I put that job on my resume? Stupid. So stupid. And why was he fixated on New Mexico rather than my more recent assignments, ones I could back up with references? It was almost as if he smelled a rat and was determined to flush it out from its hiding place.

"No, he knew it was temporary. I moved on once he found a permanent member of the team."

"Is that so?" He reached for his cell phone, drawing it toward him. "So, if I called him right now and asked for a reference, he'd back up your story?"

I wrung my hands. The game was up. Time to beg. "Please, I really need this job." My voice shook, emotion and desperation choking me. "I just need a chance. I'm a good worker. I'm not lying about that."

"Just about everything else, huh?"

He slammed the lid on the laptop shut, and my heart plummeted to the floor.

"Are you in trouble with the police?"

I shook my head. "No, sir."

That gaze landed on me again, vivid, forceful, rapacious. I squirmed under his attention. Seconds scraped by, each one feeling more like a minute. I kept quiet, too afraid that whatever I said would make matters worse. He hadn't kicked me out yet. That had to count for something.

"You bring shit to my door, and you'll wish you'd never been born."

A dart of hope lit me up, and I squared my shoulders. "I wouldn't. I—"

"You start tonight. Pay isn't much, but the tips more than make up for that. We have some pretty generous clientele. I presume you want payment in cash?" He arched that same eyebrow once again.

"Please."

He knew. He knew I was in trouble, yet he was willing to offer me a job. I hadn't a clue why, but I wasn't about to question his reasoning. I didn't care for the whys of it, only that I could earn money and take care of Chloe. I teared up, blinking furiously before they fell. Intuition told me this man had no time for waterworks.

"Be here at eight. We open at ten. You're late, you're done."

He unfolded himself from his chair, graceful as a dancer, dangerous like a predator. Wrenching the door open, he cocked his head.

"Out."

I scrambled to my feet. "Thank you, Mr. Kingcaid. You won't regret it. I promise."

He grunted for the third time in our short meeting. As I skipped toward the exit, I could have sworn I heard him say, "I already do."

The door almost hit me on the ass as I left the club and stepped into the blazing sunshine, the guy who'd just offered me a job not waiting until I was all the way through before slamming it behind me.

Jerk.

A jerk who'd just cut me a break for reasons known only to himself. He knew I wasn't legit. He knew I had something to hide. And still he offered me a job.

Maybe my luck was finally turning.

Chapter 3

Johannes

Where's the bleach?

I PEERED THROUGH THE TINY PANE OF GLASS AND WATCHED MY NEW bartender steer her jalopy onto the highway. Held together with rust and spit, it backfired as she pulled out of the parking lot sending a plume of black smoke into the air.

Jesus Christ.

Not only had I hired a woman who was clearly hiding something, but one whose transportation had little to no chance of ensuring she arrived for work on time. Better line up a few more interviews with the agency just in case and start working on a Plan B of cross-resourcing.

I made my way back to my office and opened my laptop, scanning her resume one more time. *Scant* didn't begin to cover it. Considering she'd admitted she hadn't attended college, that gave her six years between finishing high school and now to build a work history. Yet apart from a stint at her father's firm—which I didn't buy for a second, given how she'd fidgeted as she made shit up on the fly—and a few odd bartending and waitressing jobs here and there, she'd hardly worked at all.

So what *had* she been doing with her time?

I couldn't work out whether she *was* trouble, or she was *in* trouble. Either way, I didn't need the headache or the hassle.

Which begged the question of what the hell I'd been thinking when I'd given her a job at my most prestigious club? The club I'd entered into the *Hottest Nightspots in LA* competition, which ran once a year. To win that coveted top spot would propel not only Level Nine but all my clubs to a new level, one that paved the way for expansion.

Some might say I'd done a nice thing for a desperate woman. Those people didn't know me. I'd given up being nice long ago. Almost becoming a statistic kind of stripped the nice right out of a person. Well, it had with me.

The real reason was far simpler. I'd needed a bartender. The agency sent me someone pretty and whom, as Margie had said, my customers would like—much as it irked me to admit it—and my choices were limited.

Besides, in my experience, desperate people were often the hardest workers. And I had no room, or time, for slackers.

As long as she arrived on time, didn't mess with me, and did her fucking job without bringing shit to my door, then she could stay. But one sniff of trouble and she was out of here. I'd tend the fucking bar myself if it came to that.

I had an business to build, and while the clubbing side of the Kingcaid empire had started off slow, it was growing fast. Last year alone, I'd opened six new clubs, and in the next twelve months, I planned to double that, at least.

I might be damaged goods, and treat everyone with suspicion, but I could run a fucking business. From birth, success had been ingrained into me. Sadie had knocked me off course for a while, but I'd put the past behind me—to a degree—and now I wanted to pay back my father for the belief he'd shown in me and line up beside my family as an equal.

Dad's idea of starting a business might have begun as a way of giving me something to concentrate on, goals to aim for, and a company to ground me. But in the end, his "here's an expensive toy to play with" had been exactly what I'd needed to fire me up. I wanted to prove him wrong. To show him that while I might be the ugly-mutt son whose biggest claim to fame was the fact that I'd trusted the wrong woman and almost died, that I had just as much to offer the Kingcaid brand as my brothers and cousins.

I wasn't an underdog. I was a broken man who'd lost my way for a few years. That was then and this was now, and nothing would stand in my way of putting Kingcaid nightclubs on the map.

At the sound of bottles clanging from the bar, I rose to my feet and slammed the laptop closed. As I entered the main area of the nightclub, Stan's butt crack greeted me as he bent over to pick up a crate of beer.

"Fuck's sake, Stan. Pull up your pants before I have to bleach my eyes."

Stan set the crate on top of the bar, hoisted up his jeans,

and flashed me a toothy grin. "Afternoon, boss. Want to give me a hand?"

"Is that you tending your resignation, considering I pay you to manage the bar?"

Stan's grin grew. He was one of the few people outside of my family who dealt with my moods with good humor and the lack of an offense gene. It didn't matter how foul I was to him; he'd come back at me with a joke or a friendly nudge and somehow coax a glimmer of a smile out of me.

Not today, though.

"I take it you saw the glass."

His cheeks tinged pinked and he nodded. "I'll speak to the team."

I nodded curtly. "Make sure it doesn't happen again."

"You got it, boss."

I tapped a fingernail on the surface of the bar. "Andy's quit."

Stan dropped the crate he'd picked up back onto the stack and straightened. "You're fucking kidding."

"I never joke about business. Family stuff, apparently."

"Timing couldn't be worse, what with that big VIP party coming in tonight."

Yep. Nate O'Reilly, the darling of Hollywood, had chosen to celebrate his thirtieth birthday party at Level Nine. Just him and six hundred of his closest friends. The club could hold twelve hundred, but as VIPs tended to be assholes most of the time, I counted every VIP as the equivalent of three "normal" people, which meant the staff would work harder than if we were at capacity.

It was going to be a long night, especially with the new girl.

"Want me to put feelers out and call in a few favors? Get someone on a temporary basis."

I shook my head. "Already done. Woman named Ella... something. Can't recall her surname. She'll be here at eight."

Stan's blond eyebrows flew up his forehead. "That was quick."

"I don't mess around."

"True. She experienced?"

I twisted my lips and shrugged. "She's tended bar and done some waitressing."

He narrowed his eyes at me, searching for... fuck knew what. "But she hasn't worked in a place like Level Nine?"

"No."

Stan groaned. "And on a VIP night, too."

"Look at it as a challenge, Stan. I'm sure you can train her up just fine."

"And if she fucks up?"

"Then I'll fire her."

"And how will that help us tonight?"

I growled. Stan and I were always like this, but for some reason, his incessant questions were riding me today, like fire ants burrowing under my skin.

"Then I'll tend bar. Jesus Christ. Back the fuck off, or you'll find yourself out on your fucking ear."

Stan's hands shot up to either side of his face in an attempt to appease me. "Okay, okay. I'll show her the ropes and keep an extra-close eye on her. I'm sure it'll be fine."

Stan wasn't the only one who'd be keeping a close eye on the intriguing Ella... I bit my lip. What was her fucking surname?

Reyes! That was it. Ella Reyes.

"It will be. I don't hire duds." I paused. "Except for you."

Stan rolling his eyes brought a faint smile to my lips.

"Go do whatever you need to do. I've got a bar to stock."

I left him to it and returned to my office. I shifted the stacks of papers around on my desk so that they wouldn't be in view when I joined the videoconference for today's board meeting. One day soon, I really had to get around to filing this shit.

My phone buzzed against my ass. I leaned forward and retrieved it, frowning at the screen. Ash. What did he want? My brother had gotten married last year, but it hadn't slowed him down in the slightest. If anything, having a wife had spurred him on to work harder, although he took every other weekend off these days, which was quite the improvement. Ash was a workaholic. He had been for as long as I could remember. Even at school, my elder brother was the studious one, the son who'd always achieved top marks, while my younger brother, Penn, and I had messed about getting into scrapes and, well, being boys.

I swiped at the screen, bringing the phone to my ear. "Is Dad suffering from selective hearing again?"

Ash's familiar chuckle sounded in my ear. "Hello to you, too."

"You know me. No time for pleasantries."

He paused. I imagined him shaking his head. "What's Dad done now?"

"He's put a fucking board meeting in from five to six. I've lost count of the number of times I've told him that's a busy time for me. It's like he's got wool in his ears or something." Or he didn't take my business as seriously as the others. Yet more motivation to put Kingcaid nightclubs on the map and prove this business was far more than an expensive hobby.

"Actually, that's my fault."

"Yours?" I rapped a pen on my desk. "Thought you'd want to get home to the little woman. Won't she have your dinner on the table by six?"

He snickered. "Please let me be present when you say that to Kiana. I'll bring popcorn and everything."

I smiled despite a healthy dose of irritation crawling up the back of my neck. Ash's wife and I had a tumultuous relationship, partly—okay, mainly—down to me. I'd played a trick on her before she and Ash had hooked up, and our interactions had gone downhill from there. Although, once, when she'd needed help, she'd come to me. But I got the impression she tolerated me for Ash's sake rather than a desire to be friendly.

Suited me fine.

Now Penn's fiancée... she was a different prospect altogether. Gia got me. She understood me on a level that even my family struggled with. No idea why, but from our very first meeting, we'd clicked. That wasn't to say I didn't give her shit most of the time, but Gia knew how to handle me and give it back tenfold.

I'd never, ever admit this to her or anyone else, but I fucking loved Gia like the sister I'd never had. How she and Kiana were best friends remained a mystery I didn't care enough about to try to unravel.

"So, you gonna spill why you're fucking up my day?"

"Charming," Ash drawled. "And just for the record, I don't sit in my office conjuring ideas for making your life a misery, Johannes. I've invited Garen Gauthier to the meeting to talk about expanding our business relationship, and this was the only time he had free."

Gauthier was one of the CEOs of a rival business, ROGUES. They were diversified along similar lines to Kingcaid, and a while ago, Ash had signed a deal with them that benefited both companies. Gauthier handled the hotel business within ROGUES, just like Ash handled the hotel business for us. Still, I hadn't a clue what this had to do with me.

"And I have to be there because...?" I left the question dangling.

"Because you're part of the fucking family, whether you like it or not."

I flinched, glad this was a voice call and not video so Ash couldn't see my reaction to his bald statement. I was well aware I'd kept my family at arm's length since the attack that had almost claimed my life, but I'd spent so long withdrawing into myself as I'd tried to come to terms with what had happened that by the time I'd emerged through the other side, damaged, struggling, *different,* I hadn't known how to find my way back.

I still didn't know how to find my way back. The man I'd been had died on that hotel floor in a pool of blood. This new version of me was hard and abrasive, and while I knew my family grappled with the enormous change in me, their struggle was nothing compared to my own.

I shook my head of thoughts that always brought on a bout of depression and sighed.

"Fine, I'll be there. But in the future, maybe consider me and the needs of my business rather than some fucking outsider."

I hung up.

There'd been no need to end things like that, but sometimes, God help me, sometimes I just couldn't help myself.

And it always made me feel like shit.

Chapter 4

Ella

Chocolate and raspberry cookies solve all problems.

The sweet smell of freshly baked cookies greeted me as I pushed through the front door, a lightness to my chest I hadn't felt in a long time. Hope, maybe, or relief. Whichever, I'd take it. The weight of juggling paltry finances and constantly looking over my shoulder had begun to take its toll, and I felt far older than my twenty-four years.

That's what happens when you marry a drug baron.

Growing up, I'd been one of life's rarities: a true innocent, although nowadays, with a few more years on the clock, I'd describe myself as gullible.

I'd believed that people were inherently good and honest. I'd believed my husband when he'd told me he was a successful businessman. I'd enjoyed the trappings of wealth and the jealousy of my former school friends as I paraded around town showcasing the latest designer purse and wearing five-carat diamond earrings.

They said that pride came before a fall. Well, I'd fallen. Hard. And I knew, deep down, that I'd have to run for the rest of my life. But worse than that, my beloved baby, Chloe, would have to run, too. And unlike me, she was a true innocent.

Oh, my husband hadn't been physically abusive. Anything but. He'd treated me like a rare jewel, an endangered species, a coveted prize to be protected and cosseted. At least, that was how I'd seen it through ignorant eyes. Now I recognized it for what it was: control.

Mateo liked to own things, and I was just another one of his possessions. And, by extension, so was Chloe. He'd never let us go, never give up searching for me and his daughter. In his own way, I believed he loved us, but it was a tainted kind of love. He'd lost custody of his property, and he'd search the ends of the earth until he recovered what belonged to him.

I'd seen what he was capable of, how he'd reacted to those who'd tried to take what was his. That fateful night still haunted my dreams, the night a rival gang had broken into our house and tried to kidnap me and Chloe as a way to force my husband to give up some of the territory he'd stolen from them. Innocence was a beautiful thing, until the force of a thousand men ripped it away.

And once my eyes had been opened, I couldn't shut them again, couldn't pretend I didn't know how Mateo provided for the life I'd enjoyed for five years, ever since I'd walked through the wrought-iron gates of his compound in Oklahoma and sold my soul to a devil in disguise.

It had taken me six months to stash away enough money to tide me and Chloe over and make plans to run. It hadn't been easy, especially after Mateo had increased our security tenfold following that night, but with copious planning, a little bit of luck, and a child who'd slept through the entire dash for freedom, I'd done it. I'd escaped.

But I wasn't free, not really. I'd never be free. The best I could hope for was to stay one step ahead and keep my baby safe.

"I'm home," I called out, hanging my purse on the coat hook by the front door.

Ginny, my savior, appeared from the kitchen, an apron tied around her middle, and a sprinkling of flour in her gray hair. I'd met Ginny, quite by chance, the day after I'd arrived in Los Angeles. I'd taken Chloe for lunch at a diner, and to escape the flea-bitten motel room we'd stayed in the previous night. She'd spilled her milkshake all over the table, and when I'd told her I couldn't afford to buy her another, she'd burst into tears. Ginny had come to the rescue, and the next thing I knew, we were chatting like old friends and she'd offered us a place to stay.

I'd refused, of course. I didn't know this woman and she didn't know me, and after Mateo, I was naturally suspicious of people, especially those who did good deeds for no reason. But she'd worn me down, and I'd agreed to stay for a few days until I got on my feet.

That was five months ago, and every time I broached the subject of moving out, Ginny would, in a masterful display of "getting her own way," tell me that, of course, if I wanted to leave a lonely old woman rattling around a too-big house, then that was my prerogative. And then her eyes would twinkle and I'd laugh, and the subject would get shelved for another few weeks.

The truth was, I couldn't afford to move out even if I wanted to, which I didn't. Ginny was like the grandmother I'd never had—both my maternal and paternal grandparents had died when I was a little girl—and Chloe adored her. I only raised the subject every now and then to make sure Ginny had a way out. She never took it, and I didn't push.

She hadn't asked me about my past, and I hadn't come forth with any details either. Nor did I intend to. The only way to keep Chloe and me as safe as possible was to keep where I came from a secret. I couldn't afford to trust a single soul, not even one as big-hearted and kind as Ginny. Besides, it was better for her that she remained in the dark. That way, if Mateo caught up to me and I had to run again, Ginny could say with one hundred percent honesty that she knew nothing.

The only thing she could tell him was the name I'd chosen to go under: Ella Reyes. "Ella" after my mother, Eleanor, and "Reyes" after my maternal grandmother's maiden name. And if I ran again, I'd drop the name Ella Reyes faster than if I'd picked up a hot pan off the stove without protective gloves.

One thing was for sure, though: Eloise Fernandez had died six months ago. And I hoped she stayed dead.

"Well?" Ginny propped a hand on her hip. "How did it go?"

A smile inched across my face. "I start tonight."

Ginny clapped her hands, then enveloped me in a squishy hug. "I'm so proud of you!"

"Mind you, it won't be as relaxed as the last place I worked. I'll have to be on my toes a hundred percent of the time. The owner is a right stickler. Grumpy, too."

And also rather beautiful.

I pushed aside the thought. It didn't matter what he looked like or how sunny or dour his personality was. I only cared that he'd given me a chance, and I couldn't mess it up.

"Well, if anyone can win him over, it's you."

I grimaced. "Not unless I discover I have a superpower."

Ginny chuckled.

"Are you certain you're still fine to watch Chloe? I'll make sure she's bathed and in bed before I leave, and I should be home by three, so I can still take her to school."

Ginny narrowed her eyes at me in a way I'd come to understand as "brace for a lecture."

"You need to make sure you don't burn out. I can take her to school. It's no bother."

I shook my head. "I'd rather do it." Taking Chloe to and from school was nonnegotiable. I felt better knowing I'd been the one to witness her going inside and the school locking the doors. Mateo couldn't get to her there. Silly, really, especially as I'd have to leave her with Ginny when I went to work, but for me, it was all about reducing risk to a minimum.

Ginny sighed. "Girl, that stubborn attitude will bite you on the ass one day."

"I'm young. I have bags of energy. And I can take a nap during the day to make up for the lack of sleep at night."

Her eyes narrowed further, and she harrumphed in that way older people seemed to master, whereas on a younger person, it'd just sound weird. She pointed two fingers at her eyes, then swiveled them around to point them at me. "I'm watching you."

I chuckled, moving in for another hug. "Do I smell cookies?"

"Yes, you do. Chocolate and raspberry. And don't think your diversionary tactics have worked, missy, because they haven't."

She whipped around and bustled back to the kitchen. I followed, grinning and, not for the first time, thanking whatever angel had placed her in the diner that day. I wasn't sure what I'd have done if she hadn't taken us into her home. To be fair, after Mateo had almost caught us in New Mexico, I hadn't thought further ahead than getting away, but Ginny had saved us, and I'd be forever grateful to her for her act of kindness toward a stranger.

Crumbs of cookie dough and a dusting of flour covered the countertop. I reached for a cloth and began cleaning up. Ginny chuckled.

"You and your obsession with tidiness."

I grinned. "It's an affliction, I know. I just like things neat."

Ginny bent down and retrieved the cookies from the oven, tipping them onto a wire rack. I reached for one and got my wrist slapped for my troubles.

"Ow." I pulled it to my chest.

"They're too hot. And they're for Chloe. Chocolate and raspberry are her favorite."

"There's"—I made a guesstimate—"at least twenty cookies. If she eats all those, she'll have a stomachache for days."

"Go on, then," Ginny groused. "You can have one."

I snagged one, blew on it to cool it down, and took a bite. "Oh my God, Ginny, you should sell these. You'd make a fortune." I swore that Ginny's baking got better and better. I'd have to watch Chloe like a hawk in case she gobbled up the entire batch.

"Oh, away with you." She flicked her wrist, but I caught the faint blush of pink stealing over her cheeks.

I devoured the rest of the cookie while Ginny poured coffee into two mugs. "If the tips at this job work out as well as I hope they will, I'll be able to start paying you proper rent." My checkered work pattern meant I hadn't been able to contribute as much as I'd have liked to, and while Ginny's generosity was boundless, I'd feel better when I could pay my way.

Ginny busied herself with adding cream and sugar to her coffee while I waited for what I knew was coming. She lifted her cup to her lips, her eyes finally meeting mine after several sips.

"You and Chloe being here is payment enough."

I sighed. "Ginny, I—"

She cut me off with one of her famous dismissive gestures. "I never had children or grandchildren, and while I can't say I've dwelled on it all that much, as I get older, it's begun to dawn on me just how much I missed out on."

Ginny's husband had gotten hit by a car while they were on their honeymoon and Ginny had never remarried. I'd asked her once why not—thirty-five years was a long time to mourn someone—and she'd gotten this misty look in her eyes and told me that a love like she and Edward had shared was the kind of love that only came along once in a lifetime.

In a way, I envied her, although not the grief she'd

suffered. But to have loved like that must've been wonderful.

"I know you and Chloe aren't my blood, but I've come to think of you like that. I believe fate brought us together that day at the diner."

She reached across the table and squeezed my hand, and this look passed between us, one that told me if I ever wanted to talk, Ginny would listen. I wasn't ready to do that, nowhere near, but maybe one day, I might pluck up the courage to trust my instincts and share at least a little bit of what had brought me here. But it would be a long way in the future. The last thing I wanted to do was drag anyone else into my mess, especially Ginny. The less she knew, the better it was for her.

"Edward left me very well provided for, and I live a frugal life. Please, let me do this for you and Chloe."

"Oh, Ginny." I placed my hand on top of hers. "There must be something I can do to repay you."

"There is. When I'm too old to live alone and they cart me off to one of those old folks' facilities, you can come visit me." Her eyes twinkled, and she winked. "And make sure I'm not being fiddled with."

I burst out laughing. "Ginny! You're terrible."

"It happens," she defended. "I read the newspapers. There are some dreadful people out there preying on the old and vulnerable." She jabbed a finger in my direction. "It's your job to make sure my nightgown stays right where it should."

I laughed harder. Ginny was an absolute treasure. "Deal."

"Good." She pushed the plate of cookies toward me. "One more for luck on your first day at a new job."

My stomach lurched, nerves swimming through my bloodstream. I couldn't mess this up. It didn't take a genius to figure out that the brooding Mr. Kingcaid had little patience for mediocrity.

I picked up a cookie and took a bite. "For luck."

Chapter 5

Ella

No room for butterfingers in this job.

The parking lot of Level Nine was fuller than when I'd arrived earlier today for my interview. I cut the engine, sweat dripping between my boobs and along the back of my neck. The air conditioner on the car had given out weeks ago, but I had no money to get it fixed, so I had to make do with an open window and windswept hair.

I reached into the door pocket and fished out a pack of wet wipes and cleaned myself up, then readjusted the rearview mirror, pinning back the loose strands and tightening my ponytail.

Deep breath. You've got this.

My dad had once told me that if what you were doing wasn't a little bit scary, then you weren't pushing yourself hard enough.

A pang swept through my chest. I missed my dad, and my mom, but I'd made my bed, and it was up to me to lie in it.

They'd begged me not to marry Mateo, even threatening to cut me out of their lives. At the time, they'd infuriated me, but now that I was a parent myself, I understood. They'd seen what I hadn't—that Mateo wasn't a good man—and had tried to stop me from making a huge mistake in the only way they'd known how. The fact that he was fifteen years older than me had also played a part, but with hindsight, I realized it was more than that. Their experience had given them an intuition that, at eighteen, I'd lacked.

I'd been so blinded with love—or infatuation, as I now recognized it as—that I'd ignored my parents and married him anyway. In the end, I was the one who'd cut them out of my life with the precision of a surgeon's scalpel.

A while after I'd married Mateo, my parents had moved to New York but a couple of years later I'd heard they'd divorced and my mom had emigrated to France after she married a guy she'd met on vacation.

I longed to contact them, to tell them they'd been right all along, and see if there was a way to build bridges, but at the same time, I feared their rejection. I deserved it, no doubt about that, and that fear kept me from taking the first step to reconciliation.

I pushed the painful thoughts of my parents to one side and exited the car. I slammed the door. It didn't shut properly, so I opened it and tried again. This time it closed fully, and I was able to lock it. Every time I climbed into the thing, I prayed it would get me where I needed to go, especially now. Mr. Kingcaid was the kind of man who didn't give second chances. I'd lucked out that he'd given me a first chance, and I could not mess this up.

I made my way over to the same door I'd entered through earlier and pulled on the handle. It opened. I peered inside. Sounds drifted down the narrow corridor—raised voices, but not in anger, bottles clanging, the hum of a vacuum cleaner, heels clipping on the floor. Swallowing my nerves, I followed the voices, passing by the office where I'd had my interview and emerging into an enormous space.

A vast bar ran the entire length of one wall, and in the center was a polished wooden dance floor. On the opposite wall was an elevated area with decks where I assumed the DJ banged out tunes. Comfy seating lined the edges, and there was a roped-off area I guessed was for VIPs and a mezzanine level with an ornate balustrade.

Right now, it looked a little unimpressive, but I'd bet that once the lights were turned on and music blasted out of the enormous speakers, and the place heaved with clubbers, it would take on a whole different vibe.

Nerves dampened my palms, and I swiped them over my hips. I'd worn the same jeans as I had at my interview—the smartest ones I owned—and paired them with flat shoes and a fitted white shirt open at the neck. But as I scanned around, I had a horrible feeling I'd made the wrong choice.

Across from me, deep in conversation, was a group of women who had to be staff, considering the club wasn't open yet. Each of them was decked out in short skirts or dresses, plenty of cleavage on show, and heels that added a good three to four inches to their height. Their makeup was cover model perfect, and they had legs for days and long, wavy blonde locks curling down their backs.

Unlike me, a mere five foot four when I stood up straight, who had a jiggly mom belly and black hair that grew to between my shoulder blades but refused to grow another inch.

My heart tripped, embarrassment pinking my cheeks. I didn't belong here.

I spun around, ready to make my escape, and clattered into a wall made of pure muscle.

"Oof."

Mr. Kingcaid, dressed as he'd been earlier today in all black, gripped my upper arms to steady me.

"Going somewhere, Miss Reyes?"

"I-I..." I ran my teeth over my bottom lip. "No."

"Good."

He released me and stepped back, and this weird feeling came over me, almost like a sense of loss. A chuckle nearly slipped from my lips at such a ridiculous thought, but one look at the scowl on the face of my new boss, and I swallowed it back down.

"Follow me. I'll introduce you to Stan. He'll show you the ropes."

I had no idea who Stan was, and I didn't ask. All would become clear, in time. I wasn't sure whether to be grateful to the surly nightclub owner for stopping me from making a run for it or conflicted that I'd have to stay.

There was one sliver of light on the horizon. He'd seen my attire and hadn't commented, so however those women chose to dress, it wasn't a company edict.

Besides, my choices were limited. When I'd left Mateo, seventy-five percent of what I'd packed was for Chloe, and I didn't have spare cash for clothes. Not even from the thrift store.

"Stan."

Mr. Kingcaid rapped his knuckles on the bar, drawing the attention of a man in his midthirties with close-cropped dark blond hair, a goatee, and twinkling blue eyes. I immediately took to him, especially when he flashed a white-toothed smile in my direction. The difference between him and the club owner was like night and day.

Stan was sunshine even in midwinter.

Mr. Kingcaid was dark, gloomy skies, the kind of which preceded a violent thunderstorm.

"This is Ella. She's our new bartender. Show her what she needs to know." He glanced down at me. "Okay?"

I wondered what he'd say if I said no, that I wasn't okay. It wasn't a lie. I was worried I'd stand out rather than blend in and scared I'd make a mess of things and lose my job on the same day I'd gotten it.

I swallowed past a narrow throat and flicked my eyes to Stan. "All good." My voice was too brittle, all high-pitched and squeaky, but Mr. Kingcaid either didn't notice or, more likely, didn't care. He gave me a curt nod and retreated.

"Don't worry about Johannes," Stan said. "His bark is worse than his bite." He laughed. "On a good day."

So that's his name. Johannes. Such an unusual name for an American. I'd heard the African version, Yohannes, before, although it was spelled the same way, with a *J*. I wondered if there was a reason behind his parents choosing to call him that or if they'd heard it somewhere and just liked the sound of it.

Stan nudged me, interrupting my daydreams. "Come on, Ella. Let's get started. We've got a busy night ahead."

Stan wasn't wrong. From the moment the club opened its doors at ten o'clock, I didn't get a second to breathe, let alone find time to go to the bathroom.

When Stan had mentioned tonight's special event and told me who was coming, I'd gone into panic mode. Everyone who was anyone knew the name Nate O'Reilly. He was one of Hollywood's hottest properties and I'd worried I'd get starstruck and act all weird, but in the end, I'd been far too busy to pay him any attention whatsoever.

I'd caught a quick glimpse of him on the dance floor with his wife, a stunning diminutive redhead, and that was about it. She gave me hope that not all guys were into tall, leggy blondes. Then again, I had no time for romance even if my dream guy dropped at my feet and begged me to go out with him. My one and only priority was and would remain Chloe. Keeping her safe and away from the toxic environment my husband cultivated was the only thing I cared about.

"Yo, Ella, quit daydreaming." Stan gave me a dig in the side and jerked his chin toward a waiting customer.

I sprinted into action, but not before I caught Johannes standing in a dark corner staring at me, his shoulder propped against a wall. He narrowed his eyes, and my stomach dropped. I wasn't an idiot. I knew he was assessing my performance, and from what little I'd gleaned, he wouldn't hesitate to fire me if he thought I wasn't up to the job.

I finished serving my current customer and scanned the bar for anyone waiting.

Oh, hell.

Nate O'Reilly held up a finger, his arm draped around his wife's shoulder. He hit me with a brilliant smile, and I came over all of a flutter. Damn, he was handsome, the kind of good looks that caused women's ovaries to weep with joy.

Deep breath, Ella.

I took his order—a beer and a mimosa—but as I stood on tiptoes to grab a champagne flute from the top shelf, I lost my balance and dropped it. Glass shattered, splattering my legs. Thank goodness for small mercies. At least I was wearing jeans, or I might have gotten cut.

"Fuck. I mean *shit*. I mean *gosh darn it*."

I flushed beet red, dropping to a crouch to pick up the biggest shards. As I rose to my feet, Johannes stood right in front of me, a scowl drawing his eyebrows inward.

"Stan," he barked. "Serve Nate and Dex."

I licked my lips, meekly spluttering out, "They asked for a beer and a mimosa."

"No room for butterfingers in this job, Miss Reyes. Looks like your first paycheck will go toward paying for breakages."

An overwhelming need to defend myself came over me. "I've only broken this one glass."

"Which just happens to be crystal and expensive. This is an exclusive establishment. One you're clearly not used to."

A tightness spread through my chest. Looked as though I'd be back at the agency tomorrow begging for scraps.

Johannes plucked the broken glass from my hand. "You've cut yourself."

I glanced down. My palm was covered in blood. "Oh." I wavered. The sight of blood always made me woozy. Ever since that night when—

"Come with me."

Johannes gripped my elbow, propelling me along the bar and through the throngs of people. I skipped to keep up with his long strides. We entered his office, and he pointed at the same chair I'd perched on earlier today.

"Sit."

My knees folded as if he'd compelled me to obey him and I was powerless to resist. He opened one of the drawers in his desk and removed a first-aid kit. My hand began to throb, and blood still oozed from the wound. Queasy, I looked away.

Johannes crouched in front of me and drew my hand toward him. His warm touch belied the coldness in his eyes. A raft of goose bumps raced across my skin, trepidation mixed with a hint of attraction.

My new boss might be brusque and dour, but visually, he was a work of art. High, aristocratic cheekbones sculpted to perfection, a strong chin, thick dark brown hair, and ice-blue eyes that bored right through me, delving into parts I wasn't willing to share.

"Are you always this clumsy?"

I swallowed past a narrow throat. "Not usually, no. I was a bit nervous."

I left out the reason for my nervousness—namely coming face-to-face with someone famous, which, even to me, sounded ridiculous.

"It won't happen again."

He grunted, removing a few items from the box and setting them on his desk.

Ah, hell.

He planned to fire me.

I'd bet he was taking care of my injury just to avoid a lawsuit or bad publicity, or a concern that I'd leave a bad review or take to social media to call him out for being a shitty boss.

Not that I had my social media accounts any longer. I'd closed them all down the night I'd made my escape. I was completely off the grid both under my real name, Eloise Fernandez, and my assumed name, Ella Reyes.

I half expected Johannes to ask me why I wasn't on multiple social platforms. Didn't all companies research their staff that way these days? Maybe he had and he either didn't care or was biding his time to ask me why I wasn't like all other young women my age, obsessed with Instagram and Snapchat and TikTok.

I still recalled the look on the face of the woman at the agency I'd signed up with on arrival in Los Angeles when I'd told her I didn't have email or social media accounts, just a cell phone and Ginny's address. Seriously, anyone would have thought I'd had a zit on my chin the size of a planet the way she'd gaped at me.

"There. You might want to have a doctor check it over, and maybe get a shot, but that should do for now."

I glanced down at my hand, wrapped in white gauze. I'd gotten so lost in my head that I hadn't paid attention to him as he'd worked.

I flexed my fingers, then lifted my gaze to his. Cold, flat eyes met mine, but beyond the surface, trauma lurked. I recognized it all too well. Each time I looked in the mirror, that same kind of stare looked back at me. A little vacant, a lot defensive, a shield that told nosy parties to fuck off.

Maybe he'd recognized the same signs in me and that was why he hadn't delved too deeply at our interview or searched the internet for information about me.

"Am I fired?"

The question came from left field. He stared at me with narrowed eyes, then rose to his feet and closed the first-aid kit.

"Why would I fire you?"

There was a softness to his voice that surprised me. "I-I broke an expensive glass."

"That you'll pay for."

"But—"

"Do you want me to fire you?"

I shook my head. "Not at all."

"Then get back behind the bar and help out your team-mates. Injured hand or not, I expect you to work your full shift."

Tension left me in a whoosh. I still had a job. I stood, offering him a small smile.

"Thank you. For the job and the bandage."

He stiffened. "Gratitude isn't necessary, nor warranted. Now, if you wouldn't mind, I have things to do."

His curt dismissal doused me in iced water. For the briefest moment, I'd felt a connection between us, but it must have been one-sided.

By the time I reached the door and risked a glance back at him, he was sitting behind his desk, scowling at whatever was on his laptop screen.

I slipped outside and returned to work.

I'd dodged a bullet.

And I'd better make damned sure I didn't land in the line of fire again. I had a hunch that I'd used my one and only chance.

Chapter 6

Johannes

Women are either drama or death—and I'm interested in neither.

Heavy bass beats rocked the floor beneath my feet, and hundreds of bodies crammed the dance floor, grinding and humping and swaying to the music.

I scanned the crowd, my eyes landing on Nate and his wife sitting behind one of the roped-off areas. I tipped my chin, and he cocked his head, beckoning me over.

Skirting the edges of the dance floor, I slipped behind the velvet rope. I remained standing, despite Nate pushing a chair toward me with his foot.

"Everything good?" My clients' happiness mattered to me. They were the lifeblood behind whether my business thrived or died. I'd known Nate for a few months, and while

I wouldn't say we were friends—I had none—I liked the guy, and I wanted his thirtieth birthday to go well.

It didn't hurt that he had a lot of sway in this town either. His word counted for a lot. Level Nine had only been open for a year, and I was still building its reputation as *the* club in this part of town for the rich and famous to frequent. We offered top-shelf liquor and ten-thousand-dollar bottles of champagne, as well as the best DJ's and dancers, and our clients received exemplary service.

"Terrific. Your staff is looking after us well."

"Good." I glanced over at the bar, my gaze landing on Ella as she leaned forward, angling her head toward a customer to hear his order. She tucked a lock of hair behind her ear, revealing an elegant slope to her neck. I tore my gaze away, focusing on Nate. "Sorry about earlier. She's new. First shift tonight."

"No need for apologies. Accidents happen."

"Yeah."

I returned my attention to her again. The same guy reached over the bar and clasped a hand around her wrist, then traced his fingertip over the bandage I'd applied.

I flexed my jaw.

One wrong move, asshole, and you're outta here.

She said something to him, and he released her. The burning sensation in my chest receded, but irritation remained. My staff weren't there to be pawed at and hit on. They served the fucking drinks with a smile and a healthy dose of efficiency, and that was it.

"He's gone."

I blinked, pulling my gaze away from Ella to focus on Nate. "Who's gone?"

Nate chuckled. "You have. She's pretty."

"Watch it," Dex warned, digging her husband in the ribs.

Nate drew her to his side and pressed a kiss to her temple. "You're the only one for me, Titch, but Johannes here is free and single. All I'm doing is pointing out an attractive woman for his consideration."

"No consideration necessary." I forced a smile. "I don't mix business with pleasure."

What Nate didn't know was that I didn't "pleasure." Period. Not in that sense, anyway. When I got an itch that my hand couldn't solve, I'd carefully select a willing participant and scratch it. The encounters were brief, from behind, and never repeated.

"All work and no play," Nate said, grinning.

I froze for a beat, then my hand automatically moved to press against my throat. Sadie had said those exact words to me that fateful night.

Six fucking years and hearing a common and clichéd phrase still had the power to choke me, to trigger me, to send me right back to the place that still haunted my dreams.

"Enjoy the rest of your evening," I managed to grit out. "Let me or a member of the team know if you need anything."

Nate's eyes flared in surprise at my curt response to what he saw as a joke, but I didn't hang around. I lurched through the crowd, breathing heavily, heading for my office, where I could take a breath and compose myself.

Before I could get there, Stan appeared in front of me.

"What?" I snapped.

"Your admirer just arrived."

I frowned, still flustered by what Nate had said. "What fucking admir—" I trailed off, scanning the club. "Ah fuck." My gaze landed on the subject of Stan's comment. "Who did she arrive with?"

"Him."

Stan jerked his chin at a man in his forties propped up against the bar. I'd never seen him before, but something about him set my instincts on fire. He had this predatory look that set my teeth on edge. I thought about asking Nate who he was but decided against it.

"Thanks."

"Want me to handle it?"

"No. I've got it."

The woman Stan had referred to, Justine, had appeared from nowhere about six weeks ago. She'd only just turned twenty-one, according to my security personnel who had ID'd her, given that she looked closer to eighteen. Since that first night, she'd come to the club every Friday and Saturday, and sometimes on Sundays, making it clear what she wanted.

Me.

Too bad for her I wasn't available.

And even if I were, I wouldn't stick my dick anywhere near someone so young and vulnerable. At least, that was how she came across to me. She gave off an air of desperation, and as much as I had an issue with women in general, I'd never purposely go out of my way to break one.

The women I fucked knew the deal. I stated it clearly right up front, and I chose carefully. Most were late twenties to midthirties, strong females who'd been through the "Who the fuck am I?" journey, and were confident in themselves and what they wanted out of life, and out of their sexual encounters. But Justine was too young and too fragile to swim in shark-infested waters.

I'd made it clear that she'd never get what she wanted from me, but either she refused to take a hint, or she'd heard me just fine but thought she could persuade me to change my mind.

Lately, she'd upped the ante by arriving with other men, or picking one up while she was here, and putting on a show, purely for my benefit. But she was playing with fire. Whether or not she got burned wasn't my business, but for some ridiculous reason, I felt responsible for her safety. Hence I'd ensured that a member of my security detail followed her home at the end of each night and made sure whatever guy she left with didn't hurt her.

So far, she'd gotten lucky. The guys would drop her off at her home, and she'd go inside. Alone. But it only took that one who refused to take no for an answer, and while my security guys would step in if things got out of hand, I couldn't keep her safe twenty-four seven, and there were a lot of men out there who didn't like being told no.

She wasn't listening to reason.

Therefore, the time had come for me to deal with this situation once and for all, and I knew just the way to handle it.

Cruel? Yes.

Necessary? Abso-fucking-lutely.

It would also make me the villain, but I had no problem slotting into that role if it taught Justine a valuable lesson that kept her safe.

I had a word with one of my security guards and pointed

out the guy Justine had arrived with. He'd block off the guy if he tried to follow us. I made my way over to the bar and held up a finger at Ella. She nodded to acknowledge me, finished serving her current customer, and then made her way over to my location.

She dipped her chin as she approached, her moss-green eyes part submissive, part defiant. My groin heated. I had to admit, she was a pretty little thing. Hair the color of the darkest night hung past her shoulders, her cute button nose turned up at the end, and a handful of freckles were scattered across her cheeks. Small, too. I liked small women, or rather, I had, when I'd still liked women.

Maybe it had called to the latent protector that hung over the male of the species from prehistoric times.

Nowadays, it didn't matter whether they were tall or short, curvy or slim, demure or overtly sexy. I didn't do women. They were either drama or death, and I wasn't in the market for either.

"How's the hand?"

Ella startled at my question, then held out her palm and flexed her fingers. "It's fine. A bit sore, but I'll live."

"Make sure you get it checked out tomorrow."

She nibbled her lip and ducked her head. "I will."

Her reply sounded more like "I won't," but whatever. Her decision, and her problem if the cut got infected.

"Can I get you anything?"

"Yeah, water."

She pivoted, crouching to one of the low-level fridges. Her top rode up, revealing a sliver of pale skin. My dick swelled. I willed it to deflate. Executing my plan to scare off my stalker wouldn't work if I had a boner.

Ella set the water on the bar. "Anything else?"

"No, I'm good."

She paused, her lips parting as if she wanted to say something, then she nodded and bustled off to serve someone else.

I tracked her for a few seconds, impressed at how she juggled serving two customers at once. She'd caught on quickly. After a few shifts, I probably wouldn't be able to tell the difference between her and my longer-serving employees. My instincts about her from a work perspective had been right on.

Were my instincts about her being trouble, or being *in trouble*, also accurate?

Only time would tell.

I spun to face the club, resting both elbows on the bar. Justine stood about fifteen feet away, shaking her booty. Her middle-aged companion had his hands on her hips and was grinding into her. She lifted her head and her gaze found me, hunger and lust blazing from her honey-colored eyes.

My water bottle dangled from my right hand, and I swung it in the air, then cocked my head. She took the bait, shoving the guy's hands off her and nearly falling over her feet as she made a beeline for me. I set off for the staff restrooms, not needing to glance behind me to know she'd follow.

All the bathrooms in my club were separate stalls rather than one large communal restroom, including the staff facilities. Perfect for what I had in mind to teach Justine a lesson she wouldn't forget in a hurry, and with any luck, it would force her to change direction from this dangerous path she'd insisted on walking.

I slowed as I approached the first stall, waiting for her to catch up. She drew alongside me and trailed a red-tipped fingernail up my arm. I snapped my hand around her arm and shoved her into the bathroom. Kicking the door closed, I spun her to face the wall and slammed her up against it.

"How do you want it, darlin'?" I sank my teeth into her shoulder. "You like it rough, don't you?"

She groaned, sticking her hips back and grinding her ass against my flaccid dick. "Yes, Johannes. Yes," she replied breathily.

"You want my cock, don't you?"

"I do, baby. I really do."

She reached behind to feel me up. I captured both her hands and planted them on the wall.

"You want me to pound your tight little cunt?"

"Yes. Yes!"

"What about your ass? I don't have lube, so I'd be going in dry. What about it, sweetcheeks? You'd let me fuck your ass until you bled? You want me that much, huh, babe? 'Cause that's what I like. I like to make a woman bleed for me. Maybe a little knife play. A few nicks here and there. Nothing too dangerous."

She stiffened, her body tautening under my hold.

Bingo. Time to press my advantage.

"What about breath play? Would you let me choke you as I came until you almost passed out? You want to please me, don't you, darlin'?"

"I-I..."

"Sure you do. Otherwise, why else would you come to my club every weekend and give me those fuck-me eyes?" I squeezed her wrists, not too hard but hard enough that she'd feel a twinge of pain. "You said you liked it rough. You weren't lying to me, were you, babe?"

A strangled noise sounded in her throat. "Johannes, please."

She wriggled. I leaned into her.

"What about whips? Canes? Floggers? I like to dole out a little pain with my orgasms. You still wanna play, sweetcheeks?"

Lie after lie spilled from my lips, but it was all for a good cause. This girl had been giving me vibes for weeks, vibes that weren't "how about a fun roll in the hay for our mutual benefit" but more "you can do whatever you want to me and I won't fight you." If I scared the shit out of her now, it might just save her life one day or, at a minimum, save her from being violated by a predator.

Like that fuckwit she'd come with tonight.

A sob spilled from her lips. "No. That's not what I want."

I immediately released her and stepped back, giving her space. She spun around, hair awry, tears staining her cheeks.

"You're not who I thought you were."

"No?" I canted my head. "That's too bad."

"You're a freak! A monster."

I suppressed a wince. She had no idea how close to the truth she'd come with that statement. But not for the reasons she believed.

"Hmm. Depends on what kink you're into. Looks as if we're not a good match after all, huh, sweetcheeks?"

I opened the bathroom door and jerked my head. She pushed past me and disappeared into the hallway, the fast-paced clacking of her heels on the floor fading away.

I exited the bathroom.

Ah, fuck.

Ella stood outside, her hand clasped to her mouth, a look of horror streaking across her face.

I ran a hand over the top of my head, straining to recall the exact words I'd used to scare off Justine and coming up empty.

"What was that?" she snapped, her eyes filled with condemnation.

She'd already made up her mind about what had occurred between me and Justine, and although I didn't owe her an explanation, I gave her one anyway.

"It wasn't what it looked like."

"Really? And what did it look like?"

I blew out a breath. For some ungodly reason, I despised the idea that Ella would think I was some kind of abuser of women when the reality was quite the opposite.

I'd survived abuse, albeit not doled out directly by Sadie. But she'd orchestrated it. She'd pulled the strings and set the events in motion. Events I still struggled to come to terms with. Events that had left me with a physical reminder and a deep-seated mistrust of women.

"Whatever you think, you're wrong. I just saved that girl from sleepwalking into a whole heap of trouble."

"Really?" She snorted. "You rode to her rescue like a white knight. Is that it?"

Her voice, layered as it was with such derision, stiffened my spine. I folded my arms and huffed a laugh, one filled with bitterness.

"I'm no white knight. Trust me."

"No. You're not."

She whirled around and strode off, her opinion of me set in stone. And what did I do?

I let her go.

Chapter 7

Ella

First impressions aren't always right.

I RETURNED TO THE BAR, THE FULL BLADDER THAT HAD SENT ME TO the bathroom forgotten in the wake of what I'd seen.

Or thought I'd seen.

Could I have misunderstood? Had I witnessed nothing more than a lovers' tiff?

I rubbed my forehead, scanning around for the girl. I couldn't see her. Unsurprising, given how crammed it was in here, and Stan had told me earlier that this was less than half of the normal number of customers on a non-VIP night. I dreaded to think what tomorrow would bring and whether I'd cope with a massively increased workload.

If I didn't get fired first.

Johannes emerged from the corridor that led to the staff

bathrooms, hands tucked into the pockets of his black slacks, his trademark frown in place. He sought me out. Our eyes locked, and a tremor crept up both my arms and shot down my back.

Fear?

No, it wasn't that. He didn't frighten me. He confused me. He intrigued me.

He fascinated me.

"Whatever you think, you're wrong."

And what did I think?

If I truly believed he'd assaulted that girl, then I should call the police, even if I'd lose my job as a result.

I snuck another sidelong glance at him to find him still staring at me. Pulling my gaze away, I busied myself with serving customers. Once my shift finished, I'd have time to think and decide what to do.

I tried to picture the woman, her clothes, her hair color, her facial features, just in case I had to give a description to the police.

A little before two in the morning, the clubbers began to disperse, the packed crowd thinning until there were only a few stragglers left finishing up the remains of their drinks.

Waving to a customer who shouted goodbye, I set about cleaning down the bar with a couple of the other women whom I hadn't yet had much chance to engage with, but what I did know was how wrong my initial thoughts had been. They might have been blonde and leggy and beautiful, but they worked their asses off and were professional to a fault.

Tiffany—was that her name? I couldn't remember—made her way toward me, a beaming smile showing off a perfect set of white teeth. Everyone in LA seemed to have the most amazing teeth, as if it were a rite of passage or something. Mine were okay, a little crooked on the bottom, but they didn't hold a candle to Tiffany's.

"How was your first shift?"

I smiled, allowing my shoulders to droop a little. "Exhausting."

"Yeah, it's relentless. Wait until you work a normal night."

"Stan mentioned it wasn't as full as usual. I just hope I can keep up."

Tiffany winked. "You'll do fine. You catch on fast."

"Yes, she does," a deep baritone drawled from over my right shoulder.

I startled, glancing behind me. "Thank you, Mr. Kingcaid."

He tapped a fingernail on the bar. "A word, please, Miss Reyes."

"Um, I still have to finish up here."

"I got it." Tiffany removed the dishcloth from my hand and gave me a nudge. "When the boss demands that you jump, the right response is 'How high?'"

"That's good advice," Johannes said, spinning around and stalking off, his message that he expected me to follow as clear as the view through a freshly polished pane of glass.

I trudged after him, my mind racing at a million miles an hour, running scenarios on the best way to approach this conversation.

Let him talk and follow his lead, or demand that he explain himself?

Or somewhere in between?

As selfish as it sounded, I dreaded losing my job on the first day, but at the same time, I wouldn't be able to live with myself if I truly, with a hundred percent certainty, believed I'd witnessed a man assaulting a woman and I didn't step in and do the right thing.

I entered Johannes's office to find him perched on the edge of his desk. He pointed to the same chair I'd sat on twice before, but I shook my head.

"I prefer to stand."

A lie, given that my feet were killing me after being on them for six hours straight, but this way, we were more equal in height, if not in status.

"Suit yourself."

He moved around his desk and folded his elegant frame into his high-backed leather chair.

"I want to talk about earlier."

"It's none of my business."

"True, but considering the way you looked at me as if I were some kind of sexual predator, I feel I have no choice but to explain myself."

"I-I don't—"

His hand came up. "Please don't insult either of us by denying it."

I shut my mouth and waited for him to continue. He inhaled a deep breath, expelling it through his nose.

"Justine, the girl—woman—you saw me with has been coming on to me for weeks, making it abundantly clear that she's available. I tried ignoring her, but the more I did, the more she flirted with other guys, some considerably older than she is, in a bid to get my attention."

A dubious expression must have flitted across my face because he gave me a faint smile.

"I'm not being egotistical, just factual."

"Right. I mean, okay."

"She's just a kid, and she's playing with fire. Lately, her behavior has escalated, and some of her chosen companions have concerned me enough that I've had one of my security detail follow her home when she leaves with these men to make sure nothing happens to her."

I sucked in a breath, and it sounded like a gasp. I hardly knew this guy, having only met him today, but my first impressions had been of a dour, broody, hard-nosed businessman who put his own interests first—always—and cared for no one other than himself.

First impressions weren't always right—and on this occasion, I'd been way off the mark.

This woman had potentially made a nuisance of herself, and he clearly wasn't interested in a fling or anything more with her, yet he'd cared enough to make sure she got home safely.

Which meant I could have been mistaken in regard to what I'd seen earlier.

"So, before..." I coaxed.

"That was me sending a warning of what she risked if she carried on in this vein. My methods might be blunt, but they're effective."

"I see."

I wasn't sure I did, but from the look in his eyes and the set of his jaw, he'd finished explaining himself.

I grazed my teeth over my lip. "Thank you for explaining it to me."

The merest hint of a smile touched his lips, disappearing by the time I'd blinked.

"I don't need the police crawling all over my club. It's bad for business."

"Oh, I wouldn't have called the police."

Except if I hadn't believed his explanation, I probably would have, even if it cost me the financial security Level Nine had to offer. Just like Johannes didn't want the police sniffing around his club, I didn't want them sniffing around me. Staying under the radar was key to keeping one step ahead of Mateo, and that meant staying away from the authorities.

Back in Oklahoma, Mateo had the police in his pocket. For all I knew, the same could be said of Los Angeles. I had no idea how far my husband's influence reached, and I was glad I wouldn't have to take the risk of finding out.

Johannes didn't respond to my denial, just eased that tall, elegant frame of his out of the chair and gestured to the door.

Guess that's my cue to leave.

"Well, um, I'd better go and help the guys clean up. I'll see you tomorrow?." My tone lifted, making it sound more like a question than a statement.

Johannes's curt nod sent a rush of relief-soaked adrenaline speeding through my veins.

"Don't be late."

"I won't."

I turned to leave.

"Ella."

I paused, returning my attention to him. His intense

stare heated my skin, and my stomach flipped. He might scowl more than he smiled, but damn, he was gorgeous. I shifted my weight from one foot to the other.

"Yes?"

"You did well tonight. Keep it up."

My spirits soared and something akin to joy swelled in my chest. It didn't take a genius to work out that pleasing Johannes Kingcaid wasn't an easy thing to accomplish.

I offered a faint smile. "I will."

I virtually skipped back to the bar, the weight I'd carried since witnessing the scene with Johannes and the young woman lifting. My smile was broad as I rejoined the team, who'd pretty much finished clearing down the bar. The empty club had a weird vibe, as if each customer had left a piece of themselves behind, a sense of their presence.

"What can I do?" I asked Stan.

"Enjoy this."

He handed me a wad of cash. My mouth parted as I flicked through the bills. There must have been at least three hundred dollars here. Maybe more. If I made even half of this on every shift, I'd soon have a decent nest egg saved in case we had to run again.

Money made everything that much easier.

"Wow. Are you sure?"

Stan chuckled. "Course I'm sure. It's your share of the tips. You've earned that and more. Although, if you don't want it..." He showed his palm. "I'll happily take it off your hands."

I grinned, shoving the money into the front pocket of my jeans. "Not a chance."

"You did good tonight, Ella. I think you're gonna work out just fine."

Praise from Johannes and now Stan. My chest puffed out that little bit more.

"Thank you. I appreciate your support and confidence in me. I won't let you down."

"Not me you have to worry about, honey. It's him."

He jerked his chin, and when I glanced over my shoulder, my gaze fell on Johannes standing with Tiffany and one of the security team, deep in conversation. As if he sensed my eyes on him, he turned his head and met my gaze.

Something passed between us, an inexplicable connection. Tingles crept down my arms to my fingertips, and for a few seconds, nothing else existed other than me and this enigmatic, alluring, intriguing man.

I tipped up my chin and smiled. He remained stoic, his lips flat, his eyes hooded. Then he looked away and shattered the spell.

"Keep him sweet, and you're golden," Stan said.

"I'll do my best."

I said good night to the rest of the team, sending a wave at Tiffany, who waved back and gave me that perfect smile once more, and then shouted, "See you tomorrow, Ella."

I'd been wrong about several things tonight, starting with my worries that I wouldn't fit in.

I'd fit in just fine.

I might not have looked like these other women, or most of the customers who had come through those doors to celebrate Nate O'Reilly's birthday, but no one seemed to care.

I'd worried that I'd stand out, but I'd blended into my surroundings like a scorpionfish, only a lot less deadly.

Unlike the man I'd run from.

As long as I stayed hidden in the shadows, I might just be able to make a life for me and Chloe here.

And if my camouflage failed, you could bet your ass I'd be ready to run.

Chapter 8

Johannes

And just when you think you've turned a corner, you get whacked in the face.

A WEEK HAD PASSED SINCE ELLA'S FIRST SHIFT, AND SHE'D SETTLED in well. Last night, she hadn't been on the schedule, which had given me the opportunity to visit my club in San Francisco. In a normal month, I spent maybe forty percent of my time at Level Nine. The last month I'd increased that to fifty percent, mainly down to my determination to win the coveted *Hottest Nightspot* award. But since I'd employed Ella, I'd upped my time spent here to eighty percent. Couldn't have the new girl ruining my chances of winning, although from what I'd witnessed so far, I had nothing to worry about.

She was hardworking and a natural behind the bar, and the clientele seemed to like her. Some a little too much, which always caused a burning sensation in my chest, though none of them had overstepped the mark enough for me to send in security.

I put my unusual reaction to male customers getting a little overfamiliar with Ella down to a commitment to offer a safe working environment for all my employees, but especially the women. Alcohol made some men braver —or more idiotic—than normal, and inappropriate behavior or making staff members feel unsafe or uneasy was intolerable to me. Ella wasn't any different from the rest. She was new, that was all. That was why I'd altered my working patterns. Once she settled in, I'd revert to normal.

Taking up my usual vantage point, which gave me an entire view of the club, I sipped from a bottle of water and scanned the crowd. Busy night for a Thursday, but according to the figures for the last few months, attendance on Thursdays had slowly crept up and was now almost ninety percent of a weekend night. Couldn't complain about those statistics, although I'd always strive for more.

My gaze kept straying to Ella as she dashed up and down the long bar, ensuring she treated every customer like a rock star, offering them a broad smile and a bit of chitchat before moving on to the next. I couldn't fault her work rate, and apart from that first night, which I put down to nerves, she hadn't broken a single glass. And she'd grown in confidence, too.

For a long time after Sadie, I'd doubted my instincts. After all, I'd placed my trust in someone who had almost gotten me killed. Taking a chance on Ella had been a leap of faith, a risk I wouldn't have felt confident making a few months ago, especially given the importance of Level Nine to the Kingcaid nightclub brand.

Yet so far, Ella had surpassed my expectations and given me a sliver of hope that maybe I could begin to trust my instincts once more. I couldn't figure out why her, why Ella, but I'd take it. There were times over the past six years where I'd thought I'd never claw my way out of the deep, dark hole Sadie had pushed me into, but perhaps there was a chink of light, a chance, however small, of rediscovering the man I'd once been.

A scuffle broke out on the dance floor. I gestured to my security team to move in and break it up. Seconds later, they'd dealt with the issue and removed the offenders. They'd receive a lifetime ban for their troubles. There were several things I didn't tolerate at my clubs, violence being one of them. The other was drugs. If anyone was found taking drugs in any of my establishments, my staff knew to call the police. We had a zero-tolerance policy for any form of substance abuse. Sure, we served alcohol, but if a customer took it too far and got completely hammered to the point they were falling over or abusing the staff or other patrons, my security immediately removed them.

I found my gaze pulled back to the bar once more. Ella was deep in conversation with a young guy in his early to mid-twenties. She nodded, smiled, and then handed him a bottle of beer. He caught her wrist and tugged her toward him. She lost her balance and stumbled.

Rage ignited in my stomach. *Fuck no. You picked on the wrong woman, asshole.* I shoved through the crowd and grabbed the guy by the scruff of the neck. "Get your fucking hands off her."

"Johannes, it's fine. I've got this."

"No one touches my employees without their permission and gets away with it." I shoved the guy away from me. "Out."

"Johannes!" Ella snapped. "I said I've got this."

"Hey, man." The guy raised his hands beside his head. "I didn't mean anything by it."

Ed, one of my security team, dashed over, but before he could haul the soon-to-be-banned customer from my club, Ella appeared and put herself between him and me, and the man.

"Johannes, I *said* I had it under control. Please, allow me to do my job."

My eyes flew wide, my lips parting in shock, both at her reaction to what had happened and at her reaction to me. I wasn't used to people questioning my decisions. "He put his hands on you. I don't stand for that in my club."

"He didn't mean to. He just wanted to talk and couldn't hear me properly over the noise."

She was yelling now, and I couldn't say with absolute certainty that the noise was the reason.

"I really didn't mean any trouble," the guy said. "I'm sorry if I overstepped."

"See?" Ella shooed me away with a flick of her wrist. "It's all under control." She turned to face the customer. "That's fifteen dollars. For the beer." She held out her hand.

My jaw dropped. This woman was... something else.

The guy pulled out his wallet and handed over a fifty-dollar bill. "Keep the change. And thanks. I like coming here. I'd hate for a misunderstanding to ruin what's fast become my favorite nightclub in the city."

Fuck. Me.

"You're welcome." She gave him a small smile. "And thanks for the tip. Enjoy your night."

Ella skirted past me and returned to her place behind the bar. The guy gnawed his bottom lip and winced as he looked over at me. "Are we cool, man? It won't happen again. I promise."

I glanced at Ed, then nodded. Ed retreated. "We're cool." I loomed over him, leaning down to put my mouth close to his ear. "But you so much as fucking touch her again, and we will have a major fucking issue. You feel me?"

The guy backed up, nodding furiously. "Got it." He spun around and disappeared into the crowd. I sought out Ella. Almost as if she felt my attention on her, she turned her head and gazed right at me, a small curve to her lips, her mossy-green irises almost black under the dim lights. Regardless, they sparkled. And then she winked.

She winked! At me.

My stomach flipped, and a long-forgotten sensation swam through my veins. It took me a few seconds to pin it down. Desire. Too bad I didn't fuck my staff. Banging an employee would just end up awkward, and Ella was far too good at her job to risk losing her over something as pointless as sex.

I made my way over to the bar, bracing one elbow on top, and watched her as she dashed from customer to customer. I must have been there about fifteen minutes when Stan tapped her on the shoulder and jerked his chin toward the door that led to the staff quarters, signaling her turn for a fifteen-minute break. But instead of heading that way, she sashayed over to me and set a fresh bottle of ice-cold water on the bar, even though I hadn't finished my current one.

"Here. You look like you need cooling down." She smirked, and I found my lips forming a half smile.

"Just so you know, I'd have done the same for any of my employees. Male, female, or nonbinary. Doesn't matter to me. No one gets to put their hands on my staff without their express permission."

She clasped a hand to her chest. "Wow. And here was me thinking I was special." She winked again, and my insides twisted in a knot.

"Sorry to disappoint you."

"I'll live."

"Aren't you due a break?"

"Trying to get rid of me?"

"Not at all. It's your break, not mine. If you want to spend it standing there, that's your call. It's a free country."

"Is it, though?"

I arched a brow. "A political statement? Hmm. Wouldn't have thought politics interested you."

"They don't. It's just an observation. Are any of us truly free? Aren't we all slaves to our landlords, or our need to put food on the table or gas in the car? To clothe ourselves and feed our kids? Women aren't even permitted to own their bodies. The government does. Freedom is an illusion, one created to keep us all in line, to sell a lie that moving forward will result in a better life."

Whoa. I blinked. "Deep."

"Maybe." She hitched a shoulder. "Depends on your perspective and your experiences that have led you to this point, I guess."

I flattened my lips. My experiences had led me to distrust women, but this probably wasn't the best time to raise that point. Besides, I distrusted myself to a far greater extent. If I'd paid more attention, maybe I'd have read between the lines and figured out what Sadie had intended before I'd walked right into her trap.

Nor could I understand what it meant to struggle to make ends meet. Neither I nor my entire family had ever had to worry about where the next meal was coming from. I counted myself extremely fortunate, as did my entire family. Money didn't always buy happiness or good fortune, but on my dark days, I tried to remind myself that there were so many out there who had it far tougher than I did. I was proud of the fact that my family donated huge sums of money to various charities each year, although it never quite seemed like enough. There was always more to be done.

"And on that happy note, cheers." She tapped her own bottle of water against mine, then took a long drink. "Can I ask you something?"

"Depends on what it is?"

"Why do you always wear those?" She jerked her chin at my high-necked sweater. "Aren't you hot?"

In direct contrast to her question, a coldness hit my chest, and my hand automatically traveled to my throat, the ugly scar and evidence of my weakness hidden beneath the close-fitting turtleneck. I glared at her. "What I wear is none of your business, Miss Reyes. And your break is over, so I suggest you get back to work before I decide I can make do with one less nosy bartender."

I whipped away, but not before I'd witnessed a flash of profound hurt sweep across her face.

Chapter 9

Ella

Correction: First impressions are *always* right.

I spent the remainder of my shift nursing an ache in my chest caused by Johannes's biting retort to an innocent question. If the tables were turned and he'd asked me the same thing about my outfit, I'd have told him that clothes were a luxury I couldn't afford but that I tried to look as smart as my bank account permitted.

Instead, he'd bitten my head off and threatened to fire me. It seemed the more time I spent working at Level Nine, the greater my chances of getting fired grew. But no matter how much I thought about it, I couldn't for the life of me figure out how what I'd said had offended him.

Maybe he had a third nipple and worried about gaping

shirts revealing his secret. Or he had a ridiculously hairy chest, hence the high-necked sweaters. Or perhaps he was growing a replacement body part somewhere about his torso or, far more likely, a personality.

God knows he could do with a new one of those.

Pushing aside my fears of losing my job, I smiled and chatted with the customers and made certain I delivered the best service I could. If Johannes chose to fire me, I'd ensure it had nothing to do with my work and everything to do with his attitude. I couldn't control the latter, but I sure as hell could the former.

I'd bet the only reason he kept his staff was because the tips were so darned good. Ever since I'd started working here, I'd earned more money than I'd dreamed of. Even on non-weekend days, the tips were healthy. Fridays and Saturdays were on another level. I'd only worked one weekend, but Stan had assured me the wad of cash he'd pressed into my hand wasn't unusual.

As closing time neared, the club emptied out, save for a few stragglers determined to eke out the last few minutes strutting their stuff on the dance floor. I grabbed a cleaning cloth, and a few minutes later, Tiffany joined me. She'd taken me under her wing, and in the short time I'd worked here, I'd grown fond of the beautiful, leggy blonde. Guilt pricked my chest at the clichéd assumption I'd made when I'd arrived for my first shift, though there was no denying I was the odd one out. A plain Jane in a sea of stunning beauties, and I couldn't help wondering why Johannes had hired me when I was so different from the other women. Even the male bartenders were attractive. Not that it mattered. He had, and I was determined to cling to this job by my fingernails if necessary.

"You look beat," Tiffany said when I yawned for the fifth time straight. "Why don't you take off? I've got this."

As much as I'd love to take her up on the offer, after the earlier spat with Johannes, the last thing I needed was for him to think I was slacking and pushing work on the other staff members. I shook my head.

"I'm good. I like to do my fair share."

"Ella, you do more than your fair share. I thought that on your first night, and I've thought it every night since." She nudged me. "Go on. It's five minutes."

I cast a furtive glance around the empty club. I couldn't see Johannes, but knowing my luck, he'd catch me as I stepped outside and that'd be it. No more job, no more enormous tips. I couldn't risk it. Not even for five minutes.

"I'd like to finish."

Tiffany shrugged. "Suit yourself." She grabbed a cloth and ran it under the faucet, then scrubbed at a sticky cocktail stain on the bar while I put away the last of the glasses. Stan did his final checks, then handed out our tips. My eyes bugged out. Another fabulous night. It was still early days, but if this continued, then in a few months, I might even be able to afford the rent on a place of my own.

I'd miss Ginny, of course, but I owed it to Chloe to show her that it was important to work hard and reap the rewards. Kids were sponges, and I didn't want her getting the impression that someone else would take care of her. My daughter would grow up independent and able to take care of herself, and never, *ever,* allow a man to control her the way I'd allowed Mateo to control me. I'd been too immature, too blinded by his smooth, sophisticated style. Too enraptured by his extravagance. I'd loved living in luxurious surroundings and being able to have whatever I'd wanted.

I'd loved having a man to take care of me.

Then the blinders had come off, and I'd had my eyes well and truly opened. And what I'd seen had terrified me.

Chloe would grow up smarter than that. Less gullible, more suspicious and questioning of the people around her. Bad people were everywhere, waiting to take advantage of innocence to further their own ends.

Oh, I had no doubts Mateo loved me. In his own way. But his love came in the form of possession rather than protection. He believed we were his belongings. He owned us, which was the reason he'd never stop searching for us.

And I'd never stop running from him.

Tiffany walked me to my car, waiting until I'd gotten inside and driven away. She waved as I exited the parking lot and drove onto the highway. I stuck my hand out the window and waved back at her. If things were different, Tiffany could be the older sister I'd never had. But I couldn't afford friends. Closeness led to loose lips, to questions I wasn't prepared to answer.

Couldn't risk answering.

At least I didn't have those worries with my boss. He was too self-absorbed to bother about little old me. And that suited me just fine. But I couldn't deny how much I enjoyed those moments that passed between us, the ones where my stomach would turn over and my fingers would tingle with pleasure before Johannes snapped the tenuous link.

I pulled up outside Ginny's house, shut the car door as

quietly as I could, and trudged inside. The house was deathly quiet. I crept down the hallway and slipped inside Chloe's room. She'd thrown her comforter on the floor but clung tightly to her brown bear, one of the few things I'd taken when we'd fled.

Kneeling beside her bed, I brushed her ebony hair out of her eyes and leaned down to kiss her forehead. She felt a little warm, but nothing too concerning. I laid the comforter over her, gave her one last loving glance, and then tiptoed to my own room.

I peeled off my clothes, threw them in the laundry basket, and collapsed into bed.

The smell of sizzling bacon and the aroma of coffee woke me. My eyes were stuck together, and my head felt as if it weighed a hundred pounds, but I hauled myself out of bed and made it to the bathroom. My plans for today comprised of taking Chloe to school and then crashing for several hours. As much as I loved working at Level Nine, I wasn't used to late shifts and snatching my sleep in pockets of time. I'd get used to it, eventually, but right now I felt as if I were one of the walking dead, a zombified version of myself that required three strong cups of coffee before I could join the human race.

I showered, dressed, and popped my head into the kitchen to say a quick "Good morning" to Ginny before making my way to Chloe's room. It surprised me that she wasn't up already. She usually liked to help Ginny make breakfast, although *hinder* was far more accurate. Still, Ginny would give her the very grown-up job of putting napkins on the small kitchen table. She'd even taught her how to fold them all fancy, and Chloe loved it.

"Morning, pumpkin." I opened her drapes, letting light flood in. "Time to get up."

"Mommy, I don't feel so good."

I perched on the edge of her bed. She did look flushed. I felt her forehead. Hot. Too hot.

"Hold on there, baby girl." I dashed back to my room and grabbed a thermometer from the bathroom. Popping it into her mouth, I waited.

A hundred and one degrees.

Shit.

I updated Ginny and she prepared a few cold towels while I gave Chloe some medicine to hopefully reduce her fever. A hundred and one was high, but nothing to worry too much about. If it climbed higher, I'd have to call a doctor, one I couldn't afford. Goddammit. A few more weeks at Level Nine and I'd have enough money saved to pay for a couple doctors' visits.

Ginny would loan me the money from her widow's pension, but I hated the idea of taking advantage of her kindness once more.

Best thing was to hope the over-the-counter medicine and cool compresses worked.

I called Chloe's kindergarten teacher to let her know Chloe wouldn't be attending school today, then dragged a chair in from the kitchen and sat by my baby's bed, watching her like a hawk. Exhaustion swamped me, but sleep would have to wait.

Please, God, let her be okay.

Ginny pressed a cheese sandwich into my hand a short while before disappearing to the grocery store. She returned with more medicine, giving me one of her special glares when I reached for my purse.

Not for the first time, I wondered what I'd done to deserve a guardian angel like Ginny. Someone must have been looking after me the day I'd bumped into her in that diner.

I must have fallen asleep, waking to the sounds of a hacking cough. By the time I'd fully opened my eyes, Chloe had thrown up all over her comforter. She promptly burst into tears. I bathed and changed her while Ginny replaced her bedding. I gave her another dose of medicine and retook her temperature. It had come down slightly, but not nearly enough. Maybe by the morning, she'd be on the mend.

I was due on shift in an hour, but there wasn't a chance in hell I'd leave my child when she was sick, no matter what it cost me. Even so, my fingers shook as I dialed the telephone number for Level Nine, and my stomach rolled over and over as I imagined Johannes's reaction to the news that I couldn't work tonight.

If the man threatened to fire me for commenting on the clothes he wore, chances were slim that he'd forgive me for skipping work so close to my shift. Whatever happened, happened. Chloe came first. Always.

"Level Nine, Stan speaking. How can I help?"

Relief flooded me. My shoulders slumped, and I blew out a breath. Stan. Thank God.

"Hey, Stan, it's Ella. I'm so, so sorry, but I can't make it in tonight. Something's come up." I'd told no one about Chloe. Not that I'd chosen to keep her a secret on purpose, but more that the subject hadn't materialized. We were all too busy working our asses off to spend time on idle chitchat.

"It's a family emergency. I wouldn't run out on you if it wasn't serious."

I bit my lip, waiting for him to bawl me out. Or maybe Stan had the power to fire me, too.

"Ah, shit. Sorry, honey. Don't worry about it. We'll manage. You just take care of whatever problem you have, and if you can't make it in tomorrow either, you let me know."

"Thank you so much, Stan. I feel awful."

"Shit happens, babe. Life throws us curveballs, and all we can do is duck and hope we don't get smashed in the face. It's no biggie."

That was a lie. Coping with an unplanned staff absence was a huge issue in a place as popular as Level Nine. And on a Friday night, too. But what could I do?

"I'll call you tomorrow and let you know what's happening. If I can be there, I will be."

"You take care."

Stan cut the call before I could thank him. I envisaged him putting the phone down, then cursing me to hell and back. It was what I'd have been tempted to do had the situation been reversed.

At least it wasn't Johannes who'd answered the phone. Something told me his response would have been a lot worse than Stan's. God only knew what he'd say when he arrived for work tonight to find out I wasn't there.

Well, too bad. My baby needed me.

Chloe shivered as I set my phone on her nightstand. I lay beside her and pulled her to my side, humming a lullaby. Eventually, her breathing evened out and sleep pulled her under.

I lay staring at the ceiling for a few minutes, praying that when tomorrow came, my baby would be better and I would still have a job.

And if neither of those things happened... I wasn't sure what I'd do.

Chapter 10

Johannes

And there we have it.
Yet another disappointment.

I PARKED MY CAR IN MY RESERVED SPACE AT LEVEL NINE AT FIVE minutes before one. The parking lot teemed with Ferraris, Lamborghinis, and Aston Martins, and despite the club closing in an hour's time, the line to gain entry snaked around the side of the building. The clear evidence of success should please me, but after an unexpected trip to San Francisco to fire the manager for skimming, I was too tired and too pissed off to celebrate.

And now I had to find another fucking manager who met my exacting standards. In record time.

Not exactly an easy task to accomplish.

My elder brother, Asher, would have a whole host of

potential candidates lined up in thirty seconds flat. All I'd have to do was ask him for help.

Problem was, I saw that as failure, even if he wouldn't.

This was *my* business, *my* issue to solve.

I exited the vehicle and made my way to the staff entrance. As I stepped inside, a ball of anticipation weighed heavily in my stomach. It pained me to admit it, but I was looking forward to seeing Ella. I owed her an apology for last night. She wasn't to know how touchy I was about my injury, and hiding the ugly scar on my neck was the reason my closet consisted of rows upon rows of turtleneck sweaters and high-necked shirts, all in my favorite color: black.

It matched my heart.

Maybe my soul, too.

Whatever, she hadn't deserved my vitriol, nor the blunt threat to fire her, either.

But that wasn't the only reason for the fluttering in my abdomen or the way the hairs on my arms stood up as I thought of how much I wanted to see her.

It wasn't an easy thing for me to acknowledge, but fuck, I found her attractive. Maybe that was why I also found it so easy to castigate her. On some level, I didn't want to want her.

Not that it mattered.

No fucking the staff.

Quality employees were hard to find and even harder to retain. Level Nine had an exceptional reputation, but only fools rested on their laurels. This was Los Angeles, the city where everything you'd worked for could come crashing down around your ears in a microsecond.

Nothing would get in the way of my single-minded goal to win the *Hottest Nightspot in LA* award.

I emerged into the main part of the club, my eyes immediately scanning the bar.

No Ella.

I frowned. Where was she? Maybe she was on her break. I spun around and made my way to the employee break room.

Empty.

I retraced my steps, heading over to the bar. It didn't take long for Stan to notice me. He grabbed a bottle of iced water, twisted off the cap, and set it on the bar.

"Hey, man. How was San Fran?"

I shrugged. "Fine."

Stan might have been my head bartender, and if I could clone him a hundred times over, I'd be in a position to grow the business far faster. But that didn't mean I shared company business with him. Or any of my employees, for that matter. The gossip train would soon pull into the station, and everyone would know the reason for my unscheduled trip upstate.

"Where's Ella?"

"She's not in tonight."

I jerked my head back. *What did he just say?* "She isn't here? Why the hell not?"

Stan, sensing my tone, rubbed the back of his neck. "She called. Earlier today. Said she had a family emergency and couldn't work her shift tonight."

The earlier excitement I'd experienced fled in the deluge of fury that engulfed my insides. A week. She'd worked here for a fucking *week,* and already the drama had begun. And on a fucking Friday night, too.

Jesus Christ Almighty.

I was tired, irritable, and pissed at the trouble that had landed on my doorstep unexpectedly, and now I had issues with a woman I'd taken a chance on, for no other reason, I now realized, than my dick had perked up the second I'd laid eyes on her.

My dick had gotten me into a fuckload of trouble six years ago. This situation was completely different, but still, that stupid appendage had led me to make a decision I'd fast come to regret.

If I didn't like orgasms so much, I'd cut the damn thing off.

I pivoted and marched to my office, Stan's voice calling out to me fading into the sounds of the club. I pulled her resume from the overflowing filing cabinet and noted her address.

Right, Miss Reyes. Let's find out what the hell you're playing at.

Tires spinning, I gunned the gas pedal on my black Maserati and skidded onto the road. An oncoming car honked his horn as he swerved into the other lane. He pulled in front of me, then slammed on his brakes. Dick move. I pulled alongside him, and he flipped me the finger.

Ignoring him, I put my foot down. The car powered forward, engine growling. In seconds, the dick in the beat-up Chevy disappeared from view.

Forty-five minutes later, I pulled up outside a small house with a neat front yard jam-packed with colorful pots and an abundance of flowers, and a wicker mat by the front door with "Welcome" woven into the design. Funny, but given Ella's clear desperation for work, I hadn't envisaged her living somewhere like this. The house might've been small, but it was well cared for and in a pleasant neighborhood. Maybe she wasn't as poor as I'd thought.

Which, I had to admit, would make it easier to fire her. If I thought for a single second she was trying to exploit her position, or prey on Stan's good nature, she was done. Surely she couldn't think, for a heartbeat, that I was the sort of man to stand for employees who pulled a sickie every time they felt like a duvet day. And if she was, well, I was about to disillusion her.

I stepped onto the sidewalk and had almost reached the door when common sense brought me to a stop.

Yes, I was angry. My clenched fists and quivering thigh muscles told me that, but I also wasn't enough of a jerk to bang on a young woman's door at two o'clock in the morning and demand answers for why she hadn't turned up for work.

I returned to my car and drove home, but after lying on my back and staring at the ceiling for a solid hour, I gave up on sleep. Might as well get a jump on the search for a new fucking manager.

The light from the laptop screen almost blinded me. I squinted and reduced the brightness. Opening the email program, I drafted four messages to various executive recruitment consultants I'd built relationships with and included a detailed description of the kind of person I was looking for to manage the San Francisco property. My standards were high and nonnegotiable.

Which made me think. How the hell had Douglas, the guy I'd fired in San Fran, slipped through the net? I'd dropped the fucking ball on that one.

This time, I'd demand increased background checks on every potential candidate *before* I wasted my time interviewing them. Unlike bar staff, the managers of my clubs had far-reaching responsibilities.

I added a paragraph to each of the emails, mandating a deep dive on the personal, financial, and professional backgrounds of anyone they chose to put forward for consideration, then pressed Send.

Fuck, still only four o'clock.

My scar itched, a sure sign my anxiety levels were spiking. Best to get rid of some of this excess adrenaline before confronting Ella.

I dressed in athletic gear and made my way to the gym I'd had installed in the basement of my home. Running ten miles while wearing a high-necked sweater in the LA heat was only something a crazy man would do, and while I'd occupied that state of mind for a while after my attack, I wasn't in that headspace any longer.

Apart from the nightmares. When they came to me in the dead of night, I found myself right back there, on that fateful evening, searching for something I could have done that would have changed the outcome.

I caught sight of the vicious, jagged scar that ran three-quarters of the way across my neck. If the knife had sunk even one millimeter deeper, I wouldn't have made it. I ran the tip of my forefinger over the bumpy skin. I hated this thing. Hated what it signified. That I was weak, stupid, gullible. Taken in by a pretty face and a warm pussy. And all along she'd been plotting to rob me. The consequences of her actions were something I'd have to live with for the rest of my life.

And the worst scars weren't even on the outside.

I put on some lively music and jumped onto the treadmill. Five miles passed, then ten, then fifteen before my legs gave out and I stopped the machine. My body glistened with sweat, but the voices in my mind had quieted, and that sense of ants crawling over my skin had fucked off, too.

After showering, I dressed in what I called my "uniform." Black slacks, black turtleneck sweater, black Italian loafers. Before Sadie, I'd loved wearing colors. Reds, greens, blues. They complemented my dark hair and pale coloring. But wearing all black weirdly made me feel in command. I hadn't a clue why, but I wasn't about to fuck around with something that worked.

Getting jumped by a bunch of grown men, wrestled to the ground, kicked until my kidneys bled and I pissed blood for a solid two months, and then the pièce de résistance of having my throat slashed and almost bleeding to death kind of took away any sense of control. Now, everything I did was about maintaining control of every thread of my life.

At seven o'clock, with the sun just peeking over the horizon, I locked up my house and drove to my favorite coffee shop. Sitting outside, I drank a banana and passionfruit smoothie and pulled apart a croissant while the sun climbed higher in the sky. At seven thirty, I set off for Ella's, pulling up outside her house just after eight.

I climbed out, slammed the door, and made my way up the narrow path. I rapped on the door. There were sounds of someone moving around inside. When the door opened, I took a step back. A woman in her sixties with gray hair pulled back into a neat bun greeted me. Her blue eyes narrowed as she examined me from head to toe.

"Yes, young man?"

Maybe this was Ella's mother? Or maybe she'd given the agency a false address. I didn't know jack shit about her family or her background, and after the crap that had gone down with Douglas, I'd begun to regret not delving a little deeper, even if she was the most junior of employees.

Pretty face. Warm pussy. My downfall.

But that was then. This was now. And besides, Ella and Douglas were two completely different situations. Incomparable.

"Hi, Mrs..." I trailed off.

She offered me nothing other than a raised eyebrow. I prepared myself for a door slam, ready to shove my foot inside if that happened. I wasn't leaving here until I'd spoken with Ella.

"I'm looking for Ella Reyes."

A slight flare in her eyes, accompanied by a widening, told me I had the right address. That was something, at least.

"And who may I say is calling?"

Very proper.

"Johannes Kingcaid. Her boss," I added for extra impact.

"Mr. Kingcaid."

Ella appeared behind the woman. She ran a hand through hair that hadn't seen a brush this morning. Dark circles, almost reminiscent of bruises, sat beneath her eyes, and if I didn't know better, I'd say she hadn't slept in a week.

Even so, my pulse quickened, and the hairs on the back of my neck lifted. Forget pretty. Ella Reyes was a beautiful woman, and in another lifetime, I'd be asking her on a date, not contemplating firing her.

"I-I... What are you doing here?"

I folded my arms across my chest. "Coming to see why you left your teammates shorthanded last night, and whether your excuse is valid enough for you to still have a job at the end of it."

"Now hold on," the elder woman exclaimed.

"It's okay, Ginny. I've got this. You go for your walk." Ella put her hand on the woman's arm, easing her out of the way. "Please come in, Mr. Kingcaid."

She turned around and trudged down the dimly lit hallway. I edged past Ginny, who still guarded the door, glaring at me with the heat of a blast furnace, and followed, emerging into a small kitchen with a table tucked in the corner and walls tiled in a bright yellow. The front door closed, I guessed with Ginny on the other side.

I had to admit that a part of me was relieved. She had that older-woman vibe going on that reminded me of my mother. The kind who never took any crap and had a knack for making you feel about twelve with nothing more than a sharp glance and a curt word.

"Have a seat."

She waved her hand at the table. I remained standing. She gave a half shrug almost as if to say, "Suit yourself."

"Coffee?"

"I'll pass." I tracked her moving about the kitchen. "Care to explain yourself?"

Jesus, Johannes. Cut the woman some slack.

Even a jerk like me could tell she'd had a gut full of whatever shit life had thrown at her between leaving my club on Thursday night, less than thirty hours ago, and now.

Before she had a chance to answer, a child's voice called out. "Mommy."

Ella darted past me and into a room on the opposite side of the hallway. I trekked after her, pausing on the threshold.

The room was gloomy, the drapes still closed, and lying on the bed was a little girl, around five or six, maybe, with hair as dark as Ella's. She was curled into Ella's body, hacking up her lungs with a cough far too aggressive for someone her size.

Ella rocked her, kissed her hair, said soothing words in a tone too low for me to pick up. My ribs squeezed tight. On one level, I missed the intimacy of being in a relationship, of caring for someone and having them care for me. But the bigger part of me, the part Sadie had created, wouldn't allow it. "Self-preservation above all" had become my motto, indelibly inked into my being from that night forward.

The little girl's coughing fit abated, and Ella lay her back down on the bed. Innocent eyes reminiscent of Ella's turned to me.

"Who are you?"

Ella glanced over her shoulder, then returned her attention to her daughter. "That's Mommy's boss." Another glance in my direction accompanied by a raised eyebrow. "Right?"

Remorse hung over me, heavy as a thundercloud, and I nodded vigorously. "Absolutely."

Her exhaustion and worry lifted for a moment. "Would you mind giving me a moment? I won't be long."

"Of course. I'll wait for you in the kitchen."

Chapter 11

Ella

Too many questions,
and answers I refuse to give.

I gave Chloe another dose of cough medicine, stroking her hair for a few moments until she fell back to sleep. The cough had started around two o'clock this morning, and she'd been up every hour since then. Poor little mite had to be exhausted. Her fever had reduced a little more, down to one hundred degrees now. With any luck, it would come down further still today, and I wouldn't have to call for a doctor.

I hated being poor. *Hated it.* I couldn't care less about the clothes and the cars and the fancy house. Since escaping Mateo and his poisonous world, I'd come to realize that what really mattered in life was a roof over your head, food on the table, and enough money to take care of those you loved.

I had the first two thanks to Ginny, but the third was where I fell far short of what was needed. A mother's first job was to keep her baby safe, and, well, here I was making do with over-the-counter cough syrup and homemade remedies.

Johannes took up eighty percent of the space in Ginny's tiny kitchen, or that was what it seemed like to me. Or maybe it was his presence that gave me a sense of claustrophobia. At least he'd confirmed I still had a job. That was something to cling to, a sliver of good news in a sea of disasters.

Okay, maybe I was slightly exaggerating, but sleep deprivation and worry did strange things to a person.

"Sure you don't want that coffee?" I plucked a mug off the shelf and filled it to the brim with a pot Ginny had made thirty minutes earlier.

"I'm good."

I added a dash of cream and pulled out a seat at the table, sinking into it with a heavy thump. My legs were barely holding me up, and my eyes could do with matchsticks to prop them open, hence the caffeine. I'd need a ton of the stuff just to get through today. There was no chance I could work tonight. Might as well rip the Band-Aid off on that one right away.

"I won't be able to work tonight either. If that changes your mind about firing me, then go right ahead. I'm too exhausted to care."

It wasn't true. I cared. I'd had a taste of working in a top-class place and the benefits—namely, the tips—that came with employment. I didn't want to go back to waiting tables in some fleapit diner and picking up an extra dollar here and there. Landing the job at Level Nine had been the first stroke of luck I'd had in forever. Right now, my fate was in the hands of a man who, I felt it safe to say, put his own interests first. Always.

Johannes took a seat at the table. "Do you really think I'd fire you?"

"That's what you came here to do, wasn't it?"

Exhaustion also made me brave, it seemed. Or stupid. Johannes's reaction would decide which one was accurate. His lips lifted. Couldn't exactly call it a smile, but they moved in that direction.

"I admit, I wasn't happy when I arrived at the club at one o'clock this morning to find that you hadn't shown up for work."

One o'clock? Oh, so he hadn't been there for most of last night.

"I was in San Francisco dealing with some urgent business."

Ah. My question must have shown on my face. I kept quiet, waiting for him to continue.

"And I also admit that firing you was a distinct possibility if I'd discovered you didn't have a good reason for calling off work."

I opened my mouth, then shut it when his hand came up.

"But now I know you had a good reason."

He moved his chair back and crossed one long leg over the other. The movement drew my eye for a second. There was something alluring about an elegant man, and

Johannes had elegance in spades. His height helped, as did his physique and the air of mystique he carried off so well.

"Have you called a doctor?"

His blunt, unexpected question dragged me from my musings. I bit my lip, considering the best way to phrase my answer. In the end, I kept it short.

"No."

"Why not?'

My eyebrows flew up my head. Okay, there was blunt, and then there was downright none-of-your-fucking-business. "Excuse me?"

"Your daughter is clearly sick. A medical professional should see her."

The temperature of my blood shot up several degrees, mainly because he was right, and I knew he was right, and there wasn't a damned thing I could do about it. "For your information, we don't all have wads of cash idly lying around. Doctors cost money. Money I don't have."

I thought my curt response would have forced him into retreat. Instead, he doubled down.

"Can't her father pay?"

My back stiffened, and about a dozen alarms went off in my head. He was getting too personal, too close. Goddammit. I shouldn't have let him in the house. Now he knew far more about me than I was comfortable sharing. He knew I was dirt-poor. He knew I had a precious daughter. And if I didn't get him out of here right now, he'd prod and poke until he'd compelled me to tell him the precise reason her father couldn't pay her medical bills.

I might not have seen any drug dealing at Level Nine, but that didn't mean it wasn't going on. Clubs were meccas for pushers and drug users alike, and for all I knew, Johannes might have links to Mateo, however tenuous, in a six-degrees-of-separation kind of way. He had to go. Now. I set my coffee cup on the table and rose to my feet.

"My personal life is not up for discussion. I appreciate your understanding and for keeping my job open until Chloe is feeling better, but I would like you to leave."

He stared at me, his jaw locked up tight. But he didn't move. *He didn't move.*

I fisted my hands on my hips and stood taller, my back as straight as a pencil. Thank goodness he'd taken a seat. Otherwise, my attempt to make myself more intimidating would have failed miserably.

"If he's a deadbeat dad, then you should involve the authorities."

Okay, that's enough. I pointed to the door. "I asked you nicely. Now I'm telling you. Out."

Another few seconds scraped by before he eased himself out of the chair, taking his goddamn time about it. He dusted off his sweater, even though it was pristine, as always.

"Keep me informed on your expected return date. I have a business to run."

He sauntered down the hallway, a confident swagger to his walk, the kind of swagger all powerful men had. It took everything within me not to throw my coffee cup at him, but since that would make a mess and I *hated* messes, I refrained. The front door clicked shut. My legs wobbled. Gripping the edge of the table to brace myself, I cursed the stupid bug that Chloe had caught, cursed the lack of money in my purse, cursed Mateo and his illegal business.

And I cursed Johannes Kingcaid, too. For coming here uninvited and forcing me to reveal a part of my personal life I'd kept private until now. The more people knew about me, the greater the chances of Mateo finding me, and I could not allow that to happen.

I checked on Chloe. Still fast asleep, thank goodness. I pressed my hand to her forehead. Hmm, warm, but not as warm as this morning. Maybe it was blind optimism rather than reality, but her cheeks weren't quite as rosy as before. Maybe her fever was on the way out, and her hacking cough would soon follow.

Kissing her forehead, I closed the door and returned to the kitchen. The spurt of anger brought about by Johannes's probing had withered, leaving me with an emptiness inside. This life I'd been thrust into, thanks to my husband, was far from the gullible dreams of an eighteen-year-old, all starry-eyed at the fact that she'd turned the head of a wealthy man much older than she. Ahead lay a long path filled with fear and loneliness. But as long as I kept Chloe safe and out of Mateo's reach, that was all that mattered.

I made a fresh pot of coffee and stuck two slices of bread in the toaster, staring through Ginny's sunny yellow blinds at nothing in particular while I waited for them to pop. I spread a thin layer of butter across the top, then loaded them up with grape jelly and retook my seat at the table. Two bites and I'd had enough. My stomach churned with worry and anxiety both for Chloe and for how exposed I felt under the sharp blue gaze of Johannes Kingcaid.

By throwing him out, all I'd done was pique his curiosity. I should have lied. I could have made up anything. Hell, I could have told him her father was dead. That would have cut off his questioning at the knees. Besides, to me, Mateo was dead. He'd died the day I'd uncovered how he made a living and the dangers he'd introduced into our daughter's life. Into *my* life, and without giving either of us a choice in the matter.

Ugh. I could kick myself in the ass. If I'd stuck to yoga, I might've been able to. As it was, all I could do was mentally berate myself for being an idiot.

I sipped my coffee, my mind focusing in on Johannes. I'd overreacted before when it had crossed my mind that Johannes and Mateo might know each other. Of course they didn't. I hadn't seen any drug dealing at Level Nine because there was none. My mind was playing tricks. That was all. Stress and worry causing a whirlwind of implausible thoughts to run riot.

But my, what an intriguing, surly, intense man he was. So beautiful, yet empty. No, not empty.

Broken.

For all his riches in the monetary sense, that man was deeply unhappy. It was right there in his eyes. They had the same flat hollowness as mine did, although mine were also tinged with fear, whereas Johannes's were filled with recrimination.He'd either witnessed or suffered trauma.

Whatever he'd gone through, it proved the old saying right—that money didn't bring happiness. It only enhanced your life if you were already happy. And it didn't save anyone from the ravages that the hand of fate doled out at will.

Pushing thoughts of my intriguing boss aside, I discarded the half-eaten toast in the trash and went to check on Chloe.

Chapter 12

Ella

Turns out that good deeds do exist, but at what price?

I ran the almost dry cloth under the faucet, squeezing out excess water. A couple of hours after Johannes had left, Chloe's fever had spiked again, and her cough had considerably worsened, the hacking sound drawing a wince from me every time she had a coughing fit. I'd talked to Ginny, and we'd both decided that if her fever didn't break in the next hour, I'd take her to the emergency room at County. There'd be at least a four-hour wait to be seen, but what other choice did I have?

My biggest worry was having to give personal details—albeit fake ones—and that it would, somehow, lead Mateo to us. For all I knew, he had a team monitoring hospitals for a woman with a five-year-old child matching Chloe's description. I wouldn't put anything past him. If he could keep his position as the head of an international drug organization from me for all those years, then who knew how far and how deep his reach was? He could have eyes on me right this second.

I glanced over my shoulder, almost as if I expected to find him standing directly behind me, running a hand through his salt-and-pepper hair, a villainous smile on his too-handsome face.

A shudder ran through me. I dreaded to think what he'd do to me if he ever found out where I was. But I couldn't allow my fear to damage Chloe's health. She came first. Always had, always would.

One hour.

Then it was decision time.

I returned to Chloe's bedroom.

"Here," Ginny said, "I'll do it. You look dead on your feet."

Grateful, I handed the cool towel to her and went to sit down, but before my butt hit the chair, a knock at the door interrupted me.

"Who's that?" I asked.

Ginny cocked a brow. "Seeing through walls isn't something I've yet mastered."

I stuck out my tongue at her. "Funny."

"Go answer it." She jerked her chin. "And if it's Fred from next door come to ask me out on a date, again, tell him my answer is the same as the previous twelve times he's asked."

"You keeping score? Maybe Fred just needs to be a little more persistent."

Ginny wagged her finger. "You give that man ideas, and you and I will be having words."

I chuckled to myself, the moment of levity a welcome distraction, and trudged down the hallway. Poor Fred. Got to give the man ten out of ten for effort, even if it was misplaced.

I opened the door.

It wasn't Fred.

A tall, reedy-looking man with dark, curly hair and a long, thin nose, which matched his physique, was standing on Ginny's front step. Dressed in a snappy suit and a cobalt-blue tie, he carried a briefcase, one of those that door-to-door salesmen often hauled along, stuffed with household items that plenty bought but no one used.

"Yes?"

"Miss Reyes?"

I stiffened. "Who wants to know?"

His smile was meant to reassure. Didn't work on me. I folded my arms and made myself as tall as possible.

"I'm Doctor Magnusson. I'm here to see Chloe."

My head snapped back so fast I thought I might've broken my neck. I rubbed at the nape and narrowed my eyes. "Who called you?"

"Mr. Kingcaid. He said I was to come right by."

I ground my teeth. The interfering *bastard.* He knew full well I couldn't afford a damned doctor, yet he'd butted his nose in where it wasn't wanted and sent one anyway. Who the *hell* did he think he was?

And on a Saturday, too. I was almost certain that weekend visits were even more costly than weekday ones.

"I'm afraid you've had a wasted visit, Doctor Magnusson."

"Oh?" He frowned. "Do I have the wrong house?" He stepped back and checked the number stamped on the wooden porch. "I'm sure this is the right address."

"It's the right address, but you've received the wrong information."

His frown deepened. "You don't have a sick child?"

A band locked around my chest. Having a doctor standing right there, with the training and medicine to help my daughter, when I knew I couldn't afford his fee was a form of torture no one should have to endure.

"Yes, I do, but what I'm lacking, Doctor Magnusson, is the ability to pay you."

"Ah." A broad grin spread across his face, and two dimples popped, giving him a boyish look that belied his middle age. "That's all taken care of. Mr. Kingcaid gave strict instructions that all bills for Chloe's care were to go to him."

If a stiff breeze blew through at this moment, it'd knock me right over. Why would Johannes Kingcaid do something as compassionate as this? I should be grateful. Instead, a flush of annoyance made me grind my teeth. Damn man coming here, making out that he was going to fire me, poking around in my personal life and asking unwanted questions, then sending a doctor over to my house—Ginny's house—to take care of *my* daughter. All he'd done was shine a light on my appalling failure as a mother.

"May I come in?"

I blinked several times in quick succession. If I let the doctor treat Chloe, then I'd be in Johannes's debt, and powerful men like him always collected. If I turned the doctor away, I'd have to take Chloe to the ER and all the inherent risks that came with it.

My lungs crushed under the weight of an impossible choice. There was only one sensible course of action, and it was standing right in front of me.

I stood back, motioning to the doctor. "Please, come in. She's just down the hall."

Ginny's eyebrows shot north when I entered Chloe's bedroom and introduced her to Doctor Magnusson. She stared at me, questions in her eyes. I shook my head and shrugged.

Hovering like a mother hen while the doctor examined Chloe, it took Ginny's firm hand on my arm for me to back off and give the man some space. I wasn't a medical expert, but his examination couldn't have been more thorough, and twenty minutes later, he snapped his bag closed and rose to his feet.

"Chloe has a nasty case of bronchitis," he pronounced. "Nothing that a hefty dose of antibiotics won't clear up in a few days." He handed me a prescription. "I've given her a shot, just to move things along. She's to take one of these three times a day, starting four hours from now. I'll stop by tomorrow to see how she's doing. Make sure she gets plenty of fluids."

I clutched the prescription to my chest, the tension of the last twenty-four hours sliding off my shoulders like grease off a plate.

"Thank you, Doctor Magnusson." I saw him to the door, hovering on the step while he climbed into his car and drove away.

Ginny bustled up behind me, snatching the prescription

from my hand. "I'll go get this filled. You sit with Chloe. And when I get back, you can tell me everything."

Before I could stop her, she was halfway down the street. I closed the door and went to sit with Chloe while I waited for her to return.

Bronchitis. Thank goodness it wasn't anything more serious. If my indecisiveness while I balanced the risk of getting treatment for Chloe with the chance of Mateo finding out our location had resulted in Chloe's condition worsening, I'd never have forgiven myself.

I should be grateful for Johannes's action compared to my inaction, but I couldn't shake the creeping sense of outrage at his high-handed approach to something that was none of his business. And the more time that passed, the greater my annoyance grew.

As soon as I saw an improvement in Chloe, Mr. Bigshot and I would be having a conversation about boundaries—and recompense. Christ only knew how I'd pay the man back for a personal doctor visit, but he'd given me no other choice.

I refused to allow myself to be indebted to a man. Any man. Or under the control of one, either. Been there. Done that.

Got the mental scars to prove it.

After Ginny returned with Chloe's antibiotics, I gave her the rundown on what Doctor Magnusson had said and how Johannes had sent him here and offered to pay for Chloe's treatment. Ginny, who I'd come to understand was a bit of a romantic, got stars in her eyes and declared that his handling of matters that were none of his business made him some kind of prince, or a knight riding to my rescue.

At eighteen, I'd been a romantic, too. And look where that had gotten me.

No, Johannes hadn't done this out of the goodness of his heart. He'd seek payment, one way or another. And the only way to take away his power was to refund him every single cent.

Somehow.

K

Two days later, with Chloe well on the road to recovery, I steered my rust bucket onto the freeway and set off for Level Nine. I hadn't heard a peep from Johannes since I'd thrown him out of the house on Saturday morning. Not that I'd expected to.

Yet if that were true, why did I have this sense of disappointment sitting on top of my shoulders, weighing me down? And why was that feeling warring with one of impending doom when I made it clear how I felt about Johannes's enormous overstep in sending a doctor to my home and agreeing to foot the bill?

I should let it go, but I couldn't. It wasn't pride that stopped me from just being grateful and accepting his gesture. My resentment went far deeper than being prideful. If I let him usurp control on this occasion, he might think it gave him carte blanche over other parts of my life, such as a right to know more about my past, or Chloe's father. He could bring up his generosity at any moment and use it as a way of getting what he wanted.

I didn't trust him.

I didn't know him.

I could not allow him to have any hold over me, financial or otherwise.

He was my employer. He paid me to do a job, and I owed him my best efforts during my working hours. Nothing more. Nothing less.

I pulled into the parking lot, spying Johannes's car parked in its usual spot. As I'd hoped, the rest of the lot was empty. Thank goodness. From what I'd gleaned during my short tenure at Level Nine, he often came in far earlier than anyone else, and on this occasion, my guess had paid off.

As I made my way to the staff entrance around the side of the club, my courage fled. I almost turned around, got back in my car, and drove home. Only a deep-rooted need to say my piece, to set boundaries, stopped me. Didn't stop my hand from shaking as I tried the door. Dammit. Locked. I should have expected this. If I were working alone in a nightclub filled with booze, I wouldn't leave the door open either, even though Level Nine was in an exclusive neighborhood.

I rapped on the door a of couple times, then waited. After a minute went by with no answer, I thumped again, harder this time. A few seconds later, Johannes's face appeared in the small window in the door. I expected a frown or his trademark bored expression. Instead, his lips curved into an almost smile as he opened up to let me in.

"Ella. I wasn't expecting to see you. How's Chloe?"

"Better, thank you," I replied stiffly. "I need a word."

"As long as that word is 'I'm back on shift tonight,' then sure."

Was that a joke? Knowing Johannes, unlikely. "That's five words, and no."

His almost smile faded. He stood back to let me in, then shut and relocked the door. I followed him to his office, closing the door behind me despite us being the only people in the building.

"Doc worked out, then?" He sat behind his desk, motioning for me to sit, too.

It seemed churlish to remain standing, so I sat, perching my butt on the edge of the chair. "I need to get something straight."

Johannes arched a brow, gesturing to me. "Floor's yours. Spit it out before you burst."

Jerk.

I sucked in a deep breath and went for it, hands clenched into fists in my lap to stop my fingers from trembling. "I am not at all happy that you took it upon yourself to send a doctor to my house. My daughter is not your responsibility, and nor am I. You are my boss. I am your employee. That is where our relationship begins and ends. I will not be indebted to you, or to anyone else. I may be poor, Mr. Kingcaid, but I am not a charity case. I will find a way to refund you every penny for Chloe's care. I insist upon it. In the future, I'd appreciate it if you would keep out of my business."

I was almost panting by the time I'd finished blurting out his multiple discretions. I steeled myself, prepared for a terse comeback, or worse. When it came to the man sitting opposite me, his reaction to any situation was impossible to guess. I didn't regret saying my piece, or standing my ground. But I hoped it didn't blow up in my face.

Johannes cocked a brow. "Have you finished?"

I rubbed my lips together and tried to slow my galloping heart rate by taking another deep breath. I blew it out between pursed lips. "Yes."

"Good." He leaned forward, his linked hands resting on his messy desk. "What I did had nothing to do with being charitable. The last shift you worked was Thursday night. Today is Monday. You already missed an entire weekend, and I had to pull someone in from one of my other clubs, which meant leaving them shorthanded. And while I'm not an expert in childhood illnesses, from what I saw of your daughter, if we'd left her immune system to fight on its own, it would have been at least another week before you graced my club with your presence. I can't afford unplanned staff shortages for that length of time."

Oh. My lips parted, my brain scrambling for a suitable response. I *knew it!* Of course he'd sent help for his own selfish requirements. Nothing to do with seeing a sick little girl and wanting to make her better. Nor had his supposed benevolence had anything to do with my financial status and inability to afford a doctor for my child. It had all been about his business and staffing levels.

If I weren't so stunned, I'd have laughed.

Johannes, though, continued with his special brand of motivation.

"I need you back at work, pronto, or I'll have no choice but to hire a temporary bartender to fill in. And as you're just starting to be useful, to have another trainee fucking things up would be a royal pain in my ass."

Charming.

"Well." I stood and slipped my purse strap over my shoulder. "I'm glad we got that all cleared up."

"Sit down. I haven't finished."

I sat, my shoulders tense, half regretting my decision to come here at all. I should have let things be, waited for Chloe to recover, and then returned to work as if nothing had happened.

"How is Chloe doing?" he asked softly.

His change of direction couldn't have surprised me more if he'd slapped me across the face with a wet fish. "She's doing much better. Thank you."

"What was wrong with her?"

I wrinkled my brow. "The doctor didn't tell you?" I'd have thought, since Johannes was paying, he'd have gotten a report or something.

"Chloe is his patient, and as her mother, you're his client. Anders would never breach confidentiality."

I presumed Anders was Doctor Magnusson. The fact that Johannes was on first-name terms with the doctor spoke volumes about the difference between his life and mine.

"She's got bronchitis. He gave her antibiotics, and they're working well. I'd say she's ninety percent recovered already, although Doctor Magnusson has been clear that she has to take the full five-day course of medicine."

"That's good."

We sat in silence for a few seconds. I shifted in my seat. Was the conversation over? Could I go now?

"When do you think you'll be back to work?"

I suppressed a smile. The man really did have a one-track mind. "Um, Wednesday, if that's okay?"

He pursed his lips. "It'll have to do."

Jeez. He's all heart.

I risked standing for a second time, and on this occasion, he didn't order me back to my seat. "Right, then, I'll see you Wednesday." I made for the door.

"Ella."

I stopped in my tracks. "Yes?"

"Don't be late."

I allowed a smile to break this time. "No, sir."

As I left his office, I could have sworn I heard him mutter, "Fuck me," under his breath. But as that made no sense, I brushed it aside and set off for home.

K

Anxious to turn up to work early to show good faith with both Johannes and my coworkers who'd had to take up the slack during my enforced absence, I set off for Level Nine a couple of hours before my shift was due to start. Chloe was virtually back to her normal bubbly self, and while she'd pouted a little when I'd told her I had to work, one of Ginny's famous cookies, a glass of milk, and a promise of cartoons before bedtime soon had her smiling again.

Under normal circumstances, I'd have insisted on staying until she was in bed and asleep, especially as I hated to take advantage of Ginny. But at the same time, I also didn't want to take advantage of Johannes's altruism. Who knew how long it would last? Not me.

I still had no clue how I'd pay him back for the doctor's fees, or even how much they were. Considerable would be my guess, and a knot of anxiety lodged in my stomach at how long it would take me to repay every penny. Plus, that meant I wouldn't be able to put aside any cash for my escape fund. Every time I felt as if I might be one step ahead, something unforeseen happened to pull me right back into the quagmire. Most of the time, I treaded water, waiting for a riptide to drag me under.

One of these days, I'd catch a break. Maybe.

I lived in hope.

As I steered my car into Level Nine's parking lot, I cursed. Johannes's Maserati wasn't parked in its usual space. Goddammit. I'd assumed he'd be here to let me in and my early attendance would earn me a few brownie points.

I exited the car anyway and tried the staff entrance. Locked. Shit. So much for impressing the boss. I headed back to my car, but as I opened the door to get in, the throaty sound of an engine came from behind me. I turned around as Johannes drove in, parking his car in his reserved space.

Smiling, I headed over, wiping a damp strand of hair off my forehead. As I approached, he glanced out the window and held up a finger to me, a sign for me to wait. And then I realized he was talking to someone on the phone. I went to stand in the shade, running a hand along the back of my neck. Summer had arrived early this year. According to Ginny, it wasn't usually this hot until July, and it was only the third week of May.

Johannes climbed out of his car and slammed the door, his trademark scowl on full display. Was that for me? Or for whomever he'd been talking to? Or for something completely unrelated? With Johannes, I never knew.

"What are you doing here?" he snapped. "You're not due in until eight."

"Yeah, I know. But as I've missed so much, I thought I'd get a head start on prep." I flashed a grin. "Didn't think it through properly, though. Thank goodness you're here."

"Not for long."

He opened the door and stepped inside. I followed, the air-conditioning a welcome relief from the heat of the sun.

"Oh, why's that?"

He ignored me, making a beeline for his office. I paused on the threshold as he riffled through the stacks of papers on his desk, muttering curses under his breath.

"Can I help?"

"No."

More riffling. More cursing.

"You know, if you had this all filed away, it'd be easier to find what you're looking for."

"Thanks for the tip," he snarled. Then, "Got it."

He folded the stapled pieces of paper he'd retrieved from pile number one hundred and forty-three in half.

"I could get this filed away, if you want."

He stared at the paper, scanning it, paying me no attention. "Whatever," he muttered, brushing past me. "Are you sticking around?"

"Yeah, like I said, I want to get a head start on prep."

He nodded curtly. "Tell Stan I have to go to San Francisco. I'll be back tomorrow."

"Sure. Of course."

He set a key on the desk. "Lock up. You shouldn't be in

here alone with the door unlocked. Give it back to me tomorrow."

He strode down the hallway, disappeared through the staff entrance, and slammed the door hard enough to break the small window.

Hmm. Whatever had happened that required him to go to San Francisco couldn't be good. I pitied the individual on the other side of Johannes's wrath. I imagined that being on the receiving end of his temper was like being blasted with a heat gun.

I locked up, then headed for the bar, but as I passed Johannes's office, I changed my mind. The untidy space had always bothered me. I hated messes and I hated clutter. I'd bet I could have that shipshape in an hour, which would still leave me with enough time to do most of the prep before Stan arrived.

And Johannes had said it was okay when I'd suggested it.

With a sense of purpose, I got to work.

Sixty-five minutes later, I scanned the office, pride blooming in my chest. I'd filed everything away, and even made a card catalogue so that Johannes could follow my system and easily find whatever he needed. Next time he was in a hurry searching for something, he wouldn't have to wade through piles and piles of paper to find it. He'd be able to go right to it in seconds.

I wasn't sure why, but earning praise from Johannes had become like a drug. I needed it, craved it, had to have it.

And once he saw what I'd done for him, I planned to drown in it.

Chapter 13

Johannes

**It isn't easy battling the boss
when you're the underling.
So why does she manage it so effortlessly?**

"What the fuck is this?"

I gaped around my office. At least, I thought it was my office. When I'd left for San Francisco yesterday because that fucker Douglas had turned up to the club and caused a huge scene resulting in the head bartender I'd temporarily put in charge having to call the police, it'd looked like it always had. Organized chaos. I knew where everything was.

Now, I didn't have a goddamn clue.

I stomped over to the tall filing cabinet in the corner of the room and yanked open the top drawer. The first thing that caught my eye was a colorful card filled with neat handwriting. I plucked it out and stared at it.

Fuck me.

It was an indexing system. And one I easily followed, too. Hmm. Maybe I wouldn't have had so much trouble finding Douglas's signed employment contract to pass on to my lawyer so he could use it to nail that bastard's balls to the wall if I'd had this system before.

But that was beside the point.

Who the hell took it upon themselves to come into *my* office and touch *my* things?

I strode into the bar, where Stan was making the final checks ahead of the doors opening in thirty minutes. Anger bubbled in my stomach, expanded into my chest, and spewed from my tongue.

"Who the fuck has been in my office?" I roared.

Stan jumped and whacked his head on the underside of the bar. He stood up straight, rubbing the offending spot.

"What?"

"Oh, I'm sorry. Was I speaking fucking Mandarin?" My voice oozed with sarcasm. "Someone has been in my fucking office and screwed up my filing system."

I didn't have a filing system. Until now. Whatever. I still had a system of sorts. And it was mine.

Stan scratched his cheek, frowning. "I don't know what you're talking about, boss. I haven't been in your office."

"Well, someone has. And I want to know who." I set my laser-focused attention on Tiffany. "Was it you?"

Tiffany raised her palms on either side of her head. "Wasn't me. I don't even clean my apartment all that often, so there's no chance I'd volunteer to tidy up your office."

I jabbed a finger one at a time at the rest of the bar staff. "You? You? Or you?"

"It was me."

I spun around. Ella stood behind me with an armful of napkins. She must have been in the storeroom when I'd barged in here shooting my mouth. She chewed the inside of her cheek and rocked on her heels.

"I did it. I filed everything away."

A nerve thrummed in my jaw like a jackhammer. I ground my teeth and glared at her, summoning a vitriol that caught in my throat. I breathed in through my nose, letting it out slowly.

Somehow, I steadied my voice. "Give the napkins to Stan and come with me."

I retraced my steps, Ella's soft footfalls keeping pace with me. I waited for her to enter my office, then slammed the door closed. She flinched.

"Who said you could poke your nose into my personal and business affairs?"

She gave me her eyes, luminous green, like the leaves on a tree after a deluge of rain. Something shifted in my chest, a feeling of empathy. I cast it aside. I knew all too well how an odious agenda hid behind a pretty face and big, beseeching eyes.

"You did."

Whatever I'd expected her to say, that wasn't it.

"Me?" I pointed to myself as if she needed a signpost of whom I'd meant when I'd said me.

"Yes."

"And when exactly did I say this?"

"Yesterday afternoon, right before you left for San Francisco."

Puzzled, I rubbed my forehead. The conversation

remained stubbornly out of reach. I had zero recollection of giving her permission to tidy my office. I blamed Douglas and his stupid stunt, although he'd rue the day he'd threatened my staff and my business. I'd make sure of it.

"What exactly did I say?"

Her eyes shifted up and to the left. "If I remember correctly, I told you that whatever you were searching for would be easier to find if it was filed away. And then I offered to do it, and you said 'Whatever.'" She shrugged. "So I did."

I blinked, stared, blinked some more. "Let me get this straight. You took a throwaway comment I made while I was distracted as approval to come into my office and go through my fucking things?"

Her lips flattened, and she crossed her arms. Defensive mode activated.

"Forgive me, *Mr. Kingcaid*, for taking you at your word. Maybe next time, you should make your communications clearer. It's a well-known fact that if someone misunderstands your meaning or intent, that's on you, not them."

My eyes bulged, the simmering spark of irritation exploding into an inferno of rage.

"How fucking dare you! This is *my* office. Mine. Your job is out there on the floor, pouring drinks, smiling at the customers, and keeping your nose out of my fucking business."

Her chin wobbled, but she stood her ground. I had to give her credit for that. Most wilted beneath my wrath.

"I did a nice thing for you, and this is how you react? I read only what I needed to in order to categorize the papers logically. I'm not the slightest bit interested in your business. After what you did for Chloe, I wanted to pay you back in some small way while I figure out how the hell I'll settle Chloe's medical bills and still put food on the table. Next time, I won't bother."

She pivoted.

"Wait," I barked as she gripped the door handle.

She paused but remained with her back to me. I closed my eyes, releasing a slow breath through my nostrils. My anger withered as fast as it had ignited.

"I appreciate that your intentions were good ones. I'm a private person. That's all. I don't like having my shit messed with. And I don't expect repayment for Chloe's medical treatment."

She turned to face me, her eyes filled with challenge rather than submission. Heat flooded my groin at her blatant provocation. And somehow, it meant more coming from her because of her situation and how desperately she needed this job. Yet she wasn't willing to be a doormat or discard her principles for anyone.

I respected the fuck out of that.

"I'm not a charity case."

"I never said you were."

"But you think it?"

"You're in my head now?"

"Even I'm not that brave."

A smile tugged at my lips. Goddamn her.

"I don't want your money."

"What do you want, Johannes? Just what will you expect in return?"

"Nothing. Like I said, I needed you back at work. That's all. Anders' fee was cheap for ensuring that outcome."

Silence fell over us as she chewed over my words, probably weighing whether she believed me. That lack of trust in another was something I understood all too well, and I admired her for it.

"You need an assistant."

I blinked at the change of subject. As much as I hated to admit it, she had a point. The business was growing, and I couldn't keep on controlling everything. Sooner or later, I'd have to learn to delegate, although trusting anyone other than myself wasn't an easy thing for me to accomplish.

While I only had twenty clubs, it was right on the edge of manageable. But what about when that expanded to thirty, forty, a hundred? What would happen when I developed the business globally? I couldn't possibly approve every decision. Trusting my staff to do the job I paid them to do would become a necessity, not a luxury.

Maybe hiring an assistant was a good place to begin growing that trust in others. I'd almost missed a requirement to complete a form for the *Hottest Nightspot* award only a couple of weeks ago, remembering in the nick of time. And this was supposed to be my goal, my focus, yet with all the other demands on my time, it had slipped my mind. If I had an assistant, it would be his or her responsibility to ensure I kept on top of such matters.

But who? Where did I even begin?

"I can see the cogs turning in your brain."

I looked over at Ella. "Sorry, what?"

"Cogs. Brain." She tapped her temple. "I can hear them, too."

She flashed me a grin, and I found my lips stretching in response. There was something about this woman that appealed to me on more than a physical level. She wasn't in awe of me, or afraid of my moods. She stood up to me, and I had enormous respect for her courage.

It wasn't easy battling the boss when you were the underling.

"I'll be sure to take on extra fluids today for lubrication purposes."

She pressed a hand to her chest, her mouth forming a perfectly round shape. "Johannes Kingcaid, did you just make a joke?"

My lips twitched, the beginnings of a chuckle rising into my throat. I swallowed it down. Laughter wasn't something that came easily to me, but Ella's teasing had brought me closer than I'd come in a long time. The only other person who could almost drag a laugh out of me was Gia, my brother Penn's fiancée.

"I'll try not to make a habit of it."

"Oh, yes." She nodded sagely. "We can't have that. People might mistake you for human."

She winked, and a part of me I'd long since forgotten sparked to life. My heart clenched at the moment of camaraderie. Not that I'd ever outwardly show the effect she was having on me. No, I'd push it down and lock it behind a newly built wall I now realized she'd chipped away at since the day the agency had sent her to me for a job interview.

"Anyway, if you've finished yelling at me, I guess I should get back to work." She glanced at her watch. "We're about to open."

As she turned to leave for the second time, an idea

sprang to mind. I wasn't one to act on impulse, but this made total sense.

"How would you like to be my assistant?"

She froze, one foot in front of the other. Her head slowly swiveled, her hips twisting as her feet remained glued to the floor.

"Me?"

"Sure. Why not? You have the organization skills I'm lacking as you so delicately pointed out. You know me. You're not in awe of me. You're honest and will tell it to me straight. Plus, this way, you'd be able to work days and spend more time with Chloe. We could work around her schooling, and if there was a requirement for extended hours, then I'm sure we could figure something out. The pay will be more than you earn tending bar, too, and that includes the tips you're picking up."

She spun around to face me. "But... I don't have any experience."

"The only experience you need is the ability to handle me, and you seem to manage that with no trouble."

Her teeth grazed over her bottom lip. She stared at her sneakers, then lifted her chin.

"I thought we were shorthanded at the bar?"

"We are."

This time I did smile. "Your first job as my assistant is to find an adequate replacement, and ensure that nothing falls over in the meantime."

She threw back her head and laughed, and another brick popped out of the wall. Goddammit.

Thrusting out her hand, she waited for me to take it. I

hesitated, then pressed my palm to hers, thinking of anything other than how soft her skin was and how small her hand looked inside mine.

"You have yourself a deal."

Chapter 14

Johannes

This is not a date.
I repeat, this is not a date.

Ella, it turned out, was a revelation. Fifteen days had passed since I'd hired her as my assistant, and although I'd never tell her this, I'd begun to wonder how I'd coped without her. Hell, I had enough trouble admitting that fact to myself. Relying on others did not come naturally to me, and that trait had worsened after what Sadie and her hired thugs had done. Yet Ella had slipped into my life in that quiet way of hers and pried a few spinning plates from my hands, then dealt with each one with poise and efficiency.

Tonight, I had a meeting with Ryker Stone, one of the board members of ROGUES, a global behemoth a similar size to my own family firm. Ryker managed a chain of dance clubs called *Poles Apart,* and while the premise was different from my nightclub business, Ryker seemed to think there was an opportunity for us to work together. Dad had a lot of time for Ryker, and the other ROGUES board members, as did Ash. After all, my elder brother had gone into business with Garen Gauthier, who headed up the ROGUES hotel business, and it had been fruitful for both sides.

I had to admit to being intrigued by what he had to offer.

Ella popped her head inside my office door, a ready smile on her pretty face. Despite my usual stoic response, she always had a smile for me, for Stan, for everyone right down to the janitor and the driver who delivered the liquor. I admired her for that. And envied her.

"Do you need anything else before I go?"

"No, I'm good. Thanks for the prep ahead of tonight's meeting." Ella had pulled together a briefing paper on *Poles Apart,* including everything from locations to estimated turnover. Even if I didn't think they were a good fit for a joint venture, I could learn a lot from how Ryker had expanded into international markets. He'd already achieved what I was aiming for. Spending a few hours in his company couldn't hurt.

Plus, Ryker's Los Angeles branch of *Poles Apart* had won the *Hottest Nightspot* award two years running. For some reason, he hadn't entered this year, but he might have some worthwhile strategies I could emulate and put my own twist on.

I *had* to win that award. Coveted it. Could picture it sitting right there on my shelf. Physical proof of my achievements, a way to show Dad that I might've been the fuckup son whose naivety had almost cost him his life but that, like a phoenix, I'd risen from the ashes and triumphed.

That I still suffered night terrors and refused to speak to a therapist about the PTSD I'd never dealt with was another issue entirely. My business and I were two separate beings. One could succeed while the other was an utter mess.

"Okay, then, I'll see you Monday. Hope tonight goes well."

Fuck. I'd almost forgotten that it was the weekend. I worked every day regardless, but Ella had Saturdays and Sundays off.

I didn't like it. In fact, I despised it. I'd come to not only rely on her but also relish spending time with her. She was the complete opposite of me. The ice to my fire and the calm to my disquiet. I couldn't go two days without seeing her, and while that thought scared the shit out of me, the desire to bask in her light won the day.

I jumped up from my chair and followed her into the hallway outside my office. "Hey, Ella, wait up." I strode toward her. "I don't suppose you're free tonight?"

She frowned, and my fingertips itched to smooth the lines from her face. "What do you need?"

For the first time in my life, I felt awkward, almost gawky. Jesus, I hadn't felt like this even in high school when I'd plucked up the courage to ask Susie Dover out on a date. She'd turned me down, too. Last I heard, she'd gotten divorced for the third time.

Lucky escape for me.

"I thought it might be a good idea for you to accompany me this evening. As my assistant," I added hastily in case she misunderstood and assumed I meant something more. "I'd appreciate your views on Ryker as a potential business partner."

Her sweet to my salty might grease the wheels of business, too. I was known for my ability to rub people the wrong way. Plus, she was far better at this "peopling" shit than me. Take that asshole who'd grabbed her a few weeks ago. I'd been ready to break his nose and ban him for life, yet she'd dealt with him without bloodshed and had him eating out of her hand. One of many examples of her people management skills. I believed it came so naturally to her that she wasn't even cognizant of it.

"Oh." She twisted her lips to the side as if she was searching for a plausible excuse, or a polite way of saying "Hell no."

I found myself holding my breath, readying a counterargument to the anticipated refusal.

"Um, I'm not sure I'm the right person. I've made my fair share of mistakes when it comes to reading other people."

She blushed, ducking her head, almost as if she'd said more than she'd meant to. My curiosity spiked. I still knew so little about her. She kept her cards pressed close to her chest. *Takes one to know one.* I had the same affliction.

Mine came from a traumatic experience. Did Ella's come from something similar? And if so, what? Her relief when I'd offered to pay her cash at her initial interview had led me to think she didn't want to leave a trace of her existence. But why? Who was she hiding from? Chloe's father, maybe?

Not that it was any of my business. Her place in my life began and ended with her role as my assistant. Sure, she was an attractive woman. Who wouldn't think so with her thick, ebony hair and luminous, mossy green eyes that shone with an intriguing combination of innocence and experience? Her courage turned me on, too, as did her humor, her personality, her curves for days. The way she was so comfortable in her own skin, refusing to adapt to the Los Angeles cookie cutter version of a woman. Staying true to herself.

All pointless attributes. She could be my ideal woman in every way, and I still wouldn't touch her. And not only because I'd risk losing a perfectly good assistant. As ideal as she appeared on the surface, beneath the calm waters, sharks lurked.

I'd thought Sadie was the perfect woman, and look where that had gotten me. Nope. Better to keep our relationship purely professional. That way, no one got hurt.

"I've seen you with people. They warm to you with ease. Whereas I..." I shrugged.

"Turn them to stone with a single glare." She chuckled.

"I doubt my famous glare will have that effect on Ryker, even if his last name is Stone."

"No?" She laughed. "You're kidding?"

"I never joke about business."

She angled her head. "Dearest Johannes. You never joke about *anything*."

I narrowed my eyes. "You've grown confident, Miss Reyes. Some would say cocky. Or brave. I'd be careful if I were you."

"Is this your way of persuading me to spend my Friday night in your scintillating company? If so, your approach needs work."

I huffed, but inside, a nugget of warmth set up home within my chest. I'd forgotten how much fun banter could be, especially with a worthy opponent. "Are you free or not?" I deadpanned.

"Wow. How could I refuse such an enthusiastic offer?"

I swallowed the beginnings of a chuckle, an occurrence rarer than a lottery win. Or trusting a woman.

"What about Chloe?"

"I'll ask Ginny if she wouldn't mind babysitting, but I'm sure she'll be fine. If there's a problem, I'll text you. She goes to bed at seven thirty, so I need to be there for that."

"I'll pick you up at eight."

I spun on my heel and returned to my office, triumph mingling with the beginnings of a flicker of excitement.

It wasn't a date. I didn't date.

But the feeling in the pit of my stomach wasn't listening. It was too busy looking forward to the night ahead.

K

"You look... nice."

I suppressed a curse. *Nice* was the kind of word used to describe the banal, the boring, when the occasion called for politeness, something I wasn't all that familiar with. *Nice* was not the word to describe Ella Reyes.

She'd piled her midnight-black hair on top of her head, leaving a few tendrils to grace her elegant neck. A light application of makeup enhanced her natural beauty, but didn't overshadow it, and she'd poured her curves into a topaz-blue dress that, while not designer, didn't need to be. Ella could wear a trash bag, tie a piece of string around the middle, and still look like a million bucks.

"Nice? Wow. You're being a bit extravagant with the compliments. I'd dial it back if I were you."

Every day that passed, Ella's confidence grew, along with my infatuation. The day we'd met, she'd been nervous as hell, given me the impression she was ready to run at a moment's notice, and had come across as meek and submissive.

How wrong I'd been in that assessment.

In the early days, there had been flashes of bravado, such as when she'd tackled me over an imagined assault, but it was since I'd hired her as my assistant that the true metamorphosis had begun.

I'd started to think my attempts to convince myself that I wasn't interested in anything more than a business relationship had been doomed from the beginning.

"If you're looking for compliments, you've picked the wrong companion for the evening."

And with comments like that, I'll be lucky if I keep her as an assistant.

"I didn't pick you for a companion. You picked me."

Goddammit. She had an answer for everything. I wasn't used to people answering me back, but the way my dick swelled, it enjoyed her snark as much as I did.

"Shall we go?" Without waiting for her, I spun on my heel and returned to my car. I got in, without even opening her door for her.

Minus points for chivalry.

I snapped my seat belt in place, and once she'd situated herself, I pulled away from the curb.

"That color suits you. It goes well with your eyes."

I caught sight of her in my peripheral vision, her head

slowly coming around. "You were right."

I frowned. "About what?"

"You are terrible at compliments."

"I didn't say I was terrible at them. I said you'd picked the wrong companion if compliments are important to you."

"Same difference."

"I disagree."

"Of course you do."

A chuckle rumbled in the base of my throat. She was magnificent, not that I had any plans to share such thoughts. Didn't want her getting any ideas that I was a pushover, or worse, that I was interested in her in any way other than as an employee.

"Oh my God!"

I almost slammed on the brakes, my head whipping toward her. "What? What's the matter?"

"You... you laughed." She put her hand to my forehead. "Are you sick?"

I returned my attention to the road. "Jesus Christ, Ella. I thought something was seriously wrong."

"It is. You're becoming human. It's a huge worry. I think we need medical intervention."

My chest tightened. *Where have you been all my life?*

"Don't be ridiculous."

"Yeah, you're right. Cyborg it is."

Dear God, help me. Another wave of laughter crawled up from my chest. I pushed it into the pit of my stomach. Ella needed no further encouragement, and while I'd tolerated her overstepping up to now, the last thing I needed was her getting too familiar at this meeting with Ryker. Ash had called me right as I was leaving my place to wish me luck and warn me that Ryker Stone was as astute as they come and to stay on my toes.

Letting Ella distract me with her smart mouth and sunny personality would lead to disaster.

I pulled up outside the restaurant, handing the keys to the valet as I waited for Ella to join me on the sidewalk. I gestured for her to walk ahead. As we entered the building, my hand moved to the small of her back, a long-forgotten instinct driving my actions. She glanced up at me and gave me a dazzling smile.

"Thank you for inviting me."

I arched a brow. "Wait... is that... is that *gratitude*?"

"Is that... is that... another joke?"

This time, I couldn't contain the laughter I'd worked so hard to suppress. In response, Ella looked as if I'd given her what her heart desired. Her eyes shone, and her smile grew even wider.

"You should laugh more often, Johannes. It suits you."

The moment of mirth died. I cleared my throat. "This is a business meeting. No room for jokes. Please remember that you're representing Kingcaid, and we take our business interests extremely seriously."

Jesus. She'd been right about the cyborg. *Who speaks like that?*

She smoothed a hand over her dress. "Of course, Mr. Kingcaid, sir." Her words were submissive, but the twinkle in her eye was anything but.

"Sit up straight, be polite, and follow my lead."

She winked. *Winked.*

"You got it, boss."

Ah, fuck. I was doomed.

Chapter 15

Ella

When the Earth tilts on its axis, hold on for dear life.

Who am I, and what am I doing here?

Johannes's out-of-the-blue invitation to accompany him to a business meeting had completely stunned me. Not only the unexpectedness of it, but also his reasoning for it.

"I'd appreciate your views on Ryker as a potential business partner."

I was the wrong person for a task like that.

I'd married a drug baron without having a clue who he really was.

I'd been blinded to the man beneath his polished exterior until it was almost too late.

I didn't trust my instincts.

I'd been too gullible, too innocent, and I'd believed every word that had come out of my husband's mouth without questioning a single one of them.

But how could I refuse a request by my boss to accompany him to a business meeting? I was his assistant, a job I'd come to relish these past two weeks. My confidence in my abilities had grown with each passing day, and with it, the real me, Eloise, not Ella, had emerged.

When I'd run from my home with what few possessions I could carry and a few hundred dollars in my wallet, I'd made a decision to play a part.

Stay quiet, hide in the shadows, be respectful and submissive.

No one noticed the little mouse in the corner. But since Johannes had hired me as his assistant, we'd grown closer, and as a result, my true personality had crept to the fore.

For some strange reason, Johannes didn't seem to mind my sass. I'd go so far as to say he enjoyed it when I bantered with him. And the laugh he'd shared with me... it had crawled into my heart. I craved to hear it again, over and over, and know that I was the one who'd broken down his barriers.

I'd never met such a closed-off person in my entire life. No one voluntarily imprisoned themselves, and while Johannes Kingcaid had riches beyond my wildest dreams, they brought him little, if any, happiness.

I wondered what would make him happy.

The award he was hell-bent on winning?

More nightclubs?

More riches?

Who knew? I hoped that one day, he'd find that missing piece.

Maybe I could be the one to unearth it.

I laughed to myself. *Don't be silly. You're an employee. Nothing more. Nothing less.*

The hostess led us over to a table set for three in the center of the dining room. Crystal chandeliers hung from the ceiling, the silverware sparkled, and the tablecloths were pressed to perfection. The whole thing oozed elegance... and money.

How the other half lives.

How I'd lived, once. I wasn't unaccustomed to wealth. Mateo had taken me to all the best places. We'd stayed in five-star hotels, vacationed on yachts in the Gulf of Mexico, and drunk wine at ten thousand dollars a bottle. And all the while, I'd believed his lies. He profited off the misery of others, and his so-called business had put my daughter in danger.

I'd never forgive him for that.

Never forgive him for leaving us so exposed that a rival drug gang had broken into our home and tried to take me and Chloe as bargaining chips to force Mateo's hand into agreeing to relinquish the territory he'd stolen.

If Mateo hadn't come home unexpectedly after getting a tip-off that something was going down, anything could have happened.

"Ryker."

Johannes's greeting brought me back to the present. I pasted on a welcoming smile and waited for him to introduce me.

"Good to see you." The two men shook hands. "This is my assistant, Ella."

He pressed a palm to my lower back again. I savored the

warmth from his skin, the pressure of his touch. Goose bumps peppered my arms, the hairs standing on end.

"Nice to meet you, Mr. Stone."

"Ryker, please. Only my wife calls me Mr. Stone."

My eyebrows flew up my head, and I searched for an appropriate response to such a comment until I spotted the glint in his eye. I laughed, and he did, too.

"Athena, that's my wife, isn't the compliant type. She'd never stand for such a thing. Might make me call her Mrs. Stone, though." He winked, then sat.

I liked him.

Enormously.

Johannes held out my chair, and I almost choked. Was he trying to impress Ryker or just make up for his lack of chivalry earlier tonight?

Or had our lighthearted banter shifted something between us?

"Thank you." I smoothed my dress beneath my thighs and sat down.

The waiter brought over a bottle of wine I presumed Ryker had ordered before we'd arrived. I took the smallest sip. The last thing I needed was to get tipsy. This might have been outside my normal working hours, but I was still on duty, still representing Kingcaid, as Johannes had pointed out in his unique, blunt way.

I couldn't take my eyes off Johannes as he and Ryker talked about strategy and growth and how their different businesses might align in a joint venture that, from the sounds of it, would benefit both parties.

He was more animated than I'd ever seen him, his

enthusiasm contagious. Even I began to get excited about his future plans to grow across the United States and, eventually, overseas as Ryker had done with his dance clubs.

I tuned out the details of the conversation but let the tone of Johannes's voice soak through my chest and right into my heart. This was the hidden side of the man, and I felt honored he'd allowed me to witness it.

Not that I'd ever bring it up.

Knowing Johannes, he'd hit back with some barbed comment or other and ruin the illusion. But whether or not he was aware of it, he was changing right before my eyes.

The Johannes I'd met a few short weeks ago was slowly disappearing, the steps so small that they weren't noticeable on a day-to-day basis. But if I thought back to that very first meeting, how dour and gruff he'd been, how dull his eyes had looked, how desperately sad he'd come across despite his brusque manner, the transformation was remarkable.

Our dinner arrived, and my stomach rumbled. It smelled amazing. I reached for the salt at the same time as Johannes. Our fingers brushed, and a bolt of electricity shot up my arm.

His eyes cut to mine and held there for a few seconds. At that moment, we weren't in a packed restaurant surrounded by a hundred people or at a table with a business associate. We were alone in a private bubble, just him and me, and a whole heap of chemistry.

The sound of clattering dishes being collected at the table next to ours broke the spell. I blinked, dazed.

What was that?

Johannes looked as stunned as me, his eyebrows furrowing as he, I assumed, tried to process the last few seconds. Ryker, meanwhile, flicked his eyes between the two of us, a faint smile pulling at the sides of his lips.

I dabbed the napkin to my mouth. "Delicious food," I announced to no one in particular.

"You haven't tasted it yet," Ryker pointed out, that same twinkle I'd seen in his eyes earlier in the evening blazing with mischief.

"I-I mean, I'm sure it will be delicious. Sure smells lovely."

"Where were we?" Johannes asked, shifting his body away from mine.

I hadn't realized how close we'd gotten. I shuffled my chair a couple of inches to the right, too, and dug into my dinner.

Refusing dessert, I excused myself to go to the restroom. It was probably wishful thinking, but I sensed Johannes's eyes on me as I weaved through the crowded restaurant.

How had a single touch changed everything?

A heaviness gathered between my thighs, and I was certain that if I took my temperature, a doctor would diagnose me with a fever.

Sure enough, my cheeks were flushed when I looked in the mirror, the redness spreading over my neck and chest. I ran a towel underneath the faucet and dabbed myself to cool my skin.

Get a hold of yourself, woman.

I was imagining things.

Nothing had changed between us.

I'd had too much wine. That was all.

Except... I'd only had two sips.

I shook my head, rinsed my wrists under the cool water, and returned to the dining room. Johannes didn't even acknowledge me as I retook my seat.

See? It *was* my imagination running riot.

Still, for a moment, it had been nice to dream.

"Ready to go?" Johannes asked.

Oh. I'd been so caught up in my fantasies that I hadn't realized they'd wrapped up. Ryker was already on his feet.

"Yes, of course." I leaned down to pick my purse up off the floor.

Johannes stood and fastened his suit jacket, then shook Ryker's hand. "I'll be in touch."

"Great to meet you, Ella," Ryker said, holding out his hand for me to shake, too.

"And you."

"I'm sure I'll see you again sometime."

"Maybe," I murmured.

The three of us left the restaurant together. Johannes handed his ticket to the valet while a stretch limousine pulled up for Ryker. He said his final goodbyes and climbed inside.

As he pulled away, the valet pulled up in Johannes's car. I hid my surprise when Johannes opened the passenger door for me, especially as he hadn't done so on the way here.

The way he switched moods and actions made my head spin. If I lived to be a hundred, I doubted I'd ever figure out the enigmatic Johannes Kingcaid.

He rounded the hood then got in the driver's side. He

checked both ways, then pulled out of the parking lot onto the highway.

"Thank you for coming with me tonight."

"Oh, you're welcome. I enjoyed myself. And it seemed fruitful."

"It was. Very. He had some good tips to help position Level Nine for the award I'm going for, and if it all pans out, a joint venture with ROGUES will be great for me and the plans I have to grow my business." He gnawed on his lip. "This may surprise you, but I don't trust easily."

He cocked a brow, and I laughed.

"You don't say?"

We fell into a companionable silence on the drive back to Ginny's place. When he pulled up outside the house a few minutes after eleven, I was loath for the night to end.

"I had a great time. It was good to get out for a bit."

He pressed his lips together. "Can I ask you something?"

"You mean you're asking for permission?"

I hoped to draw a faint smile from him through my teasing, but he remained stoic, serious, the Johannes he showed the world ninety-five percent of the time.

"Go on."

"What are you running from?"

My chest collapsed, a gasp forcing its way to the surface. He couldn't possibly know anything. He was fishing, testing, prodding. I gathered all my courage and glared at him, shoving my hands beneath my thighs to hide the tremor in my fingers.

"I work for you. That's it. I don't owe you a damn thing."

"That's true. But the question stands."

I reached for the door. Locked. Goddamn modern cars that locked the doors automatically.

"Let me out, Johannes." My tone brooked no argument.

He grimaced. "I'm sorry. I shouldn't have pried. I hate it when people poke their noses into my business, so I have no right to poke around in someone else's."

"No. You don't."

"Please, accept my apology."

His eyes beseeched me, the expression so out of place on him that the brief flash of anger brought on by his question withered in the face of his contrition.

"We all have our secrets, Johannes. Things we'd rather remained private."

He lowered his chin to his chest. "You're right. I shouldn't have asked."

I shook my head. I craved to pull another smile from him. To hear him laugh. To feel the rush of adrenaline at his touch.

It was stupid and dangerous, but since when did human beings always take the right path?

"Maybe we should share one truth each. One of our own choosing. No follow-up questions."

"Sounds fair."

I pointed at him. "You first."

His eyes glazed, almost as if he'd retreated to a different place inside his mind. "I almost died a few years ago, and there's no white light, no angels waiting to greet you on the other side. This is it. One life, and it's pretty shitty as it goes."

Sucker-punched, I gaped at him. I'd expected him to share something glib, not a revelation as deep as that.

"How—"

He held up a hand. "You said no questions. Your turn."

I steeled myself. Could I really say the one thing I truly wanted to? Was I brave enough? And if I was, what would I do if it ruined everything?

I took a deep breath and plunged into the unknown. "I'm having feelings for you over here, and it's terrifying."

He inhaled through his nose, his eyes wide. Painful seconds scraped by.

Oh, crap. I shouldn't have said anything. I should have picked something else to share. Anything would have been better than the knife spearing my chest with every moment that passed without him saying a word.

"Sorry. Forget I spoke." I reached for the door handle for a second time.

His hand snapped around the back of my neck, and he pulled me to him. His mouth collided with mine, and the world stopped turning.

Piece by piece, I crumbled, affection I'd craved for so long without being aware of it tearing me apart. I wrapped my arms around his neck, caressing the soft hair at his nape, pressing my body closer, closer, until an atom wouldn't fit between us. Soft sweeps of his tongue against mine undid the remaining parts of me until I gave myself to him fully, showing him with my lips and my hands and my tongue that this wasn't just a kiss.

It was the beginnings of a new life. One I'd never thought possible since fleeing my home in the middle of the night carrying my child in my arms and pulling a small suitcase behind me.

Johannes hadn't just given me a job. He'd given me a future.

He'd given me hope.

His kiss wasn't a promise of more. It wasn't a promise of anything.

But it was a start.

Chapter 16

Johannes

Unexpected visitors are not what I ordered.

I WAS A COWARD, AND A TERRIBLE ONE AT THAT. SINCE ELLA AND I had kissed last Friday night, I'd done my level best to avoid her. The weekend had been easy, as she didn't work Saturdays and Sundays, and then I'd spent Monday to Wednesday visiting my other clubs in the area, and yesterday, I'd flown up to San Francisco to check on the Douglas situation.

But I couldn't avoid her any longer.

We had an important meeting to prepare for. One of the judges from the *Hottest Nightspot* committee was due to visit the club tonight, and therefore, it had to be in excellent shape. I'd asked all the staff to come in early so I could brief them, and, proof that my cowardly status was still very much alive, I made sure I turned up at the club when I knew Stan, Tiffany, and one or two of the others would be around.

I hated myself.

The cleaning staff were hard at work when I entered the main part of the nightclub. Tiffany was busy behind the bar, polishing the liquor bottles, and Stan had his ass crack on full display as he crouched to fill the fridges with beer and sodas.

I couldn't see Ella. Which meant she was, in all likelihood, in my office.

Thank goodness I came here first.

"One of these days I'll drop an ice cube down that massive ass crack of yours, Stan."

"Already beat you to it," Tiffany interjected with a gleeful grin. "Ages ago. He leapt in the air and smacked his head on the underside of the counter."

"If hiring and firing were up to me, you'd have been out on *your* ass," Stan said, rising to his feet.

"Lucky it's not, then."

She gave me an exaggerated wink, and I found my lips forming a smile. Showed how rare it was when Tiffany's eyes widened. She stared for a few seconds, then shook her head, almost as if she thought her eyes were playing tricks on her, and carried on polishing.

"When the rest of the staff gets here, let me know. I want to make sure they're all aware of what I expect of them tonight."

Stan saluted. "Will do."

Unable to put it off any longer, I trudged toward my office, praying for an urgent phone call or an attack of appendicitis. Maybe a stroke would be preferable to facing up to a woman I should *never* have kissed.

Rule number one, dickhead. Don't shit on your own doorstep.

Especially given my unusual proclivities when it came to sex with a woman—a fast fuck and an even faster goodbye.

The door to my office lay ajar. I pushed it open and entered. Ella was sitting in my chair, a typed list in front of her with boxes down the right-hand side. Some boxes had ticks inside them. Others did not.

"Hey," I ventured.

She glanced up. "Oh, there you are. Good. We have a lot to do before we open this evening. I made a list, but I'd appreciate you looking over it and making sure there aren't any glaring errors."

She thrust the list at me, then drew another one that looked identical to mine toward her.

"Items three, twelve, and fifteen are all you. I'll take most of the others, such as making sure the VIP area is up to your standards, liaising with Stan, and checking the restrooms."

"You didn't have to do all this."

She wrinkled her nose. "Yes, I did. It's my job. This award is important to you, yes?"

"Well, yes, but—"

"Then it's important to me. Now shoo. We have a lot to do and only a few hours to do it in. Ginny is taking care of Chloe, so I'm here for the long haul."

She returned her attention to the list, jotting notes in the margin. I stood there, dumbfounded. I'd spent a week avoiding her, worried what she'd say about the kiss, whether she'd expect more, or less, or, oh, I don't know, whether it'd be awkward between us.

I'd planned my responses in meticulous detail, all of them steeped in avoidance. But all that went out the window in the face of her reaction.

"Um, about last Friday."

She paused, then put down the pen and leaned back in the chair. My chair. Funnily enough, her usurping my private space didn't upset me at all.

"I wasn't going to bring it up until after tonight, but since you have..." She tapped a fingertip against her lips. "You do know that in my religion, a kiss is as good as a proposal? My parents will want to know when the wedding is so they can plan accordingly. What shall I tell them?"

My heart almost stopped beating. Panic spread through me faster than a Californian wildfire. My jaw unhinged, flapping about as if the bones had been surgically removed.

And speech proved impossible.

This was a joke, right? It had to be.

"Johannes, are you all right? You've gone awfully pale."

"I-I..."

Ella burst out laughing. "Oh my God, this is priceless. If I'd known that would be your reaction, I'd have recorded it."

Realizing I'd been had, my mood raced from outraged to impressed in less than a second. *The little wench.*

"I will find a way to pay you back."

She laughed louder. "I should have kept it going a while longer. Really gotten my money's worth."

"You're fired."

"You won't fire me. I run your life, or the business side of it at least."

True. She did. She'd taken so much work off my plate and improved a ton of processes in all my clubs, not just this one, that I'd often wondered in the last couple of weeks how I'd managed without her. Not that I planned to share my thoughts on the matter.

Especially now.

"Watch your back. Retribution will be swift and when you least expect it."

"Bring it. I can handle you."

I snorted, and she giggled again. God, that laugh, that giggle, that chuckle. I was addicted to all of them.

Careful. Watch yourself.

Ella hadn't done anything to make me think she was untrustworthy, but that didn't mean I *could* or *should* trust her.

"And about Friday," she said. "It was just a kiss. A very nice kiss, but I can see from the panicked look on your face when you brought it up, that you regret it. And that's fine. I like you. I'm not going to sit here and lie about that, but nor will what happened between us, or your obvious regret that it did, affect our working relationship." She smiled. "So chill out, okay?"

This was what I'd hoped for. To put the kiss behind us and move on as if it hadn't happened.

But if that were true, why did I feel such a crushing disappointment?

K

I arrived home at three in the morning, exhausted but also exhilarated. The night had been a roaring success. All my staff deserved a bonus, and I'd make sure they got one, too. They'd worked their asses off from the minute the doors had opened.

Especially Ella. Wonderful, amazing, funny, sassy, little-miss-organized Ella who'd thought of everything, and more besides. She'd wowed the judge, made him and his wife feel like Hollywood elite, and sent them home happy, and more than a little inebriated. As he'd left, the judge had told me to expect to hear from the committee soon.

I knew what that meant. He was going to put Level Nine through to the final two. A huge achievement.

But I wanted more.

I wanted to win.

No one remembered who came in second. Runner-up wasn't enough for me to prove to Dad that I'd overcome the challenges of the last six years and made something of my life.

To prove to Dad that I wasn't a fuckup. I was a Kingcaid. And Kingcaids were winners.

I parked the car in the garage and entered the house via the kitchen. The sound of the TV filtered through from the living room. I froze on the spot. Someone was in the fucking house. I grabbed a knife from the block on the countertop, cursing my inaction in buying and learning how to shoot a gun. After getting jumped by those thugs, I'd considered it but hadn't ever gotten around to it. And as time had passed, I'd decided not to. I wasn't a huge fan of firearms.

Fuck.

I crept down the hallway on the balls of my feet and peered into the living room, knife held aloft.

"Jesus fucking Christ!"

My younger brother, Penn, and his fiancée, Gia, were curled up on my couch, watching a black-and-white Bette Davis movie. The two of them looked at me standing there holding a butcher's knife aloft, and they laughed.

They fucking laughed.

"Easy, soldier," Gia said. "All you need is one of those *Scream* masks, and it'd be like a live-action replay of the movie."

"Nah, he's nowhere near cool enough to pull that off," Penn said.

I fizzed with rage, my hand gripping the hilt until my knuckles whitened. I'd never come so close to punching my brother, and by God, I'd come close over the years.

"Did it *ever* occur to you that coming home in the middle of the night and hearing you in my fucking house might've triggered me? You're assholes. Both of you."

I whipped around and marched back to the kitchen. Ramming the knife into the block, I grabbed a bottle of whiskey and a glass and filled it halfway. My heart rate wouldn't slow, and my stomach had tied itself in knots. I knocked back the whiskey in one swallow, then refilled my glass. My hand trembled, a sign of weakness I fucking hated. I clutched the glass hard enough to break it.

Penn appeared in the doorway, Gia hovering behind him looking the tiniest bit remorseful. Unusual for her. Gia was a free spirit who gave zero fucks. She rocked on her heels and dug Penn in the arm, prompting him to speak.

"Sorry, man. I should've thought. Didn't you get my text?"

"What fucking text?"

"The one I sent you saying we were going to stop by on the way back from seeing Mom and Dad in Seattle and should be here by eleven."

"I've been busy." I pulled my phone out of my pocket and navigated to the messaging app. Sure enough, there it was, unread. A message from Penn sent at five o'clock yesterday evening. "I missed it. You should've seen I hadn't opened it, you prick."

"When you weren't here, we let ourselves in." Penn held up a key. "I have a spare, remember?"

We all had spare keys to each other's places just in case there was an emergency.

"Fuck." I downed my second whiskey, setting the glass in the sink.

"We really are sorry," Gia said. "I feel awful."

I glowered at her. "That's a first for you."

Her dazzling smile almost blinded me. "And there he is." She skipped over to me, kissing me on the cheek. "For a second, I thought you'd cloned yourself, and the other you was almost human."

"Oh, fuck off, Gia."

She grinned, unperturbed by my rudeness. Her ability to brush off my bad moods was one of many reasons I adored her. Fucking annoying woman.

I strode across the kitchen and grabbed a bottle of water from the fridge. "What are you doing here, anyway?" I said to Penn. "You hate LA. I can count on one finger the number of times you've visited since I moved here three years ago."

Penn glanced at Gia, who gave the smallest shake of her head. "Yeah, well, maybe things have changed. Is it a crime to want to see my brother?"

"It is when you freak me the fuck out by breaking into my house."

"Ah, ah. It's not breaking in when I have a key."

"I'm changing the locks tomorrow."

"Oh, hush," Gia interjected. "Do you want us to leave?"

I stared at her sullenly. "I suppose you can stay the night, since it's so late."

"Gee, thanks. You're all heart."

"I'm going to bed. Keep the fucking noise down."

I stomped upstairs. As I reached the top, I glanced over the balustrade to the hallway below. Penn had Gia pinned against the wall, kissing the ever-loving fuck out of her.

Envy curled in my gut, my ribs squeezing tight. If Sadie hadn't fucked me over, maybe I'd have been open to finding the kind of relationship Penn had with Gia.

Maybe with Ella.

Nope. Not gonna happen.

Who'd want a man like me? One who couldn't bear to show his scars, both internal and external. I had so much emotional baggage that it'd take me a lifetime to unpack it all. And I probably wouldn't manage it even if I lived for a century.

I left them to their passion-fest and went to bed. For once, I had a dreamless night.

Chapter 17

Johannes

Fuck, are they still here?

The sounds of tinkling laughter and the smell of bacon roused me from sleep, reminding me I wasn't alone in the house. Penn and Gia hadn't left, then?

Shame.

I threw off the covers and jumped in the shower. Thirty minutes later, I tramped downstairs, scuffing a hand over my still-damp hair as I entered the kitchen.

"What's all the fucking noise?"

"Morning," Gia trilled. "Glad to see you're just as much of an asshole first thing in the morning. Although"—she pointed at the clock hanging on the wall—"it's almost noon."

Oh, shit. I rarely slept in this late. Still, I should cut myself a break, especially after last night's triumph.

I snagged a slice of toast off a stack piled on a plate in the middle of my kitchen table and reached for my keys. "I'm late. I have to go. Let yourselves out."

"Wait a goddamn minute," Penn said. "Sit your butt down." He kicked out a chair, then reached for Gia's hand, tugging her onto his lap. "We have something to ask you."

I huffed, lowering myself into the chair. "Make it quick. I have things to do. Some of us work for a living."

My rebuttal wasn't fair. Both Penn and Gia worked as hard, if not harder, than I did. Penn not only ran the Kingcaid restaurant chain, which had over four hundred outlets, but he ran an independent restaurant too—Theo's, named after his best friend, who'd died in a car accident some years ago. And Gia had opened her own Italian restaurant earlier this year and had big expansion plans.

But since when had I allowed the truth to stand in the way of a snarky remark?

"God you are salty this morning," Gia said. "Saltier than normal, if that's even possible." She pushed a coffee across the table. "Get some caffeine into you."

I ignored the gesture. "Well?" I motioned to her. "What is it?"

Penn caressed the back of Gia's neck, then touched his head to hers. "I want you to be my best man at the wedding."

I raised my eyebrows. "Me? You want *me* to be your best man?"

"That's what I said."

A band wrapped around my chest. I hadn't always been the black sheep of the family. Sure, as the middle child, I'd had one or two issues to work through, but before that night, I would've been considered a normal guy who'd lovingly fought with his brothers and enjoyed spending time with his family.

Everyone dealt with life-changing events differently. Some gutted up, faced the problems head-on, and forged forward. Others, like me, withdrew into themselves, then woke up one day and realized they didn't even recognize who they were anymore. I'd love nothing more than to find my way back to the man I once was, but I was caught in a maze, and no matter how hard I tried, the exit point eluded me.

"You should choose Ash."

A flash of hurt crossed Penn's face. "I've chosen you."

"But you were Ash's best man. That means he should be yours."

Penn scratched his nose then pinched the bridge between his thumb and forefinger. "For fuck's sake, Johannes, can't you, for once in your miserable life, just say 'Thank you'? Why is everything a battle with you?"

Because my life is a constant battle.

Gia drummed her fingers on my table. "You're doing it, Johannes. Whether you like it or not. So pull on your big girl pants and stop your whining."

Gia. The woman who *always* called it as she saw it. She'd used the term *girl* on purpose, just to needle me.

I adored her. Didn't stop me scowling at her, though.

"When is this fucking wedding, anyway?"

If it interfered with the *Hottest Nightclub* award dinner, I knew which one I'd pick.

"We're thinking in the fall, when the leaves are all gold and orange and bronze. Late September."

I grunted.

"Besides," Penn continued. "If you're my best man, that means Ash can be yours and we all get a turn."

"Then he'd better prepare himself to miss out on the best-man shit, hadn't he? Tell him that and maybe he'll change his mind."

"Johannes." Penn sighed. "You can't let what that bitch Sadie did ruin the rest of your life. You—"

I snapped my hand in the air. "Stop, Penn. Just stop." I pushed back my chair and stood. "I'll be your fucking best man, okay? Just tell me where I have to be and when, and I'll be there."

"And said with so much grace." A smirk tugged at Gia's full lips. "We're lucky to have you."

I shook my head. "Don't forget to lock up when you leave."

"Our flight doesn't leave until tomorrow," Gia said, looking far too smug for my liking. "So you're stuck with us for another night."

"Just as well I'll be at work, then."

I turned and walked away. I got as far as the door leading into the hallway when Gia spoke again.

"We'll swing by the club and pick you up for dinner. Seven o'clock."

Hands on my hips, I pivoted. "I don't have time for dinner."

Her face softened. "Please, Johannes. For me."

I ground my teeth. Goddamn woman knew which buttons to press. I was awful to her, yet she read me easier than anyone in my family. It was like she knew, on an instinctual level, that my sniping attitude was the only thing holding the crumbling walls inside me together.

"Fine. Seven it is. But I have to be back at the club before ten."

"Done." Gia dusted off her hands. "Can't wait to spend time in your sparkling company."

Penn snickered. Gia grinned. I grimaced.

Fuckers. Both of them.

K

"I hope you're hungry." Gia sashayed into my office, trailing a finger over my desk as if she were checking for dust. "So this is where the Johannes Kingcaid magic happens, huh?"

I grabbed my jacket off the coat hanger. "Where are we going, anyway?"

"Ask Gia," Penn said. "She booked it, but she won't tell me where."

"We are going..." She paused theatrically. "To Hard Rock Cafe."

"No." I shook my head. "I hate chain restaurants."

"Yes," she insisted. "It's the most amazing place. So much fun, and Lord knows, you need to have some fun." Gia linked her arm through mine, tugging me toward the door. "Have you even been to one?"

"No."

"Then you can't judge, can you?"

Damn woman is intractable.

"Fine. On your own head be it."

"That's the spirit."

"Has anyone ever mentioned that you're the most frustrating woman in the world?" I drawled.

Penn chuckled. "Yeah. Me. Regularly."

He received a sharp dig in the ribs for his troubles. "You love me."

Catching her around the waist, he kissed her hard on the lips. "Yeah, I do."

"Jesus," I muttered. "Can we just get this fucking dinner over with?"

I pointed to the door, and at that exact moment, it opened and Ella walked in. She startled when she realized I wasn't alone.

"Oh, sorry to interrupt. I wasn't aware you had company."

My stomach flipped, and my pulse increased to double time. God, she was beautiful with her windswept ebony tresses and her makeup-free face. I yearned to kiss her again, to feel those plump lips against mine, to taste her if only to remind myself of what I could never have.

"What are you doing here?" I snapped. "You don't work Saturdays."

"I-I know. I just..."

She trailed off, her eyes falling away from mine and staring at the floor. The air around me stilled, silence cloaking me. The only sound was my thunderous heartbeat pounding in my ears. I hadn't expected to see her, and now here she was, standing before me, a sight I'd begun to crave.

I caught Gia raising her eyebrows in my peripheral vision, her gaze volleying between me and Ella. And then she nodded as if she'd found an answer to an unasked question.

"Hi, I'm Gia, Johannes's soon-to-be sister-in-law, and this is his brother, Penn." She stuck out her hand for Ella to shake. "And you are?"

"Um, I'm Ella. His assistant."

Gia glanced at Penn, then at me, and then back at Ella. "Assistant. Is that right? Well, you're not an assistant tonight, Ella. You're his date. We're going to Hard Rock Cafe and three is a terrible number. You've arrived in the nick of time."

"What?" I barked. "No. That's completely inappropriate."

Ella's face crumpled as if I'd crushed it underneath my boot. "Yeah, I have to get home anyway. I only stopped by for..." Once again, she didn't finish her thought.

"Nonsense," Gia pronounced. "We'll only be a couple of hours, especially as Cinders here has to be back at his castle before ten."

Ella's eyes widened. She'd never heard anyone talk to me the way Gia did, because no one spoke to me like that.

Except... sometimes Ella did.

"That's decided then," Gia said, even though neither Ella nor I had spoken. "I have a craving for an enormous burger and a craft beer."

She linked her arm through Penn's and paraded out of my office, leaving me and Ella behind.

"You don't have to come," I said. "Gia's a force of nature. You shouldn't let her bully you."

"Would you rather I went home?"

No. No, I fucking wouldn't.

"Don't you have to get back to Chloe?"

"I'm sure Ginny won't mind if I stay out for dinner. I can text her to make sure." She nibbled her lip. "But if this is uncomfortable for you, then—"

"I'd love for you to come," I whispered.

Her smile dazzled me. "Then let's go."

I drove Ella in my car, following Penn and Gia in their rental. That way, if I decided to cut the night short—highly probable—I didn't have to rely on them for a ride. Ella kept quiet on the drive, other than shooting me the occasional glance before staring out the window. Suited me. I wasn't in the mood for idle chitchat either.

When was I ever?

Hard Rock Cafe was everything I'd dreaded and more. Kids ran amok, their parents too busy filling their faces to discipline their offspring, music blasted from a hundred speakers, and the smell of burgers and fries turned my stomach.

And then I saw Ella's face, shining with excitement as she chatted with Gia, and I swallowed my antipathy. That smile was worth every drop of discomfort. I could suck it up for a couple of hours if it made her happy.

Wait...

When had I started to care about her happiness?

Before I could ponder the obtrusive thought, a host dressed in a black uniform came over to greet us, then led us to a booth.

Gia and Penn slid along one bench, leaving the other one free for me and Ella. She sat first, shuffling over to the far side. As I sat down, my thigh touched hers, and a zing of electricity shot straight to my groin. I shuffled a few inches to my right, putting a reasonable amount of space between us.

Ella shuffled to her right, too, pressing our thighs together once more.

Okay, then.

Semi-hard-on it is.

Chapter 18

Ella

Wow. Talk about calling it as you see it.

"Time for a trip to the ladies' room." Gia cocked her head at me. "Keep me company, Ella?"

"Why do women always go to the restroom in pairs?" Penn queried, wiping his mouth after polishing off the biggest hamburger I'd ever seen.

"Duh." Gia elbowed him in the ribs. "We want to gossip about men, of course."

I glanced at Johannes. He'd been quiet on the ride over here, which I presumed was discomfort at having me join his family for dinner.

The thought made my chest ache.

Then again, he had said he'd love for me to come along, despite Gia pushing him into it, so he couldn't be *that* uncomfortable. From what I'd gleaned these past few weeks, Johannes wasn't the kind of man to put himself out. He didn't care enough about hurting feelings to suffer for the sake of another.

Yet he seemed... different somehow. I couldn't put my finger on it. While his avoidance techniques since he'd kissed me after meeting Ryker Stone hadn't gone unnoticed, he wasn't the same man I'd met all those weeks ago.

At first, his choice to avoid me had stung, until I'd figured out that he was probably spooked at how spontaneously it had happened. That was when I'd decided to keep it light rather than barrage him with questions that put him under pressure to respond.

He stood to let me out, staring at the floor instead of at me, but as I slipped by him, I could have sworn he moved his arm, and our pinkie fingers touched. My stomach flipped. Maybe he'd decided not to avoid me any longer and to tackle our growing attraction to one another head-on.

I hoped so. Because for the last week, I'd dreamed about his lips on mine every night, and the thought of never kissing him again wasn't something I wanted to even contemplate. With him, though, I had to tread carefully. The truth he'd shared with me about almost dying had led me to revisit my initial impression that he'd suffered some kind of trauma. Johannes reminded me of the thoroughbred horses Mateo had kept.

One wrong move and he'd bolt.

God, some days I forgot I was still married. I had no business striking up any kind of relationship, especially when it had no future. I wasn't a free woman, and I would never *be* free. I couldn't divorce Mateo without revealing where I was. My circumstances trapped me in limbo, with no potential for escape.

Next month, I'd turn twenty-five, the prime of most people's lives, yet mine was effectively over. Like Ginny, I'd spend the rest of my days alone. But unlike Ginny, I'd never know what it was like to fall in love so deeply that another man couldn't ever match up to the love she'd lost.

I almost laughed at my fanciful musings. Johannes had kissed me once, and his actions since then had made it clear he wasn't interested in kissing me again. And here I was, getting all up in my head and ruing a loss of something I'd never had in the first place.

Besides, a relationship would only complicate things, a thought I'd had several times, and my priority was, and always would be, protecting Chloe and keeping her—and myself—out of Mateo's clutches.

Gia linked my arm as if we were lifelong friends and not acquaintances who'd only met this evening. I liked her enormously. She had this ability to make everyone in her orbit feel special, and small talk—something I'd always struggled with—was her forte.

She pushed open the door to the ladies' room, and as soon as it shut, she rounded on me.

"Okay, fess up. What's with you and Johannes?"

My head jerked back. "What do you mean?"

"I mean that my grouchy, sullen, withdrawn soon-to-be brother-in-law can't stop sneaking glances at you when he thinks no one is watching, and the look on his face when he does..." She fanned herself. "Phew."

"Nonsense," I scoffed, while secretly celebrating inside. I hadn't noticed him looking at me. I'd looked at him, though. A lot. "I'm his assistant. I don't even know what I'm doing here."

Gia canted her head. "Oh, sweetie, you don't? Then let me enlighten you. Johannes is a complicated man who doesn't date, ever. He has a tongue sharper than a samurai sword and enough baggage to fill the cargo hold on an Airbus A380. Yet when he looks at you, it's as if he's won the love lottery."

She stuck her hands in the back pockets of her jeans. "Please tell me he isn't off base, because although he's a dick and we needle each other all the time, I adore the bones of him. He's like a second brother to me, and soon, he'll be a real brother. So if you're not where he is, then please, tell him. And soon. Before he gets in too deep."

"I-I..."

Words failed me. She couldn't have this right. And what did she mean about him not dating? Had he, like Ginny, loved and lost? Was that the reason for the dead eyes and spiky attitude designed to keep everyone at a distance? Was that what he'd meant when he'd said he'd almost died?

"We kissed," I confessed. "Once. Over a week ago. And he's pretty much avoided me since then."

Gia pulled in her lips and nodded. "Of course he has." She rolled her eyes. "Like I said. He's a dick."

I chuckled. Gia sure called it as she saw it.

"The question is, do you like him?"

The door opened, and a gaggle of girls piled in. One of them wore a pink-and-white sash with "Bride-to-be" emblazoned across the middle, and all of them wore tiaras and were weaving around as if they'd drunk their weight in tequila.

Maybe they had.

Gia grabbed me by the arm and led me outside. Huh? So the trip to the restroom had nothing to do with the need to empty her bladder and everything to do with grilling me on Johannes.

"Too noisy in there." She jerked her chin at the ladies room door. "You were saying?"

I grinned. She was good, but two could play at that game. "I don't think I was saying anything."

She wagged her finger at me. "Uh-uh, missy. If my best friend, Kee, were here now, she'd tell you to fess up before I bring out the big guns. I'm relentless, and you, my dear Ella, have no chance of not telling me what I want to know."

Yeah, I liked Gia. She was the sort of woman you wanted on your side. And her bluntness might help me break down Johannes. Maybe.

"Yes, I like him. Too much."

Her hand whipped through the air, the gesture dismissive. "No such thing. But if I can offer you a piece of advice..."

"Go for it."

"If you want him, then you're going to need a lot of patience. Johannes has a traumatic past, and it's shaped the man he is today. He doesn't trust easily, if at all, and he has mastered avoiding any kind of emotions. They're locked up so tight behind walls of concrete that it'll take a long time to knock them down."

I knew it.

The eyes never lied, and Johannes's were steeped in suffering. As were mine. But if Gia saw in me what I'd seen in Johannes, she didn't let on.

"Don't ask me," she stated, even though I hadn't spoken. "It's not up to me to tell you. It's up to Johannes. And believe me, you're in for a wait before he'll share his past. He might look at you as if you're all his fantasies rolled into one cute-as-a-button package, but that doesn't mean he trusts you."

"I understand."

Gia squealed, then squished me in a tight hug. "This is so exciting. He deserves happiness, and I have a feeling you're it."

My heart sank.

No, I wasn't.

Not until I found a way to escape Mateo for good, if such a way even existed.

But what if... what if I could gather the courage to tell Johannes about my past.

No.

Not until he shared his. Given what Gia had said, if he told me about his past, then I'd know that he fully trusted me, and only then could I take the leap of faith needed to share my story.

Besides, all this could be moot. Gia might've read the situation all wrong. As much as my fingers itched to test her theory, Johannes would have to make the first move. Or second move since, technically, he'd made the first move when he'd kissed me.

We strolled back to our table. Penn and Johannes

appeared deep in conversation, and as we approached, I heard Penn ask about me.

I put out a hand to stop Gia, curious as to how Johannes would reply to his brother if he thought I wouldn't hear his response.

We all know what they say about eavesdroppers.

His voice rang out, clear and true. "She's just my assistant. Nothing more. I'm being nice. That's all."

My heart plummeted to my feet.

So Gia had read it wrong after all. I had no right to feel this rush of disappointment, but it came at me so fast that it stole my breath.

Penn laughed. "Bullshit. You're never nice. I saw the way you've been looking at her all night. Don't be an asshole. Just admit you like this girl."

"Yeah, Johannes," Gia said, butting her hip against Penn's shoulder for him to move over. "Tell us. Or better still, tell Ella."

Floor, please open up and swallow me whole.

Heat flooded my face until it felt as if I'd been cooked under the same grill as Penn's burger. I didn't dare look at Johannes. Or sit down. Or move.

"Fuck off, Gia," Johannes growled. "You're assholes, both of you."

Gia threw back her head and laughed, unperturbed by Johannes's barked curse.

"Yeah, but you love us."

"The way one loves a bout of gastric flu," he snapped. "Ella, for Christ's sake, sit down."

I slid onto the bench, my back as straight as a rod of steel. As my butt hit the seat, "We Will Rock You" by Queen started to play. The entire restaurant erupted as the staff jumped up onto the bar and began to clap and stamp their feet.

"Yessss!" Gia exclaimed.

"Kill me now," Johannes muttered.

"Oh shut up," Gia said. "This is *awesome.* I love it when they do this. It's a Hard Rock tradition."

She kissed Penn hard on the mouth, then skipped over to the bar. Seconds later, one of the bartenders reached down and helped her up. Displaying the kind of confidence I would sell a kidney for, she joined right in, shimmying her hips, shaking her boobs, and clapping and stomping and singing louder than anyone else.

"You do realize you're marrying that," Johannes said.

Penn's smile almost split his face wide open. "` Yeah, I do. Isn't she fantastic?"

"That's one word for her."

Relieved that Gia had diverted attention away from me and Johannes, I clapped in time to the song, stamping my feet along with ninety-nine percent of the restaurant, Johannes being the one percent who flatly refused to join in.

"You're allowed to have fun, you know," I said, grinning in an attempt to coax him from underneath the black cloud that hovered over his head.

"This isn't what I'd call fun."

"Johannes's idea of fun is plucking out his leg hairs with tweezers," Penn shouted, his eyes still locked on his fiancée shaking her booty.

Johannes's glower deepened. I shifted in my seat.

"We can go if you want," I said.

He looked down at me, and his eyes softened a little. "Do you want to leave?"

I shook my head.

"Then we'll stay."

"But you're not enjoying yourself."

"Says who?"

"You did, just now." I drummed my fingers on the table. "If you are having a good time, maybe let your face know."

One side of his mouth lifted in as close to a smile as Johannes ever got. "You're a brave woman."

"Or maybe your bad-boy act doesn't scare me. Sticks and stones and all that." I shrugged.

Johannes stared at me as if he wanted to reply, but the words on his tongue never made it into the open when the song ended and Gia skipped back to our table, where she promptly threw herself into Penn's lap, gripped his face in her hands, and kissed him for a good ten seconds.

"Time for the check," Johannes said. "Before my steak comes back up."

Gia broke off from kissing Penn and flipped her middle finger. "Don't worry. You'll be rid of us tomorrow."

"Thank fuck for small mercies. Let yourselves out in the morning."

I chuckled. Their banter was steeped in rudeness that neither side appeared the slightest bit bothered by. In fact, I'd say they relished it. The more vicious, the better. And Penn, who seemed like a really mellow guy, just sat on the sidelines as if relaxing in front of the TV and watching a UFC match.

Imagining these two in a fighting cage... my money was on Gia to emerge triumphant.

"You may scoff at my 'lovedupness,' dear brother," Penn said. "But one of these days, it'll be your turn."

His eyes shifted to me, then back to Johannes.

Johannes's face darkened, and a nerve thrummed in his cheek. "Not happening." He tapped me on the shoulder with the back of his hand, gesturing for me to stand. "Let's go. Penn can get the check."

"Gee, thanks."

"Don't mention it."

"Fabulous to meet you, Ella," Gia said. "Maybe you can come to our wedding as Johannes's plus-one?" She fluttered her eyelashes at him. "After all, he's *such* a catch."

"Fucking hell," Johannes muttered.

I think I have a crush on Gia.

I beamed at her. "Great to meet you both. Have a safe trip home."

Johannes hustled me from the restaurant, and seconds later, we were speeding down Hollywood Boulevard as if we were running from the cops.

"Easy," I cautioned. "I'd like to get home in one piece."

He backed off the gas, and the car slowed. "Sorry."

A few silent seconds edged by.

"I liked them."

He grunted.

A few more seconds passed.

I sighed. "Can I ask you something?"

"Depends on what it is."

"Well, how will I know?"

He side-eyed me, then returned his attention to the road. "If there's the remotest chance it's intrusive, then I'd advise you to refrain."

I should heed his warning. But then Gia's observation of the way Johannes had looked at me tonight made me feel brave. Or stupid.

"Why don't you think you'll ever find someone?"

He locked his jaw. "Intrusive."

"I'm aware."

"Then back the fuck off."

"Do I mean anything to you at all?"

His hands tightened on the wheel, his knuckles turning white. "We hardly know each other."

"I'm aware," I parroted.

"And you're an employee."

"Also true."

"I don't get involved with employees."

"According to Gia, you don't get involved with anyone."

His nostrils flared. "Gia has a big fucking mouth. She also hasn't a fucking clue what she's talking about."

"I think she knows you pretty well." I covered his hand with mine. "I'd like to get to know you, too."

He ripped his hand from beneath mine, setting a clenched fist on his thigh. "I don't do relationships."

"Why?"

He braked hard, and the car slewed to a stop. The sudden movement threw me forward in my seat, and the belt snapped into action.

"Get out."

I gaped at him, then glanced through the windshield. I recognized our location. It was at least five miles from Ginny's house.

"Johannes," I pleaded. "I'm miles from home."

"You should have thought of that." He stared straight ahead. "Out."

"You can't be serious."

"Deadly. Call an Uber, walk, get the bus. I don't care. Just get out of my fucking car."

My legs felt weak as my feet hit the sidewalk. I took a few steps then looked over my shoulder. Johannes hadn't moved, his face stony, his hands gripping the steering wheel. I shook my head and set off walking. I hadn't gone far when the sound of a car door slamming reached me, and hurried footsteps closed in.

"Ella, wait."

I stopped walking, but I kept my back to him.

"Fuck, I'm sorry. I'm..."

He trailed off. I slowly pivoted, my heart twisting at his stricken expression. He scuffed a hand over the top of his head.

"Shit. I-I'm just... I can't—"

I touched his arm, the need to soothe him overcoming my confusion and disbelief that he'd let a woman walk home alone after dark. Except, looking at his face, I knew he wouldn't have let me get far.

"We all have complications in our lives, Johannes. Things in our pasts that we'd rather stayed there. But if we don't open ourselves up, even a tiny bit, to human emotion, human contact, to touch, then who are we?"

He palmed his neck, muttered, "Fuck," under his breath, and the next thing I knew, his mouth was on mine.

I melted as he threaded his fingers into my hair, angling me to better suit him. My spine arched, and he planted a palm against my lower back, supporting me.

Everything tingled, from the top of my head to the tips of my toes. My blood set on fire, my lungs stopped working. But my heart... my heart sang.

He pulled away, his breaths coming as fast as mine.

"Call Ginny," he rasped. "Tell her you'll be home before Chloe wakes in the morning." He bit my earlobe. "Tonight, you're mine."

Chapter 19

Johannes

What the fuck am I doing?

I held Ella's hand on the ride over to my house. Neither of us spoke, and I was still in some kind of stupor, having gone from throwing her out of my car, all because her questions had hit a tad too close to home, to inviting her to spend the night at my house. In my bed. I could only pray I wasn't making a gigantic mistake.

As I steered the car onto my road, I groaned. Penn's rental car was parked on the street. Amid blind anger and potent desire, it had slipped my mind that they were staying at my place. They must have left the restaurant soon after us and driven straight back here. At least the fucker had left my driveway free.

But that left me with a problem. There wasn't a chance I'd fuck Ella while Gia and Penn were right down the hall.

Knowing those kinky bastards, they'd have a glass pressed up against my door, listening to every pant, every grunt, every sound. Plus, Gia's smugness wasn't something I had the patience for.

I turned the car around.

"Wrong turn?" Ella asked.

"Unwanted visitors." I pointed at my house as we passed. "That's my place. And that black Mercedes is Penn's rental car."

"Oh." She peered through the window at my home. "Modest home for a billionaire."

I shrugged. "It's just me. I hardly need a mansion with eight bedrooms and twelve and a half bathrooms." Not to mention those places were meccas for the underbelly of society. Showing off my wealth had almost gotten me killed. I'd made a stupid immature mistake when I'd been too young to know any better.

Now, I knew better. Which was the reason I lived in a three-bedroom home in a family-oriented neighborhood, chose not to own a dozen sports cars, and left getting ferried around in limousines to Ash.

"It's nice." She nibbled her lip. "We can't go to Ginny's."

"No." I pressed the phone button on the car and scrolled down the screen until I reached the number I was looking for. I hit Dial.

"Thank you for calling Kingcaid Los Angeles. Nichole speaking, how can I help you?"

"Hi, Nichole. This is Johannes Kingcaid." They knew me well at this particular branch, and I'd met Nichole several times. "Is the penthouse suite free tonight?" If it wasn't, then I'd stay in Ash's suite. He kept one in the hotels he visited the most. If I had the choice, though, I'd rather not.

"Oh, hi, Mr. Kingcaid. Let me check for you real quick." A pause. "Yes, it is."

"Great. Hold it for me. I'll be there shortly."

"Of course, sir. Will you need anything else?"

I pressed Mute and glanced at Ella, whose eyes were bugging out of her head. "Walk of shame, or do you want me to have our designer-store manager drop off a selection of clothes?"

"Designer clothes?" She shook her head, glancing down at her jeans and blouse combo. "I'm good."

I unmuted the call. "Nothing, thanks, Nichole."

Cutting the connection, I reached for Ella's hand again. Her fingers trembled in mine. "Second thoughts?" I asked.

"No. None." She smiled at me. "Penthouse, huh? There are some benefits to being a billionaire, then."

My own lips curved a little. "When the situation calls for it."

"It's nice not to have to worry about money, huh?"

"Oh, I worry about money." I flashed a sidelong glance at her. "When Dad put me in charge of building the Kingcaid nightclub business a few years ago, he had these grand plans to open a branch in every big city in the US, and move internationally within three years. But I didn't want to do that. Throwing money at things is all well and good, but where's the sense of achievement if you get your success that way? I want to make it on my own steam, so I run my business separate from my own personal fortune and the fortune of my family. Every branch must be profitable in its own right within twelve months. I cross-subsidize from the more successful clubs during the startup phase, but after that, those clubs have to stand on their own or they're done."

I stopped rambling, then realized she hadn't said a thing. I risked another glance. Ella was staring at me. Her lips were parted, and she blinked a few times in succession. "What?"

"You... I... Just that you've never shared your thoughts like that. Not with me. Your drive and your determination to succeed on your own are inspiring, Johannes."

She brought our joined hands to her lips and kissed the tips of my fingers. The hairs on the back of my neck stood on end, my groin warmed, and something akin to pride swelled in my chest at her praise.

"Thanks."

She chuckled. "This is so weird."

I frowned. "Weird how?"

"This. Us." She waved her free hand between us. "I'm not sure how we got here, but I'm glad we have."

"I'm unconventional."

"You can say that again."

She laughed once more. I'd come to relish her laughs, almost as if each one she shared with me shored up a damaged piece of my soul while simultaneously putting another crack in the walls I'd built. She was dangerous, yet instead of running away, I craved to nestle closer, to steal her innate goodness and keep it for my own selfish needs.

The valet strode forward as I pulled up outside the hotel. He opened Ella's door and held out a hand to guide her. I joined them, took her hand, and gave him my keys.

"Ready?" I posed the question as a way of giving her a final exit strategy.

"So ready," she whispered.

Tingles fired through my veins, and prickles crept over my skin as I struggled to control the Neanderthal inside me that yearned to be inside her right fucking now.

Nichole was serving another guest, but as she saw me approach, she set a key card on the desk without breaking her attention away from the customer. I picked it up and led Ella over to the elevators. The doors closed with just the two of us inside, and the intimacy of the moment enveloped me. My dick hardened, and my fingers itched to explore her firm, round tits, her enticing curves, her lips, her soft skin.

She shuffled from her left foot to her right and gazed up at me from beneath her lashes. I ran my teeth over my bottom lip.

"I'm not touching you here."

She blinked. "Why not?"

"Because if I do, I won't stop."

Her pink tongue darted to dampen her lips.

Fuck. She's trying to kill me.

"Maybe you don't have to stop." The elevator dinged. Ella smirked. "Saved by the bell."

I led her through the welcome foyer and into the penthouse. She took in the opulent surroundings and the view of downtown Los Angeles through the floor-to-ceiling windows, lights sparkling in the dusk.

"This is gorgeous."

"You're gorgeous." I pulled her to me, encircling her waist as I lowered my head to kiss her. A raft of feelings coursed through me at her sigh, the way her body fused with mine, the hitch in her breath as I breached her lips with my tongue.

And with those feelings came fear. I could not, *would not*, allow myself to get in too deep. I'd told her I didn't do relationships, yet she'd come here with me anyway. To fuck. That was all. Not to have a deep and meaningful conversation or to share the painful shit of our pasts. We were here to scratch an itch that had developed between us over these past few weeks.

I unfastened her jeans, pushing them and her panties past her knees. My fingers sought her heat, a groan rumbling through my chest as I slid two inside her.

"So wet, so ready," I murmured, my lips forging a path from her ear to the slope of her shoulder. I strummed her clit, and she responded beautifully, clenching around my fingers.

"God, yes," she gasped. "Christ, I'm there. I'm already fucking there." A long groan spilled from her lips and she thrust her hands into my hair, tugging on the roots as she orgasmed less than twenty seconds after I'd first touched her.

I held back a smile that threatened. "You needed that."

Drowsy eyes found mine, swimming with satisfaction. "You have no idea."

Her honesty forced a chuckle from me, the sound alien, yet it felt appropriate. No, not appropriate. It felt right. I slipped my hands around her waist and kissed her, fusing her body to mine. And then a thought hit me from left field. Fuck!

"I don't have a condom."

Kingcaid hotels weren't in the business of renting rooms

by the hour, so boxes of condoms weren't part of the complimentary toiletries we provided to our guests. And as I rarely had sex, carrying around a spare rubber in my wallet wasn't something I thought about. I planned my liaisons. This wasn't planned.

"I'm on birth control."

"You sure?"

"Yes." She reached for the button on my pants. I spun her around and bent her over the couch, freeing myself in seconds.

"Not like this." She glanced over her shoulder. "I want to see you, to touch you."

A coldness hit my core. This was the point where she walked out. I braced myself. "This is how I do it."

I'd made a mistake. I shouldn't have brought her here. My stomach lurched. I usually had these conversations long before I pushed my fingers inside a woman, bringing her to a rapid climax. I made a point of being clear about my proclivities. With Ella, though, I'd gotten caught up in the moment.

Fuck.

"Why?"

My erection deflated. I stood up. Backed away. Shoved my dick in my pants and zipped up. "Forget it. I'll take you home."

Standing, jeans and panties still around her ankles, she made no attempt to dress herself as she turned to face me.

"Johannes." She reached out a hand. "Come here."

I stared at her hand for so long that she let it fall to her side. God. I was a bastard. Hurt and confusion streamed across her face, and still I stood there, mute.

"You only have sex from behind?"

"Yes."

She ran her gaze over me. "And clothed."

"Yes."

She nodded as if she understood. She didn't understand. She couldn't possibly understand. How could she when I'd withheld all the pertinent facts? Reasons that would explain my reticence to expose myself, emotionally more than physically. The problem was, in my head, they were so tied together that they were basically the same thing.

"Is there a mirror around here?"

I frowned. "In the master bath. Why?"

"Where is that?"

I pointed to a door to the left of the bank of windows. "That's the master bedroom. It's through there."

She kicked off her jeans and panties, unbuttoned her blouse and slipped it down her arms, and unfastened her bra, where it, too, joined the heap of her clothes. My deflated dick sprang to life so fast, I felt dizzy.

"Jesus," I hissed, letting my eyes travel over her nakedness. The tips of my fingers tingled, the urge to touch her, to trace her body with my hands and my tongue and my mouth causing a carnal urge so powerful that I almost came without her laying a hand on me.

"I want you." She looked me straight in the eye, unwavering, brave, hot as hell. "And I know you want me. If having sex from behind is what makes you comfortable, then that's what we'll do. But I want to see you." She hitched a shoulder. "If that has to be in a mirror rather than face-to-face, then so be it."

"Ella," I breathed. "Fuck."

Her attention slipped to my groin, to where the outline of my dick was visible through my pants. She took my hand and led me over to the bedroom. I ceded control to her, the experience unusual yet oddly erotic. Her eyes went to the bed, but only for a moment. Bypassing the comfortable mattress and luxurious silk sheets, she entered the bathroom and planted both hands on either side of the sink. Her eyes met mine in the mirror, a comforting smile gracing her lips.

"Is this okay?"

I closed my eyes, taking a deep breath through my nose. Strange thoughts crowded my mind, ones I'd never had with any other sexual partner since Sadie. I wished I could strip off my clothes, lay her down on the enormous bed, and explore every inch of her while she did the same to me. Pipe dreams, stupid fantasies that my emotionally stunted brain would never allow. I hated the scar across my neck, not only for its physical abhorrence, but also for what it demonstrated.

Weakness. Stupidity. Naivety.

Every time I looked at the raised, ugly skin, it triggered me, taking me back to that night. The pain from being repeatedly punched and kicked, the sickly smell of fear filling my nostrils. Realizing the woman I was in love with had orchestrated the entire assault. The searing agony as the blade sliced through my flesh. The warm rush of blood spurting from my neck as I lay on the floor knowing I was about to die.

I snapped my eyes open, fixating on Ella standing with her hands braced on the bathroom counter, waiting for me to fuck her. Willing to let me fuck her the way I needed to.

The only way I knew how to. Putting me and my feelings ahead of her own.

I'd done nothing to deserve her benevolence, yet she freely gave it to me anyway.

"Kiss me," she murmured, twisting to look over her shoulder, her eyes hooded and heavy with lust.

The last thread of my resolve snapped. I ran my palm down the smooth skin of her back until I reached the curve of her ass. Sliding one hand over her abdomen, I angled her head with my other hand, allowing my mouth to take hers. Our tongues dueled until she surrendered to me, permitting me to take back the control I'd loaned to her. I unzipped my pants and pulled out my cock. I closed my hand around my shaft. A deep, husky groan rumbled through my chest.

Breaking our kiss, I bent my knees, lined up the head of my cock, and thrust inside her. She snatched a breath, pushing back into me.

God. So good. So fucking good.

I thrust again until I was seated to the root, and then I stopped. Our eyes met in the mirror, hers deep pools of emotion I didn't deserve and hadn't earned. Sex for me was a physical release, not an emotional connection. But with Ella, there was a shifting inside my chest, a yearning for something deeper. Something *more.*

I ran my nose along her neck, breathing in the faint scent of her perfume. "Are you okay?"

"I'm okay." She lifted her hand and cupped the back of my neck. "More than okay."

That was it. The moment when I lost control. I gripped her hips and pounded into her. Over and over and over until my vision blurred, my balls tightened, and all I could feel was Ella's walls sheathing my cock, her snatched breaths filling my chest, her beautiful face flushed, and her eyes glossy.

"God, Ella. Fuck." I released one of her hips, reaching around her to play with her clit. I wasn't so far gone that I thought only of my own pleasure, although it was a close-run thing. I refused to come until she had. But Christ, I hoped it didn't take long.

"Are you there?" I asked as her walls rippled around my dick.

"Almost. God. Faster. Yes, that's it. Right there. Don't stop. God, don't stop."

She exploded, her clit vibrating beneath my thumb, her body twitching as an orgasm charged through her.

"God, Johannes, yes!"

Her cry made me feel like a fucking king. I let go, emptying inside her. I couldn't stop coming. My climax went on and on and on until I was sure I'd lose consciousness if it didn't stop soon.

The scent of raw sex enveloped me as I slowly came down from the kind of erotic high I'd never thought I'd experience again. I sought out Ella's flushed face in the mirror, an unbidden smile stretching across my face, one I hardly recognized yet couldn't stop from forming. I placed a kiss on her shoulder as I pulled out of her and wrapped my arms around her waist, tighter and tighter, loath to let her go.

"Thank you," I whispered, overcome with emotions I didn't have names for.

She turned in my arms, capturing my face in her hands. "No. Thank you. For showing me a piece of you."

Chapter 20

Ella

Intimacy is a dangerous game for people like us.

Weary yet fulfilled, I collapsed onto the softest, comfiest bed I'd ever lain on. Johannes crawled into the space beside me, his all-black attire in direct contrast to my pale nakedness.

My curiosity was off the charts, but no matter how much intimacy we'd shared, I suspected that if I even tentatively broached the subject of why he only had sex from behind, or his reasons for remaining fully clothed during the act, he'd clam up and we'd lose the tenuous connection we'd built.

I wasn't ready to let him go yet. Not even close.

This taciturn, complicated man sprawled beside me

carried so much pain within him. Of that I was a hundred percent certain. But if I stood a chance of winning his trust, I had to do that through my actions, by showing him I was someone he could confide in, when he was ready, and not before.

Badgering him for answers would have the opposite effect.

Besides, who was I to talk? I had more secrets than the CIA, yet he hadn't pressured me to spill all the gory details.

Should I tell him everything?

No.

I wasn't ready, and neither was he. To hear my story, or to share his own.

And what if he called me on my stupidity and naivety for being so blind about Mateo's true colors? I already thought those awful things about myself. I didn't need someone pointing out my biggest flaws and making it obvious that what I thought of as my worst traits were, in fact, real.

"Do you want something to drink? Or eat?"

Johannes sounded tentative, almost as if he'd never spent time with a woman after they'd slept together.

Maybe he hadn't.

"Some water would be good."

He climbed off the bed and disappeared into the living area of the suite. Less than a minute later, he returned with two bottles of water.

He loosened the cap and handed one to me. That small, kind act set off a swarm of butterflies in my stomach. For all his broodiness, he had an almost sensitive quality, that somewhere within him, hidden too deep to mine, was the kind of empathy a woman could drown in if he ever allowed it to surface. The amateur psychologist in me wondered whether, in spite of his radiating "keep away" vibes, underneath it all, he was desperate for love. To give it, and receive it.

His relationship with his brother had intrigued me, and with Gia, too. It was as if he was determined to push them away with his barbed comments and sullen refusal to join in with any kind of fun activity, yet at the same time, he craved their approval, their acceptance.

"Thank you." I drank a third of the bottle, then set it on the nightstand.

"Are you cold?" He pulled the sheets over me without waiting for an answer.

I pushed them off. "Are you scared of looking at my nakedness in case it tempts you for a second time?"

He swallowed, his eyes shifting to my boobs. "No."

"No you're not scared, or no, you're not tempted?"

His tongue dampened his lips. "I'm not scared."

"But you are tempted?"

"I'm just a man. You're a beautiful woman. I'm constantly tempted."

I rolled onto my side and snuggled against him. He stiffened, but I persisted, running my hand over his abdomen. The muscles flexed beneath my palm.

"Do you have a six-pack?"

He let out a huff of air. I wasn't sure if it was through irritation or humor.

"I work out and watch my diet. So yes, I do."

"Can I see?"

I was pushing him when I'd promised myself that I wouldn't. I blamed the devil on my shoulder, egging me on. But I craved a deeper connection, some skin-to-skin contact. I braced for him to throw me off and stomp out of the room, or blurt that he was taking me home.

Or just ignore me.

He grasped my wrist and removed my hand, and my heart sank a little. Until he gripped the hem of his sweater and pulled it up to his chest, revealing smooth, pale skin and those delicious ridges of muscle I found irresistible.

"There. Happy now?"

I pressed the flat of my hand to his abdomen. He flinched, but he didn't push me away or tell me to stop touching him. I grew a little braver. "Can I kiss them?"

"You're talking about muscles as if they're sentient beings."

"My clit wants me to kiss them."

His full lips twitched. "Does it now?"

"Yeah. It's pulsing. That's a sure sign it wants me to kiss them."

He smiled, and elation coursed through me.

"Well, I wouldn't want to disappoint your clit."

"Now who's talking about body parts as sentient beings?"

"You're a bad influence."

"So, can I kiss them or not?"

He laced his fingers together and braced them behind his head. "Be my guest."

I kissed all six individually, pressing my thighs together to relieve the ache between my legs. Johannes shuddered every time my lips touched his skin.

"You're not used to this, are you?"

"Used to what?"

"Intimacy."

His face darkened, his eyes turning to stone. "No."

"Do you dislike it?"

He paused, staring at the ceiling for a few moments. Eventually, he gave me his attention.

"With you, maybe not."

For Johannes, that was a huge admission.

An enormous step.

The more time I spent with this intriguing man, the greater my understanding of him grew.

"Have you ever slept with a woman face-to-face and unclothed?"

He rolled onto his side and tucked both hands beneath his head. In that moment, he looked boyish, his usual harsh features softening. His eyes glazed as he looked at me, as if he was physically here but his mind was somewhere else.

"Yes."

"How long ago was that?"

He made a frustrated noise. "You do like to push, don't you?"

"Meh." I shrugged. "You've had your dick in my pussy. I think that entitles me to ask a question or two."

He snort-laughed, and I almost fell off the bed. God, he was transforming right before my eyes.

I only hoped it would last.

"Truth for a truth."

I grimaced. Last time, I'd avoided sharing a snippet of my past, even though he'd shared a snippet of his. Something told me I wouldn't get away with it a second time.

"Okay." I motioned to him. "You answer mine first."

"A little over six years ago."

Six years?

His comment in the car right before we'd kissed fired into my mind.

"*I almost died a few years ago*".

"A few" could be six.

Were the two things connected?

I wrinkled my nose, curiosity pushing me to ask a follow-up question.

"What happened?"

He shook his head. "A truth for a truth. You asked for a time. I gave it to you. My turn."

Dammit.

I logged away the nugget of information for the next time we played this game.

If, in fact, we did.

I held my breath, bracing for what was to come.

"Who are you running from?"

My stomach dropped.

I'd hoped he wouldn't go there, wouldn't focus on that particular subject. But he had, and I couldn't blame him.

Earlier, drowning in post-orgasmic bliss, I'd considered telling him about Mateo, but now that he'd opened the door, I couldn't do it. I couldn't walk through it.

The risk was too great.

"My parents." The lie tripped off my tongue so easily and rotted me from the inside. I hated myself for it. "And I'm not running as such. More that I don't need their brand of control in my life, or in Chloe's."

"I thought you were going to say Chloe's father."

My pulse rocketed tenfold, and another lie spilled out. "Chloe's father was a one-night mistake. I never saw the guy again."

Buy it. Buy the lie.

Please, Johannes, stop digging.

"Then you're better off without him. If he doesn't want to be a father to his child, then he's a worthless piece of shit."

"I'm definitely better off." *At last, a truth.* "Can we change the subject?"

He tucked a lock of hair behind my ear, and a piece of my heart cracked. "Whatever you want."

I searched for a safer subject, one that didn't involve our pasts, our presents, or, God forbid, our futures.

"Tell me something fun."

He arched a brow. "This is me. I don't do fun."

"True." I nodded sagely. He dug me in the ribs, and I squealed. "Ow." I prodded him in the chest. "Tit for tat."

His eyes lowered. I lifted his chin. "Eyes up here, mister."

"You were the one who mentioned tits."

I giggled. With every minute that passed, my adoration and admiration for this complex man grew.

"Not that kind of tit."

"Ella, yours are the only kind of tits that matter."

"Ugh. You're so frustrating. Okay, forget fun. Tell me something interesting."

"Okay, although whether this fits the bill is anyone's guess. Our family name used to be the far more common Kincaid rather than Kingcaid."

"Oh? When did it change?"

"Centuries ago, when the British ruled America. One of my ancestors, a man named Robert Kincaid, fell in love with the King's daughter. He thought he stood more of a chance to win the hand of the princess if his name sounded more regal, so he changed it to Kingcaid."

"And did he win the hand of the King's daughter?"

"Sadly, no, but he kept the name and later went on to marry a duke's daughter, so maybe the change of surname did help him marry into the aristocracy in the end."

"Wow. Fascinating. I know nothing about my ancestry."

"I'm not particularly interested myself. I'd rather live in the present. The past is done, and the future is uncertain. Now is the only time we can count on. But my father loves that story. He tells it at almost every dinner party, despite my mother's exasperation."

It was the first time he'd mentioned his parents to me, and the fond way he spoke about them caused an arc of pain to rip through me.

To distract myself, I traced my fingertips over his defined cheekbone, but as I moved close to the neckline of his sweater, he caught my fingers in a viselike grip.

"Don't."

My heart tripped.

Whatever he was hiding lay beneath that sweater. His eyes begged me to back off, not to push or continue on this path. Out of respect for him, and out of guilt for my earlier lie, I refrained, nodding. His audible sigh of relief cut me deeply.

"Let's get some sleep."

He pulled the sheets over me, but not himself. Leaning closer, he kissed my forehead. "Night, Ella."

I swallowed my hurt. "Good night."

Turning away from him, I closed my eyes, hoping he'd move in and hold me.

He didn't.

Chapter 21

Johannes

Stay in the safe zone.

I WOKE WITH ELLA DRAPED OVER ME, HER LEG THROWN OVER MINE, her pussy fused to my hip, and her midnight tresses spilling all over my chest. I'd had a dreamless night, a minor miracle and a major relief. Trying to explain why I woke up drenched in sweat and panting like I'd run the two-hundred-meter sprint wouldn't have been easy.

I shouldn't have let her stay, but after the way we'd left things last night, I didn't want her to think I was punishing her for being curious. Instead, I punished myself by sleeping beside her and risking a nightmare and all the questions that would come with that.

The biggest punishment was lying next to her all night and not touching her. It was my penance for being a coward.

"Ella." I eased her off me, and she let out this adorable

sound, a cross between a purr and a moan. She stretched and the sheet slipped.

Goddammit. My eyes locked on her tits, the rosy nipples erect from the air-conditioning. My mouth watered, eager to taste her, to suck the hard buds into my mouth, to explore her smooth skin with my hands and my tongue. To make her mine.

Her eyelids fluttered, glazed at first, then clearing as she focused in on my face. She smiled. "Good morning."

A shift occurred in my chest, a dangerous fluttering, a yearning to wake up beside her every morning and have her say those words to me. I shut it down.

"It's five o'clock. We should get going. You don't want to be late for Chloe." I went to get out of bed. Her hand on my shoulder stopped me.

"Wait."

I faced her. She stretched out her arms, beckoning to me. "Come here."

"Ella." I sighed.

"Johannes, don't make me morning-mad. You wouldn't like morning-mad Ella."

She was teasing me. I saw it in the twinkling in her eyes, the faint pout to her lips, the way she cocked her head to the side, the move steeped in challenge. I succumbed. Lying down beside her, I let her put her arms around me and pull me close. God, she felt like warmth on a winter's night, and despite my reservations, I snuggled closer. Not since Sadie had I lain beside a woman the morning after sex. Of course, I now knew that the intimacy we'd shared and the love she'd showered on me had all been a lie.

Was Ella lying? Or was the way she tightened her hold

on me and kissed the top of my head real?

Trust. Such a fragile commodity. So easily shattered. Not so easily rebuilt.

"I have an idea."

"It's too early for ideas."

"Not this one."

I lifted my head and looked at her. "Let's hear it."

She nibbled at the corner of her mouth. "It's easier to show you."

Tossing the sheet to the side, she pushed me onto my back and straddled me. The next thing I knew, she was rubbing her pussy against my cock. It responded, hardening in seconds.

"Ella." My tone was soaked in warning, but Ella just smiled. She rocked her hips. Back and forth. Back and forth. And then she gripped both her tits and pushed them together, rubbing her thumbs over the hardened points. A soft moan spilled out of her.

Fuck. I'm dead.

"You don't have to take your clothes off."

She raised herself up and unzipped me, reaching inside my pants to remove my cock. The moment she touched me, my resolve crumbled.

"Christ, Ella." I gripped her hips, helping guide her onto me. She sighed with such contentment as I filled her that my heart tripped. Me. I'd made her sigh like that. I'd given her that look of pure pleasure.

"It's like you were made for me," she breathed. "You fit just right."

God help me.

"I'm not made for anyone," I gritted out, thrusting up

into her.

"I don't believe that." She gasped when I angled her to help me hit the right spot. "God, yes!"

I'd never been with a woman so vocal in telling me what she liked, what turned her on, and it turned me the fuck on. I sat up and sucked her nipple into my mouth, swirling my tongue around the tip.

"Kiss me," she demanded. "Kiss me like you mean it."

I took her mouth, ferociously, spearing her with my tongue, biting her lips. She clawed at my back, her nails breaking through my sweater, driving me to the edge of madness.

I flipped her over, lifted her ass and pounded into her, a violent need to possess, to own every inch of her, powering through me. The sight of her lying there, her hair an unruly tangle, her eyes wild and heady with desire, her lips swollen from my assault, undid me.

God she was beautiful.

One night and I was addicted.

My head screamed *danger*, but my cock was in charge and it screamed *more*.

I rolled her clit between my thumb and forefinger, somehow maintaining my rhythm. Her pants and gasps and pleas for faster, slower, harder, softer brought me to the edge of orgasm. I couldn't control it. My balls tightened, seconds from exploding.

"Fuck, Ella, please. Come."

She shattered, pulsing along my shaft. I followed her into the abyss, falling, absorbed by the pleasure, immersed in the tingles racing up and down my spine. I slumped forward, holding her close. Just for a few seconds. As wrong as it was, I took that moment for myself, a chance to pretend that I was the old me. The carefree me. The undamaged and lovable me.

Too soon, reality crowded in, and I rolled off of her, my chest heaving as I fought to regain my breath.

Erotic.

Sensual.

Addictive.

This was supposed to be one night. One. Night. But the thought of this being the last time I came inside her, the last time she came for me... No. One night wasn't enough. I needed more.

Dammit, I'd *have* more.

If she'd have me.

She curled onto her side and pressed a palm to my chest, right over the heart Sadie had ripped out. It beat strong and true beneath her hand. For the first time since I'd woken up in that hospital bed hooked up to machines and with my parents' tearful faces looming over me, I started to believe that the deep scars I carried within me might heal. One day.

"I'm proud of you."

I peered down at her, my throat tightening. "For what?" I knew, but I hungered for her to tell me, because that might make it real.

"For proving to yourself that your beliefs, while valid, can be challenged. You can overcome whatever holds you back."

My mouth dried up, and I rolled my tongue across the inside of my upper lip to moisten it.

"I don't know what happened to you, and I'm not asking you to share. That's your business. But what I am saying is that you're strong enough to overcome your demons, to not let them rule you. All you have to do is try. And you did."

I shifted my gaze to the ceiling, her words sitting on my chest like a lump of lead. "It was just a fuck. Don't turn it into a philosophy."

I flinched at the harshness and cruelty of that statement. But I was a harsh and cruel man. Or I could be when I chose to. Sadie had created me, and when she had, the thoughtful, empathetic man of my youth had died, and a brute had risen from the ashes.

Closing off my emotions and keeping others at bay was how I survived. And I couldn't allow Ella to chip away at my protective walls any more than she already had.

"We should go." I climbed off the bed, and this time she let me. I didn't dare look at her, afraid to see hurt painted across her pretty face. I shoved my feet into my shoes, but when I heard no movement from Ella, I had no choice but to face her and the aftereffects of my comment.

My eyes went to hers.

And she...

She greeted me with a cocky smirk.

What?

"Johannes, you and I both know that what happened here was far more than just a fuck for you *and* me. But you keep on believing those lies. Stay in your safe zone. It's fine by me. When you're ready to adult, I'll be here."

She got up and padded into the bathroom, buck naked, hips swaying.

I stared after her, my mouth agape, my dick springing to life at the sight of her curves. Stupid thing didn't understand what had just happened.

And neither did I.

But one thing was for sure. I'd better find out.

After thirty of the longest minutes of my life, I pulled up outside Level Nine where she'd left her car overnight. We hadn't spoken a word on the journey over here, but every time I'd risked a sidelong glance at her, that faint smirk had remained in place.

Goddamn woman.

After the assault, my parents, my brothers, and my doctors had pleaded with me to go to therapy, but I'd steadfastly refused. Talking to a stranger about the worst moment of my life and how I shared a sliver of culpability for ending up there wasn't high on my list of priorities.

It didn't even make the top one hundred—and it never had.

But the last twelve hours had shined a light on so many things, not least my conceding to Ella's firm yet gentle coaxing to fuck face-to-face, or her calling me out and me sitting there and taking it without challenge. The barbed comment of "it was just a fuck" had been my reaction to the discomfort she'd made me feel, how she'd forced me to think, to see things I hadn't been prepared to acknowledge.

Christ, my head hurt.

"Thanks for the ride." She opened the car door, glancing back at me, that goddamn smirk still tugging at her lips. "I'll see you tomorrow."

Without waiting for a reply—probably because she guessed she wouldn't get one—she strolled over to her rust bucket of a car and climbed inside, then pulled away.

Not once did she look back at me.

Chapter 22

Ella

Who are you, and what have you done with Johannes Kingcaid?

It both saddened and frustrated me to find that Johannes acted the same following our night together as he had after the first time we'd kissed.

He disappeared.

"Taking care of issues at my other clubs" was the note he'd left on the desk for me when I'd arrived at work on Monday morning, but I knew the truth.

God, I could shake the damned idiot until his teeth fell out.

The man had locked down his emotions so tight, and then promptly lost the key. Or, more likely, buried it under a ton of concrete. But I'd pry them open, force him to face up to them if it killed me. He meant too much. He could say that what we'd shared was just a fuck, and he could even convince himself it was true, but he'd never convince me.

Feelings were odd things. Sometimes they hit you like a truck, out of the blue. Other times they crept up on you slowly, tapping lightly on your shoulder until you paid them the attention they demanded. But ignoring them never worked. Sooner or later, they'd break through.

My feelings for Johannes had built slowly over time. If I thought back to my interview, I'd considered him attractive yet brusque and far too grumpy for my type, but gradually, I'd seen past the outer shell he showed to the world to the man beneath. He had a multitude of issues, and I had more than enough of my own to contend with without taking on his as well. But there was just something about him that compelled me to cast aside common sense and leap into the unknown.

I was mature enough to recognize what was happening. I was falling for him. Which meant that soon I'd owe him the truth.

I dreaded it. I hated that I'd taken the coward's way out and lied to him about my parents, about Mateo, about the fact that I was a married woman on the run from a drug baron. I had a horrible feeling that when I finally told him the truth, he'd run for real.

And who would blame him if he did?

Friday came around, and I still hadn't seen Johannes. I turned up for work at my usual time of nine o'clock, ready to tackle the mountain of paperwork that never seemed to diminish. I didn't mind, though. Keeping busy stopped me from thinking about him and what I'd do if this was his way of ending things before they'd even begun.

I entered his office and hung my coat on the hook behind the door. Dropping my bag onto the desk, I sat in his chair and got to work. Engrossed, I lost track of time, so when someone cleared their throat, I jumped and banged my knee on the underside of the desk.

"Ow!" I glowered at Johannes standing with his shoulder propped against the door frame. "The wanderer returns, I see."

"Want me to rub that for you?" He cocked a brow.

"No." My scowl deepened. I grabbed a pile of paperwork and pushed it to the edge of his desk. "I need you to sign these."

"Sure." He swaggered over as if he hadn't slept with me—twice—then spent almost a week avoiding me. *Dealing with stuff at his other clubs my ass.* He snagged my pen out of my hand and scrawled his illegible signature on every sheet of paper without reading a single one.

"You shouldn't sign things without reading them," I scolded. "I could be trying to steal your fortune."

"But you're not."

"How can you be so sure?"

He signed the last sheet, dropped the pen, and pushed them back to my side of the desk. "Because I know you."

I snorted. "Is that what you think?"

"You are salty this morning." He sat in the guest chair, crossing his ankle over the opposing knee. "And yes, I do know you. Not your background, or your past, or where you went to school, or how you like your eggs in the morning. I know the important things. Your morals, your integrity." He smirked, his eyes filled with heat as he stared at my breasts. "Your body."

A shiver of delight trickled down my spine, but I kept my expression stoic. He'd run out on me—and nothing he said would convince me otherwise—and now he turned up here all almost smiles and direct come-ons.

No.

I wasn't having it.

"Hardly." I snorted. "After all, it was just a fuck."

He flinched, and I inwardly cheered. Good. I'd hit him where it hurt. Maybe now he'd grow the hell up and engage in an adult conversation.

"I apologize." He grimaced. "What I said was uncalled for."

I kept quiet. *Let him do the talking.*

He shifted in his seat. "It was also a lie, as you so eloquently pointed out to me that night."

Still I said nothing.

He breathed noisily through his nose. "Cut me some slack, Ella. I'm trying to make it up to you."

"By disappearing all week?"

A faint blush stole across his cheeks. *Well, I never.* I didn't think Johannes was capable of shame. There was hope for him yet.

"I admit that I took some time away to think things through. I..." He rubbed his fingers over his lips. "What happened between us wasn't normal for me. I was... unprepared for how I felt, both during sex and afterward. And so I—"

"And how did you feel?"

Push that button, girl.

His eyes widened and he shifted again, his discomfort

with my forthright questioning evident. He ran his palm over his stubbled cheek.

"Confused, elated, turned on, surprised." He shrugged. "Scared."

"Of what?"

His eyes glazed over as if a memory had appeared and pulled him back in time. The odds were that Johannes's issues began six years ago, the last time he'd slept face-to-face with a woman. I bet he'd trusted her, and she'd hurt him in some way, and the result had been him shutting off his emotions and hiding behind this cold, unfeeling exterior. But it wasn't the real him, and the cracks were starting to show.

I liked to think I had something to do with that.

But breaking Johannes wide open all at once would only send him into retreat. He had to be carefully pried open, like a scallop shell. Slowly and with great care to avoid damaging the precious goods inside.

"I don't trust easily."

"Nor do I."

"And I don't like to expose myself."

"That's good. We don't need the cops stopping by to arrest you for indecency."

He did a double take, and then he burst out laughing. It wasn't a contained chuckle, or a faint smirk. It was a full-on belly laugh that fizzed through my insides. I'd done that. I'd made him laugh so freely. Euphoria spread through my veins.

"God, you are wonderful."

I nodded. "I know this. I've just been waiting for you to catch up."

He gestured to me, then patted his lap. “Come here.”

I scooched around the desk, hitched up my skirt, and straddled him. He groaned as my pussy brushed his cock.

“Do you think this chair would collapse under a vigorous sex session?”

I considered his question. “Probably.”

“Hmm.” He combed his fingers through my hair. “Maybe we should wait until we’re on the plane, then.”

I blinked, convinced I’d misheard him. “Plane? What plane?”

“My cousin Nolen runs our casino business out of Las Vegas. He wants to talk to me about opening a Kingcaid nightclub in our flagship hotel there, and I want you to accompany me.”

“Las Vegas?” I parroted. “A business trip?”

“Partly.” He ran his hands up the outside of my thighs. “A little pleasure thrown in.”

“For how long?”

“Three days.”

I shook my head. “I can’t leave Chloe for three days. It’s not possible. And she has school on Monday. I always take her to school.”

“I don’t expect you to leave her.”

I narrowed my eyes. “You want me to bring a five-year-old child on a business-slash-pleasure trip?”

“Vegas is an adult playground, that’s true, but I’m sure we can occupy her. There’s a terrific pool at the hotel that I’m certain she’d love.”

I angled my head. “I’m not sure, Johannes. It seems pointless to come all that way only for me and Chloe to sit by the pool while you conduct your business. And like I said, she has school on Monday."

"She's five. Missing one day won't damage her education."

"What do you know about five-year-olds?" I challenged.

He quirked an eyebrow. "Well, since I behaved like one this week, quite a lot."

I chuckled. Whatever soul-searching Johannes had done during his time away, I approved. He was almost like a different man. Both versions turned me on, but this one was a lot easier to be around.

"We could arrange childcare, or"—he tapped a finger against his lips—"even better, bring Ginny."

"Ginny." I broke into a smile. "She would love Vegas, I'm sure. And I bet it's been a good long while since she had a break away."

"Then it's settled. Vegas, here we come."

K

"Wow," Ginny murmured in my ear as Johannes disappeared into the cockpit to talk to the pilot. "Look at this."

"I'm looking," I whispered back, my eyes wide as I gazed around the sumptuous interior of the Kingcaid private jet. Talk about opulence. The leather was butter-soft, the wood paneling polished to perfection, and the thick carpeting felt like walking on air. I'd flown first class commercially with Mateo, once, but this was riches on a completely different scale.

Chloe tugged on my hand, and I crouched to her level. "You okay, little bug?"

"Are we really going to fly, Mommy? Up in the air?"

"We are, baby girl." I flicked the end of her nose, and she giggled. "Are you excited?"

"Yes!" She pulled away from me and went skipping down the aisle. I chased after her, concerned about breakages or sticky fingers ruining the expensive furnishings. I caught up to her as she disappeared through a door behind the galley. Inside was a double bed, a small nightstand and dresser, and a partially ajar door that led to a bathroom.

"Ah, I see you found the bedroom," Johannes murmured in my ear, too quiet for Chloe to pick up on, and rested his hands on my hips. "Maybe next time."

A fluttering set off low in my belly, and I grew heavy between my legs. I was about to turn around when Chloe threw herself onto the bed.

"Chloe, no." I made a grab for her, lifting her into my arms. "That's naughty."

"It's fine," Johannes said, running a fingertip up my bare arm. "Diving onto beds is fun. Right, Chloe?"

"Yes!" she announced, wriggling for me to put her down. The moment I did, she repeated what I'd just scolded her for.

Little Miss Mischief.

I was about to reprimand her again when Johannes flung himself onto the bed right next to her. The two of them promptly burst into laughter. My heart clenched. Mateo hadn't ever played with Chloe. He was the one who'd insisted we start a family right away, and then when she'd been born, he'd shown hardly any interest in her whatsoever. Unless it suited his purposes, and then he was Father of the Year.

At the time, I didn't pick up on it, too enamored with this vastly more experienced man who appeared in control of everything, but in time, it irked me that he wouldn't bathe her or play with her or read to her at night, leaving a hundred percent of the child-rearing to me. When Chloe was two, he'd broached the subject of us having another baby. I'd told him we'd discuss it when he took a real interest in the one we already had.

He hadn't liked that one bit.

No one stood up to Mateo Fernandez.

As punishment, he'd locked me in my room for a week and refused to allow me to see Chloe.

After that, I'd made sure I religiously took my birth control pills and kept them hidden from him. When I'd failed to fall pregnant, he'd stopped asking, and a while later, the compound had been stormed, setting off a chain reaction for everything that had come afterward.

I settled Chloe in the seat next to mine, right beside the window so she could look out as we took off. This was her first flight and I wanted to make sure she remembered it forever. Johannes sat opposite, with Ginny beside him in the window seat.

Ginny and Chloe looked out the window as the plane sped down the runway, Chloe squealing with delight and Ginny muttering prayers under her breath.

I locked eyes with Johannes, dragging my teeth playfully over my bottom lip. "Here's to good business."

He licked his lips and played footsie with me under the table that separated us. "And great pleasure."

Chapter 23

Johannes

This woman will be either my downfall or my savior.

The intense Vegas heat hit us the second we stepped off the plane. The limousine Nolen had sent waited at the bottom of the steps, KINGCAID CASINOS emblazoned on the side.

I rolled my eyes. Nolen never was one to pass up a chance to advertise.

"I guess this is us," Ella said, jerking her chin at the limo. "Although, I could be wrong." She grinned, nudging me gently with her elbow.

I'd come to relish her teasing, her sass, her keen wit and sharp mind. The only thing that still bothered me was the uncanny ability she had to read me as easily as a large-print book. I prided myself on being the one member of our family that no one could read. They never knew which version of me would turn up. The dour, brooding, taciturn one, or the dour, brooding, cutting one with a tongue as sharp as a samurai sword.

But Ella had brought out a third side of me, and it terrified and thrilled me in equal measure. Thrilled because I'd started to believe in her and that was a path I'd avoided walking down for more than six years, and terrified because I still didn't trust her enough to share my past and what had changed me from a fun-loving, enthusiastic, positive man into a surly beast who, in Ash's words, liked to play with his food—namely, hurting others for his own entertainment.

He wasn't wrong.

Except now, he might just be, and I wasn't ready to face up to the change. I liked hiding behind barriers. It stopped people from getting close and poking around in places they weren't welcome. Ella hadn't removed those barriers, but she'd made a dent in them. A significant dent. And the closer we grew, the more of the real Ella she allowed me to see.

She consumed my thoughts for large parts of the day. But would allowing her in, letting her see the real me in all my damaged glory, be my downfall?

I'd done a lot of soul-searching the week I'd stayed away from her. I hadn't wanted to, but keeping my distance had been the only way to maintain a clear head and figure out the right course of action for me, and for her. But taking that irrevocable step and sharing my past with her was a bridge too far. I was enamored with her, but I didn't fully trust her, and until I did, I couldn't risk baring my soul, only to have the guts of me ripped out for a second time.

I'd been hurt too much to allow that to happen. Sadie

had given me one gift—self-preservation—while stealing so many others.

"Goodness me, it's like being boiled alive," Ginny said as I held out my hand to help her down the steps of the plane. I caught the soft look in Ella's eyes, one of approval. That wasn't why I did it. I still had some manners, but I'd take the silent praise all day long if it meant I got to enjoy that sweep of pleasure through my midsection.

"How do people live like this?" Ginny wafted a hand in front of her face.

"They get used to it, I guess," I said as we stepped onto the tarmac. "Give me the ocean any day."

"Me too," Ginny said. "Although, the damned government make us pay for the privilege of being close to nature's miracle." She raised her eyes to the sky. "Who made them king of the world?"

I chuckled. "Beats me."

The four of us climbed into the car, breathing a sigh of relief as the doors closed, shutting out the heat and blasting us with the air-conditioning. The airport was right next to the strip. It would only take us about ten minutes to arrive at Kingcaid Las Vegas. During the journey, I pointed out the various world-famous hotels, and Ella, Ginny, and even Chloe gawped out the window in excitement.

I'd seen Las Vegas many times. It didn't hold me in awe any longer, but to see it through their eyes was like experiencing it again for the first time. Vegas was one of those places where you had to be there to truly appreciate its size and grandeur. Something that looked to be right across the street could take forty-five minutes to get to. Nothing was close by in Vegas. Caesars Palace alone took up a half mile of prime real estate.

The car pulled up outside the entranceway of the hotel that Nolen ran. I explained to Ella that although my elder brother, Ash, ran our hotel business, Nolen ran this business, and the hotel we had in downtown Vegas, in its entirety. The casinos were so linked to the hotels here that it made sense to separate them from the rest of the Kingcaid hotel chain. It was the same in Reno, and Atlantic City, and Monaco, and all the other casino locations. They all came under Nolen's umbrella.

As we exited the car, Nolen came through the sliding doors, dressed in a three-piece suit, a red tie, and a crisp white shirt. He always looked as if he'd stepped straight off the catwalk. He came toward me, all genial smile and white teeth. He clapped me on the upper arm and shook my hand.

"Glad you made it. Flight okay?"

"All good." I motioned to Ella. "This is my assistant, Ella Reyes. Ella, this is my cousin, Nolen."

"Nice to meet you." She shook his hand. "This is my daughter, Chloe, and Ginny, my friend. I hope we're not inconveniencing you by arriving en masse."

"Not at all." Nolen's gaze dropped to where my hand pressed against Ella's lower back. He arched a brow. "I've put you in a three-bedroom suite, so you all get your own space." He stared at me pointedly. I stared right back, my message clear. *Mind your own fucking business.*

"I've put another bed in your room, Ella, for Chloe." He crouched, tweaking Chloe's nose. "Well, aren't you as cute as a button?"

Chloe giggled. I scowled. Fucking Nolen and his easy-going manner that made everyone like him. He'd always been the same, even when we were kids. I couldn't remember a time when he'd lost his temper or gotten into a fight or thrown a tantrum over something and nothing. He was just Nolen Kingcaid, carefree, tolerant, and likable.

"Come on, I'll take you up and let you get settled. The bellhop will bring your bags. Once you've freshened up, I'd like to show you the space I'm thinking of, Johannes."

"How did it become available?" I asked as Nolen strode into a waiting elevator and held the doors open until we'd all gotten in.

"The previous occupants pulled out. Said it wasn't viable at the rents I was charging." He snorted a laugh. "What bullsh—" He broke off, sending an apologetic grin in Ella's direction. "Sorry, darling. Forgot about the little ears and all that. I mean what garbage. A nightclub at one of the top hotels in Vegas is a money-making machine, if you know what you're doing."

"Which I do," I stated.

Ella's pinkie touched mine. Electricity shot up my arm. I glanced down at her, then took her hand and squeezed it.

"Precisely." He lightly punched me on the arm. "And it's better to keep it in the family, right?"

"True." I smiled a little. "But if you think you're getting exorbitant rents out of me, you're mistaken."

Nolen chuckled. "It's all up for negotiation."

"Don't expect an easy ride."

"Nor you." He winked. The elevator pinged and the doors opened. "Follow me." He strode down the hallway and opened a door at the far end, motioning for us to enter. "I hope this is sufficient."

"Sufficient?" Ella repeated as she stepped inside the lavish suite. "It's beautiful." She dropped her purse onto a nearby chair and crossed the room to the floor-to-ceiling windows overlooking the Las Vegas Strip. "Look at that view."

"Yeah, pretty awesome, huh?" Nolen said. "I never tire of it."

I joined her, peering down at the street below. People as small as ants from all the way up here filled the sidewalks, and a never-ending procession of cars inched their way past the towering hotels. Probably quicker to walk, given the weight of traffic.

"Want to freshen up?" I asked, touching my hand to hers again, briefly. "And then maybe we could grab some lunch before Nolen steals me away."

"As long as he doesn't steal you for long," Ella whispered, her voice thick with promise.

A shiver of pleasure crept up my spine. "I'll make sure of it."

Lunch consisted of hamburgers and fries at Chloe's insistence. I hadn't been around kids all that much, but, minute by minute, Chloe was burrowing into my chest and prodding at the edges of my heart.

Just like her mother.

Watching Ella parent Chloe, the way she gently guided her, took care of her, scolded her when necessary, tightened my chest. I'd never even considered a future that included a relationship, let alone a kid, yet I found myself daydreaming about what it might feel like to be a father figure to Chloe, to maybe one day have kids of my own.

It wouldn't happen. I had too many issues preventing

me from opening myself up to the kind of scrutiny a deep and meaningful relationship required. Ella didn't even know about Sadie, or the night that had changed the course of my life. And the worst of it was that, as I sat here, I had no intention of telling her anytime soon.

And that reticence spoke volumes about my readiness, or capability, of engaging in an adult relationship.

It left me with only one option: keep my wits about me and enjoy it while it lasted.

"Shall we go?" Nolen suggested, dropping his napkin on top of his plate. "I have a meeting at five that I can't miss. I'll try to join you for dinner, but I might not make it."

"Not a problem," I said breezily, pleased that he couldn't make it. I'd rather spend one-on-one time with Ella. Ginny had already promised to stay in the suite with Chloe while we went out and explored a little of Vegas. In fact, when I'd broached the subject, she'd looked rather thrilled at the prospect of putting her feet up and renting the latest blockbuster from the hotel's extensive selection.

As we rounded the table, Nolen stiffened. "Ah, shit," he muttered. "Brace for impact."

I followed his gaze to a stunning-looking woman dressed in a sharp suit and pencil-thin high heels on a collision course with us. Her wavy, light brown hair fell past her waist, and her copper eyes bored into Nolen, blazing with a hatred that made even me stop and pause, and I'd perfected that look.

"There she is, the love of my life." Nolen greeted the woman with a beaming smile.

"Drop dead" was her retort as she prodded him in the chest. "You're an asshole."

I huffed a laugh, but she didn't even flinch, her ire solely locked on my cousin. I caught Ella's wide eyed stare, and another chuckle escaped me.

"Shh," Nolen scolded, glancing back at our table. "We have children present."

The woman briefly glanced at Chloe, then turned her venomous glare back on Nolen. "You won't get away with this."

"I already have," he drawled.

Ah, must be a business deal they were both vying for. Vegas was a hugely competitive city, with billionaires contending for prime real estate in an area that, when compared to Los Angeles, was pretty small.

"Does Jason know?" she snapped.

Jason. I looked at Nolen and then at the woman, and suddenly put it all together. "Marlowe?"

Marlowe Beck was the older sister of Nolen's best friend, Jason. They'd grown up together, been inseparable, and Nolen had had a huge crush on Marlowe. She'd moved away to college, and he, at sixteen, two years younger than her, had thought it was the end of the world. After he'd finished college, he'd moved to Vegas with Jason, and they'd gone into business together. I hadn't seen Marlowe since she was eighteen.

She peered at me, almost as if she hadn't noticed my presence until I'd spoken. "Johannes?" She looked me up and down. "Goodness me, you've changed."

Ella appeared at my side, a clear case of staking her claim. Fuck, she was utterly magnificent. I touched her elbow in an act of reassurance. "Yeah, well, I was only thirteen the last time you saw me."

Marlowe laughed. "That's true. I guess we've all changed." Her eyes turned cold again as she set them on Nolen. "Some more than others."

"I love you, too," Nolen declared.

"You'd better watch your back, Nolen. I won't take this lying down."

"Shame." He raked his gaze over her. "You'd look fantastic lying beneath me."

"And you'd look terrific lying in a shallow grave," she replied.

Ella inhaled a sharp breath, while I laughed again. "If this is the kind of entertainment Vegas has to offer, then I'm looking forward to a show or two."

"Your cousin is vile." She glanced at Ella. "My apologies. You're not seeing me on my best day." She gave us both a curt nod. "Great to see you, Johannes."

And with that, she swept by, striding across the restaurant with the confidence of a woman who utterly believed in herself.

"Wow," Ella whispered. "She's... feisty."

"But beautiful." Nolen stared after Marlowe for a few seconds, then sighed. "Sorry about that. Shall we continue?"

I squeezed Ella's arm. "Won't be long." I set off walking with Nolen, noting his quiet contemplation.

"So what happened with you and Marlowe? As I recall, you had a crush on her when we were kids."

Nolen looked at me, and his happy-go-lucky mask slipped, exposing rawness underneath. "I don't know. I've never figured it out. I kissed her for the first time at my college homecoming, and she was all for hooking up, then later that night, she told me I was just a boy and she was only interested in men. Not long afterward, she married some douche lawyer. Then about twelve months ago, she got divorced and Jason brought her into the business. I'd hoped the intervening decade would have softened her attitude toward me, but she soon divested me of that opinion." He laughed, the sound brittle and steeped in hurt.

"Yet instead of asking her what you supposedly did, you decide to, what, steal business from underneath her nose?"

"I *have* asked her. She refuses to tell me. Jason hasn't a clue either. And I didn't steal anything."

"She doesn't seem to think so."

He narrowed his eyes. "How about you concentrate on your own love life and leave me to concentrate on mine?"

"I don't have a love life."

Nolen smirked. "Sure you don't."

"She's my assistant."

"Who you're banging."

"That means nothing."

"It does when you look at her like you do."

"And how is that, exactly?"

"Like you're in love, dear cousin." He made a heart shape with his hands.

"Bullshit," I scoffed. "We've had sex. Twice. That's it."

"So?" Nolen shrugged. "I haven't had sex with Marlowe even once, yet I know she's the one for me."

"I think Marlowe needs a little convincing."

Nolen chuckled. "I thought you'd lost your sense of humor." He clapped me on the shoulder. "It's good to see the man I grew up with making a comeback. Love is a great healer."

“I’m not in love,” I said through gritted teeth. “I’ve been in love, and this isn’t that.”

Nolen’s jaw flexed. “No, it isn’t. And thank fuck for small mercies.”

He tapped a key card against a door and opened it, gesturing for me to go in first. The second I walked inside, my mind fired off a hundred ideas for what I could do with this space.

“Wow.”

“Right?” Nolen nodded. “And I figured we could add a second level and put the VIP spaces above the main dance floor.”

I’d had exactly the same thought, especially with the height of the ceiling. It was crying out for that kind of enhancement.

“So,” Nolen said. “Shall we talk numbers? And then you can spend the weekend with your girl pretending you’re not in love with her.”

My stomach flipped, and my heart skipped a couple of beats. “Marlowe was right,” I said. “You are an asshole.”

Chapter 24

Ella

What are the chances?

I TUCKED CHLOE'S BEDSHEETS TIGHT AROUND HER AND KISSED HER forehead. "Night, baby girl. You be good for Ginny. I won't be long."

"I will."

She snuggled further down into the bed, clutching her new teddy bear. My heart had soared when Johannes had produced it after he'd returned from his business meeting with Nolen, and Chloe had instantly fallen in love with it, pronouncing it her new favorite. I hadn't missed the pride and delight that had crossed Johannes's face either, and for the first time since my life had imploded, I'd begun to dream of a different future than the one prescribed by my life with Mateo.

A future with Johannes.

But neither of us could commit to that while we were keeping so much of our real selves hidden. It was like walking on the edge of a cliff, the stones loose beneath our feet. Both of us were afraid of falling, and neither one seemed prepared to make the first move in case that resulted in disaster.

Not for the first time, I considered taking the lead and making the first move. Telling him everything and opening myself up might encourage him to open up, too. Yes, I'd previously thought otherwise, but one of us had to be brave. Might as well be me. It was a risk, but life was full of them. I had some money stashed away. If it went badly, I could run.

Decision made. First chance I got after we returned to Los Angeles, I'd tell him everything and hope my honesty didn't bring about the end of us. I just wanted to have this one special weekend first. Maybe that was a little selfish of me, but I couldn't bring myself to take the chance of ruining these few days away.

"Mommy."

I turned back to Chloe. "Yes, little bug?"

"Leave a light on."

I nodded, turning down the dimmer to a soft glow. I blew her a kiss and closed the door.

"Well, look at you." Ginny heaved herself out of the chair, rubbing at her lower back. "Pretty as a picture."

I smiled, smoothing a hand over my lime-green dress that finished just above the knee. I'd gotten it last week at a thrift store, one of those that occasionally had a real gem and if you were lucky, you'd happen upon it. It had cost me ten dollars, but it looked like it was worth twenty times that, if not more.

"Thanks, Ginny. Are you sure you don't mind babysitting Chloe?"

Despite what she'd said about relishing a night in, we were in Vegas, and I'd hate for her to think she wasn't entitled to go out and enjoy herself, too, even if Johannes's idea to bring her was to provide childcare. There was always room service. And if he didn't like that, tough.

"Are you kidding me? Have you sat on that couch? It's like relaxing into an angel's wings. Not that I've ever done that, but I have an imagination." She patted my arm. "You're young, beautiful, and in Las Vegas, the city of sin." She winked. "And you have a rather handsome young man to sin with. So take advantage and go enjoy yourself."

Heat rushed to my face, and I ducked my chin to hide my blush. "I'll try."

The door to Johannes's bedroom opened, and he strode out in his customary black turtleneck and matching black slacks. I shook my head.

"It's a hundred degrees outside."

"And the restaurant will be closer to sixty."

Always quick with an answer to his unsuitable attire. But now wasn't the time for pushing. After I'd told him the truth, then I'd have the right to demand the same from him. Until that time came, I had no intention of spoiling what I hoped would be a magical evening.

He held out his hand, and Ginny's eyes went all soft as she pressed a palm to her chest. She was such an old romantic. I checked that she had contact details in case Chloe needed me. She rolled her eyes, muttered something about not being senile yet, and turned on the TV. Her message for me to stop fussing and just go couldn't have come across any louder if she'd yelled it.

"Where are we going?"

"Somewhere Nolen won't gate-crash our dinner. If we eat at the hotel, at some point, he's going to turn up and ruin my evening."

A limousine waited outside the front entrance of the hotel. Johannes guided me inside, then climbed in beside me. My mind went to the transformation from the man I'd first met to the one sitting beside me. Sometimes I wondered whether he had an identical twin and they'd switched places when I hadn't been looking.

"Drink?" He opened a mahogany door set into the side panel of the car. Behind it was a fully stocked bar.

"Is this your limousine?"

"It belongs to the hotel. VIP guests have several for their personal use."

"I'll have a tonic water if it's available."

He poured me a drink and one for himself—it looked like whiskey—then sat back and threaded his fingers through mine.

"I'm glad you're here."

"Me, too. Thank you for inviting me."

He leaned toward me, his eyes on my mouth. "The pleasure is all mine."

I managed a breath before his lips, so soft and warm, captured mine. His kiss was unhurried, as if we had all the time in the world. I traced the tip of my tongue along his bottom lip and curved a hand around the nape of his neck, pulling him to me. His fingertips crept up my thigh, taking my dress with him.

"Open your legs," he murmured.

I fired a glance at the driver. Huh. When had the privacy screen gone up?

"He can't see us, and he can't hear us. Now open your legs."

My breath caught in my throat at the command in his voice, the lust in his eyes, and the feel of his warm palm on my skin. I complied, spreading myself wide. He moved at a leisurely pace, moving higher, higher, and the entire time, his eyes never left mine.

"This turns you on."

A statement, not a question, and one that even if I wanted to deny it, the overwhelming evidence would make me a liar. "You turn me on."

His eyes gleamed, and his fingers snuck inside my panties, stroking me with a firm, determined motion. On each upward stroke, he swirled his fingertip around my clit, but as I raised my hips, seeking more friction, he denied me.

"Kiss me." The intimacy of his gaze, the intensity of it, was too much. If he kissed me, I could hide.

"No."

He rubbed me again, his tongue dampening his lips as I parted mine on an inhale.

"Why not?" I gasped as he slid a finger inside me.

"Because you're going to come all over my fingers while looking right into my eyes. I want to watch you, to see your pleasure and know I made it happen."

He added a second finger, his thumb playing me, the pressure in my lower abdomen growing until I couldn't hold on. I peaked, hovering on the precipice. And then I fell, gasping at the power of my climax.

"Look at me, Ella," Johannes growled.

Did I close my eyes? I couldn't remember.

"That's better. Good girl. Just like that. Fuck, you're stunning."

The initial swell receded, replaced with aftershocks that went on and on. Johannes stilled, his eyes alight as he felt every pulse until, finally, they stopped. He withdrew his fingers, dipped them in his glass of whiskey, and then pressed them to my lips.

"Open up, beautiful."

Dear God. I thought men like this only appeared in the movies, or in books, not in real life. Then again, the only previous experience I had was Mateo, and sensuality wasn't really his forte.

I pushed all thoughts of *him* from my mind. He wasn't stealing this moment from me. I opened my mouth, and Johannes slipped his fingers inside. I closed my lips around him and swirled my tongue across his skin, tasting the sweetness of myself with the mellowness of the whiskey.

"We're here, sir," a voice came over the intercom.

"Perfect timing," Johannes murmured, easing his fingers from my mouth a second before the rear door opened.

I tugged down my dress, heat flooding my face at the idea that the valet might have copped an eyeful. His gaze remained averted as I exited the limo. Probably used to being discreet.

Johannes joined me, and with his hand pressed to the small of my back, he walked me inside the restaurant. I spied the name *Fiore* emblazoned across the entranceway as we entered. Italian, my favorite food.

My orgasm still buzzed through me, leaving me with a

weakness in my knees and heat running through my veins. I leaned into Johannes for support as he gave his name to the host, who then led us to our table, holding out my chair for me. Johannes waited for me to sit before he did. The host handed us both hardbacked menus and said our server would be over shortly.

He wasn't kidding. I didn't even have time to worry about being underdressed for such an exclusive restaurant, or whether the women dolled up in their finery and dripping with jewels could tell my outfit had come from a thrift store, before the server arrived.

Johannes waved him away with a flick of his wrist. The man backed up, murmuring apologies. I opened my menu and almost choked. These prices were insane. I'd eaten in nice restaurants with Mateo, but nothing as exorbitant as this.

"Johannes, have you seen—"

"Don't finish that sentence," he interrupted. "I don't want to hear it."

"But—"

"One more word and I will bend you over my knee." He arched a brow, making me laugh.

"I'm not five."

His eyes met mine and slowly traveled down until they landed on my cleavage. "No, you most certainly are not."

I wriggled in my seat. "Stop it."

"Not a chance."

He dragged his gaze away and opened his menu. Seconds later, he closed it with a snap.

"What are you having?" I asked.

"Arancini followed by pappardelle mimmo."

I'd eaten arancini, but I'd never heard of that entrée.

"What's that?"

"It's pasta with lobster, scallops, and truffle. Delicious."

My mouth watered. "It sounds it. I'll have the same."

He smirked. "Good choice."

Beckoning to the server, he put in our food order and requested a bottle of wine and some mineral water.

Bet even that costs more than my dress.

I shook out my napkin and tried to tell myself that Johannes didn't seem to care how I was dressed or how much my outfit cost. Apart from the few moments when he'd perused the menu, he hadn't taken his eyes off me since we'd sat down. And every time I met the intensity of his fierce ice-blue gaze, I found myself pressing my thighs together to relieve the ache between my legs. I'd have thought the orgasm in the limo would've helped.

Seems not.

The arancini was divine, and as the server placed the entrée in front of me and the delicious smells reached my nose, my mouth filled with saliva. But before I could dig in, someone called my name.

My real name.

Eloise.

Not Ella.

My entire body froze as I searched for the source of my potential destruction. Oh shit. Bustling toward me was a girl I'd gone to school with. Arabella Finlay. Back then, she'd had a big mouth and an even bigger rack, and nothing had changed.

How is this happening?

"Oh my God! It is you!" she screeched, drawing the

attention of the entire restaurant. I slid down in my chair, praying for the expensive oak flooring to open up and suck me into the bowels of hell.

"What are the chances, Eloise?" She leaned over to hug me, crushing me with her enormous breasts and treating me as if we'd been besties when, in fact, she'd not thought me worthy enough to include in her circle of bullies. "You look amazing, darling. Amazing." She ran her gaze over me. "Dior? Gucci? No, don't tell me. It's Valentino, isn't it?"

Forcing a small smile, I nodded. "Great guess, Arabella. You look... well."

"Oh, I know." She turned to Johannes, and her whole demeanor shifted into seduction mode. As good as undressing him with her eyes, her gaze slowly traveled the full length of his body, and she crossed her arms so her tits squished even closer together.

I clenched my hands into fists, stuffing them into my lap. Only Johannes's flat, bored gaze when he stared back at her stopped me from smacking her one and screaming "Back off, bitch. He's mine."

"And who might this delicious man be? I thought you ran off with that older guy."

My blood turned to ice, my breathing quick and shallow as I risked a glance at Johannes. His expression was unreadable except for the smallest flare in his eyes.

I ignored her question. If Johannes didn't introduce himself, then I wasn't about to. "No, you must be mistaken."

She shook her head. "No. I'm sure it was you. The school gossip train was in full flow over it. Rumor was that he'd knocked you up and your parents made him marry you."

Ah, finally something I can dispute from a position of truth.

"He didn't knock me up, and my parents never made me marry him." My voice came out small. "It was a brief fling. That's all. I haven't seen him in years."

And... back to the lies.

"Oh." She refocused her attention on Johannes. "Well, your choices certainly improved." She flashed him a grin. He didn't return it, his stare glacial. Arabella's smile fell.

"Well, I must dash. I've got my own hottie waiting for me."

She gestured somewhere behind her, but I couldn't see whom she was referring to. I pitied the poor soul, whoever he was.

"Toodles."

She wiggled her fingers as if we were children and, without waiting for a reply, bustled off, having dropped a bomb in the middle of my life and leaving me to pick up the pieces. I toyed with my napkin, folding and refolding it before laying it on my lap. I couldn't look at him, or rather, didn't dare to.

"Sorry about her. She's—"

"Why did she call you Eloise?"

His question went right to my heart. It spluttered, then skipped a beat. Then another. Dots appeared before my eyes, my head woozy.

Tell him, my inner consciousness screamed. *Tell him everything.*

I opened my mouth, but instead of the truth, lies spilled out.

"It—Ella—is my middle name. I don't like 'Eloise.'" A blush stole across my cheeks. "So I go by Ella now."

He tapped a fingertip against his lips. "And this older

guy she mentioned? Is he Chloe's father?"

"No! I told you. Chloe's father was a one-night thing."

More lies. They drowned me, sucking me down like quicksand. It was too late to back out now. I had to see this through to the bitter end.

"The older guy was nothing. Nobody. A teenage rebellious streak. It fizzled out."

He peered at me, his eyes narrowing. I cut him off before he could hit me with a barrage of questions I could see burgeoning.

"Just drop it, okay? I never liked Arabella at school, and I haven't changed my opinion. We all have a past." I stared at him pointedly. "Don't we, Johannes?"

It was an unfair shot, but I took it anyway. If he was going to poke around in my past, then by God, I'd poke around in his.

He flexed his jaw. "Yes, we do."

I picked up the glass of wine I'd hardly touched and drank half of it in one go. My hand shook, and I doubted my legs would hold me up if I tried to stand.

"Don't let her ruin the evening." I made myself smile even though I was far closer to tears. "I nearly punched her when she eye-fucked you."

At last, his lips curved. Only a minuscule amount, but I'd take it.

"If I'd known that, I'd have egged her on. I'd pay good money to watch you go into battle to save my honor."

I laughed and held out my wineglass to him. "To keeping your honor intact."

To my relief, he picked up his glass and touched it to mine. "And to me stripping you of yours."

Chapter 25

Johannes

Enough lies. It's time for the truth.

Ella breathed steadily beside me, the lights from the city that never stopped casting a faint glow across the bed. I lay on my side, watching her for a few moments, Nolen's smug certainty that I'd fallen for her echoing around in my head.

I hated the thought of it, but he might've been closer to the truth than I was ready to admit.

Before that obnoxious woman had interrupted us this evening, I'd considered telling her about Sadie and what had happened to me. I hadn't been a hundred percent sold on it, but depending on how the night unfolded, I'd seen it as a possibility. I'd concocted a fantasy of how she'd react, her deft fingers removing my sweater, tracing my scar with her hands and her lips. Telling me it didn't matter to her. That she'd make it all better.

Then her own secrets had unraveled, and I'd galloped into retreat.

Ella or Eloise?

Maybe Ella *was* her middle name, but she'd lied to me about her reason for choosing to use it as her given moniker. It had nothing to do with preference and everything to do with her hiding something.

Or hiding *from* someone.

I'd originally bought the story about her parents. Not everyone was lucky enough to have parents like mine. Lots of families were estranged. But after tonight... nah.

She'd lied.

She'd lied about escaping her parents, and she'd lied about her name.

What else had she lied about?

Prickles crept up my neck, a horrible sense of history repeating itself crawling over my skin. Whatever Ella was hiding, I intended to find out. If she couldn't even trust me with the truth of her name, then I was right not to trust her with the truth of my past.

With the ugliness of my scar.

On most occasions, I relished being right. On this occasion, it was up there with one of the worst things that had ever happened to me.

I eased back the covers and slipped out of bed. Grabbing my phone off the nightstand, I padded across the wall-to-wall carpeting and into the living area of the suite. The drapes were open, the dazzling lights of the Las Vegas Strip throwing enough illumination in the room to fool some into thinking it was daytime. I checked my watch. One oh five in the morning. Late to call Seattle, but not excessively so. Ash often worked into the night.

I dialed his number, pacing as it rang out.

"If you're ringing for anything other than to tell me you're in jail and you want me to bail you out, you can hang up now."

"Has marriage turned you old before your time, brother?"

Ash sighed. "What do you want, Johannes? I've got a six o'clock start in the morning."

I plowed straight in. Ash wasn't fond of beating around the bush any more than I was. "I need the name of a private detective. A good one. And I thought you might have a contact."

"Why would I know any private detectives?"

"Didn't you hire one to watch that sleazeball Forster? The guy who felt up Kiana at her interview?"

He sucked in a breath. "How do you know about that?"

"I know everything." Dad had told me in passing one day, but why tell Ash all my secrets?

"What do you need him for?"

I thought about lying, or just refusing to answer, but for some unknown reason, the idea of offloading and having someone else validate my concerns loosened my tongue. In hushed tones, I briefed him on Ella, from the moment she'd arrived at my club, her face awash with relief at both the job offer and remuneration in cash, to what had happened tonight at Fiore. Ash listened without interruption, waiting until I'd finished to offer his opinion.

"Be careful, Johannes. If you go poking around in this

girl's affairs without her permission, you might push her away rather than keeping her close."

He had a point. One I'd already considered and decided to ignore. Uncovering the truth was more important. I couldn't risk this turning into another Sadie situation. To have a woman fool me once was one thing, but to walk blindly into it for a second time?

Not a fucking chance.

"Noted. So, can I have the goddamn number or not?"

"Jesus, you really can be a sullen jerk." I heard the smile in his voice. "It's your funeral. If it all goes south, don't come crying to me."

I snorted. "As if. Text it to me." I hung up, and a few seconds later, the number came through.

My finger hovered over the Call button. Calling my brother this late at night was one thing, but calling a stranger, one whose help I needed, was another.

I'd have to wait until morning.

I returned to the bedroom, but no matter how hard I tried, I couldn't sleep. At five o'clock, I gave up. Normally, when insomnia kicked my ass, I'd head to my private gym and exhaust myself on the treadmill, but the suite didn't have its own gym, and I had no intention of visiting the hotel one dressed in a high-necked sweater.

Instead, I left Ella a note in case she woke, and then went downstairs to the space Nolen wanted me to rent and turn into another nightclub. I tapped the key card Nolen had given to me against the door, and went inside. Wandering around the periphery, I allowed my mind the freedom to innovate, envisaging what it could look like. Each one of my clubs brought something different to the clubbing scene. I wasn't interested in creating a chain of identical nightclubs. I wanted my customers to have a unique experience at each establishment they visited.

I lost track of time as I jotted notes on my phone and sent a few emails to previous construction firms who'd decked out some of my other clubs. The sooner I moved things along, the better. A buzz fizzed through my veins, a burgeoning excitement that came at the start of every new adventure. Soon the buzz would disappear, replaced with stress and anxiety as I dealt with problem after problem, culminating in an opening night where I'd bite my nails until they bled. But right now, in this moment, the possibilities outweighed the negatives.

The next time I looked at my watch, it had turned seven o'clock. I called the private detective.

Thirty minutes later, having told him everything I knew—which wasn't much—he promised he'd get back to me as soon as he'd uncovered anything. I could be way off the mark, but the way my intuition had fired up after last night, stoking the embers of suspicion that had been there for a while, I didn't think I was.

When I arrived back at our suite, Ella was sitting in the center of the living room playing with Chloe, the giant bear I'd bought for the little girl sitting right beside her as if he, too, was playing the game. The smile Ella gave me tightened my chest. God, whatever she was hiding, I hoped to Christ it wasn't an unforgivable secret. Like Sadie.

I couldn't bear it… the idea that I'd allowed another woman to scale the walls I'd built after *her*, only to find I'd made the same mistake twice.

No.

Ella wasn't Sadie. I had to believe that.

"Morning." She beamed. "Come, join us."

"Johannes!" Chloe scrambled to her feet and raced toward me. She clamped her little arms around my legs and held on tight. Emotions swirled inside my chest. Tension, worry, fear, joy, surprise. A slew of them battering me until I couldn't think straight. "Play with me."

I sought out Ella whose surprise matched my own. Then her eyebrows lowered, and her eyes misted over, and she pressed a hand to her chest as if she was afraid her heart would burst right out of it.

"What are we playing?" I peeled Chloe's hands from around my legs and guided her back to her mother, then folded myself onto the floor.

"The bear's tea party." She handed me a pretend cup. I took it from her and sipped, wondering who the fuck I was right now. Only a few months ago, I'd have scoffed at the idea of me drinking pretend tea out of a pretend cup with a five-year-old kid who wasn't mine, and enjoying every second. But now...

Please don't be another Sadie. Please...

"Do you like it? I made it special."

I caught Ella's smirk and returned it with one of my own. "Delicious."

"Where have you been?" Ella asked, peering up at me from beneath her lashes. "Your note didn't say."

"I went to take another look at the potential nightclub. Made a few notes." I left out the part where I'd asked a private detective to invade her privacy. "Should be a real moneymaker if I get it right."

"You'll get it right."

My chest swelled at her pride and belief in me, then collapsed just as fast. "Have you eaten?"

"No. We were waiting for you. Ginny's still asleep, I think."

"I'll order room service, unless you'd rather eat in one of the restaurants?"

"Here is fine." She inched her hand across the carpeted space between us and touched the tips of my fingers with hers. "I like the privacy."

My abdomen clenched. The merest touch from this woman, and I turned to putty in her hands. *Focus.* Until I heard from the detective, I couldn't allow myself to fall any harder.

"I'll call down and order. Anything particular you want to eat?"

"Pancakes!" Chloe announced.

"He wasn't asking you." Ella flicked the end of her nose, making Chloe laugh.

"Bear wants pancakes."

"Does he now?" I arched a brow. "Well then, that makes all the difference."

I ruffled her hair and picked up the house phone, ordering a selection of breakfast items, then went to get a shower. As I soaped myself, an impossible dream nudged its way into my mind. That of Ella sliding open the shower door, climbing in behind me, soaping my body, my cock, maybe going to her knees and taking me into her mouth.

My hand found its way to my shaft, and I tugged hard. Once, twice, three times. I moved faster, locking in my mind the image of Ella at my feet. Her rosy lips closing around the head, her tongue playing with the slit at the top, her warm hands cupping my balls and squeezing just the right amount.

I bit my wrist as I came, jets of cum hitting the wall before the cascading water washed it away.

Please, fuck, please don't let the detective find anything bad.

I dried off, ran a comb through my hair, leaving it damp, and dressed in my customary uniform of a turtleneck sweater and slacks. As I went back into the living area, a knock sounded at the door. I crossed the room and invited the room service attendant inside. He set breakfast up on the dining table, much to Chloe's delight, who squealed at every item he unveiled. Her bubbling excitement must have woken Ginny, who padded out of her room, bleary eyed, and dressed in a set of Thor pajamas.

I only just managed to quash my laughter. Or so I thought.

"Listen, young man. I like Thor. What woman doesn't want a man who can wield a big hammer?" She waggled her eyebrows.

Her double entendre hit me and Ella square in the chest. We both burst out laughing. The room service attendant blushed and backed out of the room. And as for Chloe, well, she was far more interested in the bear-shaped pancakes I'd asked the kitchen to make than why the adults in the room were laughing.

"Look, Mommy." She picked up a pancake and brandished it in Ella's face. "It's Bear. It's Bear, Mommy."

Ella looked over at me and mouthed "Thank you." I nodded, although I had done nothing other than ask. The chef had come up with the goods somehow. *I must remember to tell Nolen.*

"They are amazing." She pulled out a chair and made Chloe sit down. "Not too much syrup, Chloe. And have some fruit."

I poured a coffee, spooned some scrambled eggs onto a plate, and took the seat opposite, where I had a better vantage point from which to watch Ella mother her child. It was oddly addictive, the way she encouraged but didn't instruct, coaxed rather than bossed, and managed to get the outcome she desired—namely, reducing the pancake intake in favor of fruit.

A master of manipulation.

I clenched my fists. Fuck. A horrible sense of foreboding crept across the back of my neck. I wasn't letting her out of my sight today. Or tomorrow. Or any day until I heard back from the detective. Sadie had disappeared into the night, leaving me to pick up the pieces.

I would not allow Ella to do the same thing.

"Ginny, would you mind taking Chloe to the pool this morning? I need Ella's help with something."

Ella angled her head, one eyebrow raised. "What do you need help with?"

"Nolen." I smiled a little, forcing myself to behave normally. "He needs some gentle persuasion in eating more fruit than pancakes."

She caught on to my false reasoning without the need for further explanation. Throwing back her head, she laughed.

"I think your cousin might be a little trickier to coax."

"True. But I think you're up to the job."

"In that case"—she tucked her chin into her chest and blinked up at me—"I'd love to help."

Ella and I met Nolen in one of the many bars dotted around the hotel, and less than an hour later, we'd settled on a deal including a sliding scale rental agreement that allowed me time to build the brand and the business before paying full price for this amount of space in a prime Las Vegas location.

If Ella had expected a family member to cut me some slack, she'd had her eyes opened. Nolen, like all the Kingcaids, struck a hard bargain and did zero favors regardless of whether or not you shared DNA. Sometimes our family went in harder on negotiations *because* they shared your DNA.

"I'm not sure how that happened, but I think I've just been had," Nolen said, draining his glass of iced water.

I withheld a chuckle. "Stop with the drama. It's a fair deal."

"Yeah, for you."

I rolled my eyes, and he laughed.

"I'll have my lawyer draw up the contracts. It'll only take twenty-four hours or so. You'll be able to sign them before you leave Monday morning."

"Sounds good." I stood, cocking my head to Ella. "Well, we should go relieve Ginny. Catch you later."

Halfway toward the swimming pool area, my phone rang. My blood ran cold as the caller ID scrolled across the screen.

"I need to take this." I jerked my head to the coffee shop in the lobby. "Go grab yourself a coffee. I won't be long."

She frowned but agreed, giving me the occasional

worried glance over her shoulder as she trekked across the expanse of marble.

I answered the call, my heart thudding in my chest. "Kingcaid."

"Mr. Kingcaid. I have news."

Chapter 26

Ella

Safety is an illusion.

I SIPPED MY LATTE, MY ANXIETY RATCHETING UP AS I WATCHED Johannes pace up and down, his spine stiffening with each traverse of the lobby. I hoped it wasn't to do with the nightclub award he'd put so much work into getting. No, they weren't due to announce the winner for a few days yet, so that couldn't be the reason for his obvious agitation.

He glanced over his shoulder at me, a deep scowl drawing his eyebrows inward. I smiled. He turned away. My stomach flipped, and I tapped my fingers against the side of the cup until the noise of nails on ceramic got on my nerves. I switched to tearing up paper napkins instead.

Eventually, he cut the call and slid the phone into his pocket, but he still kept his back to me, lifting a hand to run his fingers through his hair.

I pushed the cup away and rose to my feet, heading toward him. When I got within a few feet, he pivoted.

"What's wrong?"

His lips thinned to a white slash, and in two steps, he'd reached me. Taking a firm grip of my elbow, he propelled me toward the bank of elevators.

"Johannes, what's going on?"

"Not here," he growled.

He jabbed a finger at the elevator call button, anger coming off him in violent waves. I wrenched out of his grip, taking a step away as the elevator doors opened.

"I am not going anywhere with you until you tell me what's happened. Is it the award?" If it was, then I couldn't figure out how I'd ended up as the target of his fury. Unless I'd somehow done something to jeopardize his success. But I had no idea what that could be.

"The award?" He frowned. "No, it's not the fucking award. Now get in the elevator."

"No."

I spun on my heel and strode across the lobby. *Choose to be alone with an angry man? No, thanks*. Johannes hadn't shown me a single sign that he had it within him to mistreat a woman, but everyone had a first time. And I didn't plan on being his.

"Ella, wait." He caught up to me and made a grab for my arm.

I showed him my palms. "No. Now you tell me what's going on, right here, right now, or I'm getting Chloe and Ginny and I'm going home."

His nostrils flared, hands clenched into fists by his sides. "Come up to the suite."

"No. I'm not going anywhere with you when you're in this state. Now either spit out what's gotten you all riled up, or I'm leaving."

He jutted his chin forward. "Fine. Just when were you planning to tell me you're married, Ella? Or should I say 'Eloise Fernandez'?"

My blood ran cold, and my heart thudded. *How had he found out?* The phone call. It had to be the phone call. But who was on the other end? Mateo? Oh God, maybe Johannes's nightclub business had ties to Mateo somehow. I'd thought that once, because of the drug connection that a lot of nighttime venues seemed to have, but when I hadn't seen any sign of it at Level Nine, I'd put the fear to the back of my mind.

If there was any chance that phone call had been from Mateo, then I needed to go. Now.

"Where's Chloe?" Why was I asking that when I knew the answer? By the pool. With Ginny. "I have to go." I sprinted across the lobby toward the recreational areas at the back of the hotel. Why the fuck were Vegas hotels so goddamn big? I hadn't gotten very far when Johannes hauled me to a stop.

"Wait. Fuck, Ella, just wait."

"I don't have time to wait. I have to go. He'll be coming for me."

"Who? Your husband?" His anger had morphed into confusion. "Just tell me what's going on."

"Who were you on the phone with?"

"A private detective." His cheeks reddened. "I hired him to look into your background."

It wasn't Mateo. He hadn't found me. My shoulders

sagged, and air pushed out of my lungs in a rush, flattening them. I pitched forward, bracing my hands on my knees, panting as if I'd sprinted up a flight of stairs.

"Oh God."

"Ella." Johannes took hold of my hands and helped me to stand upright. "Please, just fucking talk to me."

As my panic subsided, outrage moved in. He'd hired a *private detective* to spy on me.

How dare he? How fucking dare he!

"You asshole," I hissed. "How could you do that? What has my personal business got to do with you?" I prodded him in the chest, conscious that we were drawing odd looks from passersby. I didn't care. "How long have you been snooping into my life? A week, a month, since the day I came for an interview?"

"Since this morning. After the whole name thing last night, I grew suspicious, and so I asked a business contact to see what he could find out."

My jaw dropped. A few hours. That was all it had taken to uncover the truth about me, about where I came from. About whom I was married to. Dear God, I'd been so stupid. So naïve. And if this private detective could find things out about me so easily, then Mateo could, too. I thought I was safe living in a big city, but I wasn't. Nowhere was safe. The only thing I could do was keep moving.

"He's who you're running from, isn't he? He's Chloe's dad."

"Go away." I shoved at him. "Just leave me alone. I need time to think."

"Please talk to me."

"No!" I shoved him again. "You could have just asked me, but instead you went snooping behind my back."

"I *did* ask. And you lied to me. Ella isn't your middle name. And your real name is Eloise."

"My name is Ella Reyes," I insisted. "That's who I am now."

He showed me his palms. "Okay, okay. Ella it is. But please, come upstairs with me and we can talk."

I shook my head. "I'm going nowhere with you. You betrayed me."

His eyes hardened, and he flexed his jaw. "I betrayed *you?* How the fuck do you think I feel knowing that you didn't trust me enough to tell me this? And to think I almost trusted you with—" He broke off, his lips sealing shut.

"Almost trusted me with what?"

"Nothing. Forget it."

Secrets. Dangerous things that, in the end, always spilled out. And when they did, carnage ensued.

"You should have told me. I could have helped you. I *can* help you."

"I don't need your help."

"Yes, you fucking do."

All the fight in me fled, leaving me weakened and exhausted. "I need time to think. Space. Give me that, please."

"Fine." His voice softened. "Whatever you need. You take the suite. I'll make myself scarce for a few hours."

He cupped my face, brushing his thumb over my cheekbone. The tender touch made me want to cry.

"But I won't give up on you. On us. When you're ready, I

want you to tell me everything, and we'll form a plan. But I guarantee that you and Chloe are safe."

I wished I could believe that. But after his private detective had found out my real name and my marital status in a mere few hours, it was only a matter of time before Mateo found me.

"Safety is an illusion, Johannes."

As I walked away, I felt the heat from his stare on the back of my neck. But when I turned around, he'd gone.

Instead of going up to the suite, I headed for the swimming pool. Mateo might not have found me, but the need to keep Chloe close trumped any and all logic. The pool deck was jam-packed with sun worshippers, the pool filled with people standing around in groups chatting and drinking. I weaved through the crammed-together sunbeds toward the children's pool and play area. The heat from the sun bore down on me, and I squinted, ruing the lack of a hat and a pair of shades.

Chloe and Ginny weren't at the pool. They must have gone inside to escape the heat. I didn't blame them. I'd only been out here for a few minutes, and I'd had enough already.

I returned inside and took the elevator up to the suite. Johannes's revelation wouldn't stop racing around in my head. He knew I was married, and he knew my real name, but he didn't know the truth of why I'd left. I should have told him. He was right about that. But when your life was on the line, you traded nothing for safety.

And besides, Johannes had his own secrets that he'd kept to himself.

Both of us were culpable.

Neither of us was willing to trust the other.

The question was, where did we go from here?

I didn't have an answer.

The light on the door turned green as I touched the key card to the black plate. I pushed it open and entered.

"Chloe! Ginny!"

Silence greeted me. Hmm. Maybe they'd gone for a bite to eat, or for a ride on the Monorail that ran the length of the Strip. Chloe had mentioned that this morning. She'd never been on one before. Neither had I. Hopefully, I'd get time before we returned to Los Angeles.

If I stuck around.

Whatever happened, I needed to tell Johannes everything, and he had to do the same. Without a complete clearing of the air, we wouldn't be able to move forward.

I kicked off my shoes and tossed my purse onto the couch. My hair fell in my eyes, and I reaffixed the hairpin I used to keep it off my face then padded over to Chloe's bedroom in case she and Ginny had returned and were taking a nap. I stepped inside. Empty. I turned around, but as I did, a movement from my left caught my eye. A man emerged from the shadows, and the bottom fell out of my world.

"Hello, Eloise," Mateo said, moving closer. "I've missed you."

I backed into the living room, assessing my options. I wouldn't make it to the door. My phone was in my purse, out of reach all the way over there on the couch, and the house phone was as fruitless as the door. Johannes wouldn't return for a while, and I hadn't a clue where Ginny and Chloe were.

Oh God.

My mouth went dry.

He had them.

"Where are they?" I whispered, my throat raw. "Where's Chloe?"

"She's safe." He strolled toward me with the confidence of a man who knew he'd cornered his prey and was deciding whether to toy with it for a while or end its miserable life where it stood.

Me. I was the prey. I always had been.

"Ginny?"

"The old lady?" He arched a brow. "She'll live. Might wake up with a bit of a headache, though."

My stomach lurched, nausea sloshing around, crawling into my chest, my throat. I swallowed. *Keep calm. Think. Don't do anything stupid.*

"How did you find me?"

"With difficulty." He smiled, but it didn't reach his eyes. "But then I had a stroke of luck. A business associate was at Fiore last night, and he saw you flaunting yourself with another fucking man." His voice rose with each word, and by the end, he was screaming, spittle gathering at the corners of his mouth.

I flinched, backing up. He followed, his face painted in fury, the rage of a man who'd had his prized possession stolen from him, only to find it damaged when he recovered it.

Johannes. I had to keep Johannes safe. Make out he meant nothing to me.

"He's no one, Mateo. Not like that. He's my boss. I had to earn money to eat, to feed and clothe Chloe, to keep a roof over our heads."

"No, you fucking *didn't*!" he hollered. "You had a home, the finest clothes, top chefs catering to your every whim. You had it all, Eloise."

"I was a prisoner!" I yelled back. "And you lied to me our entire marriage. You and your fucking drugs almost got Chloe killed." He flinched, but I powered on. "I will *never* forgive you for putting our daughter in danger. Never."

"That shouldn't have happened. I told you I'd take care of it, and I did."

"Oh, yeah." I laughed bitterly, the vision of bodies and blood running on a loop inside my head. The sounds of gunfire. *Pop, pop, pop*. Me inside the closet, holding Chloe, my hands clamped over her ears as I tried to protect her from the worst of it.

"Yeah, you took care of it all right, Mateo. Until the next time."

"There won't be a fucking next time."

I laughed. I couldn't help it. His blindness to the dangers of his chosen business astounded me. "There will *always* be a next time. And I will not have my daughter brought up in that environment."

He cornered me, boxing me in between the dining table and the wall. No way out.

"You don't have a fucking choice."

He grabbed me, spinning me around. I fought. God, I fought. Lashing out with my hands and feet. He grunted as I kicked his shin. He pressed a white cloth over my mouth and nose. My eyes closed.

Darkness.

Chapter 27

Johannes

This time, I'm not going down without a fight.

HOW ANYONE WALKED DOWN THE LAS VEGAS STRIP IN THE BLAZING heat of the day bewildered me, yet people crammed the sidewalks, every inch of space taken.

Going for a walk had been a terrible idea.

I ducked into the nearest hotel and took a seat in the lobby. How long should I give her? An hour? Two? Longer? Ash had warned me that I could lose her by delving into her private life without permission, but in typical me fashion, I hadn't listened to my wise older brother. I'd pressed on, intrigued at first, then outraged that she'd lied to me about something as important as a ring on her fucking finger.

I should have known better. I should have remembered how she'd acted at our first meeting. How skittish she'd been, her relief when I'd offered to pay her in cash. The fear lodged deep in her eyes. How shuttered she became whenever I mentioned Chloe's father.

And as soon as the private detective had told me he'd found out her real name using some kind of facial recognition technology that I didn't understand, and uncovered a marriage certificate but no divorce certificate, I'd seen red. Kingcaid's didn't cheat, and nor were we homewreckers. Dad had drummed that into each of us since we'd gone on our first dates as teenagers. Yet Ella—Eloise—had forced that upon me without my knowledge.

But if I had an ounce of common sense, I'd have paused and asked myself why she had kept her marital status a secret. Why she was hiding from him. So far, I knew very little other than his name, Mateo Fernandez, and that he lived in Oklahoma. It wasn't him I was interested in. It was her. Regardless, I'd asked the detective to keep digging and see what he could come up with. The more knowledge I had, then the better equipped I was to help Ella.

Fuck it.

I wouldn't lose her. Not over this. Everything was fixable.

I rose to my feet and exited through the sliding doors and back onto the Strip. Fifteen minutes later, I walked into Kingcaid Las Vegas. My heart thudded as I strode down the hallway toward our suite, the mixture of hurt and outrage on her face as we'd argued nipping at my insides.

"Ella," I called out as I entered. "We need to t—"

Pain exploded in my head, and I found myself sprawled on the carpet. Something wet dripped down my face. I touched it, looking at my fingers. Red. Blood. I leapt to my feet.

Two men came toward me. Meaty fists rather than sharp knives. Las Vegas rather than London.

But my brain couldn't separate the two.

I froze.

My heart rate rocketed, causing shooting pains to race across my chest. I couldn't catch my breath.

Move! Do something.

My body refused to obey. It was six years ago, and once again, I was outnumbered, helpless, and at the mercy of another.

No.

Not again.

Never again.

I was *not* helpless. And I refused to go down without a fight.

I braced myself, my belligerent stare daring them to take me on, my legs apart, my hands clenched into fists.

They made their move.

And I made mine.

I lost count of the punches I took and how many I threw. Tangled legs and arms and blood. Pain. And still I refused to go down, to let them win. To let *her* win.

Fuck you, Sadie. Fuck. You.

Ella. This was to do with Ella. But she wasn't Sadie. Not her. She was different.

Where is she? This was her husband's doing. I was convinced of it. I felt myself weakening. Running out of time. One last push. One last try. I threw myself at the man closest to me. He fell against the other one, and the two of them crashed into the thick wooden coffee table in the center of the living room.

Crack.

Stillness.

Not moving.

Blood ran into my eyes, turning my vision red. I fell to my knees, my head swimming. *Don't pass out. Stay alert.* I shook my head. Agony shot through my skull. *Ow.* No shaking. I crawled across the room to the house phone. I picked it up.

"Send help," I gasped into the handset.

I collapsed to the floor and passed out.

K

"Johannes."

I groaned as the deep voice penetrated the tendrils of fog that clouded my brain. But as much as I tried to break through, they were like chains holding me captive. I attempted to open my eyes. Managed a crack.

"Too bright," I croaked, shutting them again.

Jesus. Everything hurt, from the tips of my toes to the top of my head. Was I even alive? Yeah, I must be. If I were dead, I wouldn't be in agony.

Like an exhausted runner crossing the finish line, my memory staggered back to life. The two men waiting for me in my hotel room. They attacked me, but I fought back. Why were they there?

Oh God.

Ella.

"Fuck. Ella." I forced my eyes to open. Nolen hovered over me, his face awash with relief.

"Jesus, man, thank Christ. You scared the shit out of me."

"Where's Ella?" My voice sounded stronger this time, less raspy.

"Easy, bud." He put his hand on my shoulder. "You look a right fucking mess. Best stay away from mirrors until that bruising has gone down."

"Stop stalling, Nolen. Where is she?" I tried to sit up. Failed. *Fuck, what the hell is wrong with me?*

Nolen grimaced. "I don't know, bud. No sign of her. I've got security going through the CCTV. If she's on it, we'll find her." He grimaced again. "Chloe's gone too."

He had them. The husband. It was the only explanation. I curled my hands into fists.

"What about Ginny?"

"She's okay. I had the doctor check her over. Someone dumped her in an alley a few blocks away from here. She has no clue who it was or why she was targeted. Just that she got into an elevator with Chloe and two men followed them inside, and that's the last she remembers."

"Ella's husband is behind this," I said dully.

Nolen's eyebrows shot up his forehead. "Husband? She's married? But I thought you and—"

"I only just found out. She ran away from him, took Chloe, and came to LA. She's been hiding ever since, but somehow he found her."

"Why did she leave him?"

I shook my head. "I don't know."

We hadn't gotten that far, and it was all my fault.

Fuck.

I'd handled this badly.

If only I'd gently coaxed the answers from her instead of going behind her back and hiring a private detective.

If only I'd told her about what had happened to me, she might have felt able to open up about her own situation.

Sharing the worst time of my life would have shown her I trusted her, and in turn, she might have trusted me. My secrecy had encouraged her to keep her secret. Unlike mine, hers was a real and current danger, and keeping it had left her exposed. If she'd told me, I could have put a ring of security around her, made sure she wasn't exposed while we'd figured out what to do. Together.

You're a fucking idiot, Kingcaid. And now you've lost her, and you don't have a clue where he's taken her.

What if I never saw her again?

No, I refused to even consider the possibility. I had the resources to search every inch of this fucking country, every inch of the entire world if I had to, and I'd use every single cent I owned to find her and Chloe. They belonged with me. Not him. Not a man she'd run from. I'd seen the relief in her eyes right before her anger had hit when I'd told her the phone call had been from the private detective. She'd assumed it'd been from her husband, and it had terrified her.

As soon as I found her, I'd tell her everything. I owed her that much.

I scrubbed a hand over my face, then took in the room. I was still in the hotel suite. At least Nolen hadn't taken me to the hospital. Getting out of those places was a fucking nightmare. I should know. I'd been stuck in that one in England for weeks, long after I'd felt well enough to leave.

"Help me out of this bed."

Nolen put both hands on my shoulders and pressed me into the mattress. "You're going nowhere until you've rested up. The doc will be back again shortly. He asked me to message him as soon as you were awake."

"No, I—"

"Don't push me on this, Johannes. If he'd had his way, you'd be in the hospital, but knowing how much you hate those places, I insisted that he treat you here. Besides, you're no good to Ella in this state."

I collapsed against the stack of pillows, my energy sapping despite the minimal movement. He had a point, and I hated that he did, but I could barely sit up, let alone go chasing after Ella.

"I have to find her, Nolen."

"You love her." He repeated what he'd said earlier, which I'd vehemently denied. This time, there was no point in denials. No point in lying.

"Yes, I do."

He squeezed my shoulder. "We'll find her."

The doctor arrived before I could respond. He spent fifteen minutes running his tests before he pronounced a concussion and prescribed bed rest for twenty-four hours. He gave me a sheet of paper with a list of things to look out for, and strict instructions to call him if any of them materialized.

Nolen reappeared after the doctor left. In all the worry about Ella, I'd forgotten to ask him what had happened to those men. I remembered throwing myself at one of them and he'd fallen and taken the other one with him.

"What's the verdict?" he asked.

"I'll live. Cuts, bruises, a concussion. Back on my feet in twenty-four hours. Nolen, what happened to the men who attacked me?"

He grimaced. "Yeah, about that. I wanted to wait until the doc had seen you first."

"And he has. What gives?"

"The police want to talk to you." He grimaced again. "There's nothing to worry about. It's a straightforward case of self-defense. But"—he shrugged—"procedure, you know."

"But what's happened to them? Surely the police can put the squeeze on them and find out where Ella is."

A third grimace. "'Fraid not, cous. One's dead, and the other one's on a ventilator with a bleed on the brain. Might not recover."

I closed my eyes. *Fuck.* "I threw myself at one, and he fell and hit his head on the table. He took the other one down with him. It was an accident."

"Damn fucking straight it was. *They* attacked *you*, not the other way around. You defended yourself." He perched on the edge of the mattress and gave me a pitiful look. "Must've..." He broke off, lowering his gaze. "Brought back memories of that night." He looked at me again, tentative and wary. "You holding up okay?"

Before Ella, I'd have snarled at him and spat out a sarcastic retort. Used aggression as a form of defense. But she'd changed everything for me. My love for her had changed everything.

"I froze. For a few seconds, I was right back in that hotel room in London. But then I thought, *No fucking way*. I wasn't going to let this happen to me again. I refused to be a victim, to lie down and die. I remember little else, just receiving and throwing punches, and then the crash into the coffee table and crawling to the phone to call for help."

Shock widened Nolen's eyes. He hadn't expected me to be that open. I'd trained my family well. If they asked about that night, or Sadie, or how I was doing, or whether I'd finally decided to accept professional help, I'd hit back with cruel words intended to shut them up, to make them leave me alone. And it had worked. They'd stopped asking, and I'd withdrawn further into myself, morphing into a man I didn't recognize. Sadie had trapped me in that time, that moment.

And Ella had set me free.

"I'm so sorry, Johannes."

"Help me find her. That's all I ask."

"I will. Promise."

Chapter 28

Ella

This is all my fault.

I REGAINED CONSCIOUSNESS TO SURROUNDINGS I RECOGNIZED ALL too well. The wallpaper covering the walls mocked me, and the familiar sheets and silk bedspread imprisoned me. Fear crawled into my throat, little barbs that clung to the tender skin and refused to let go.

Just like Mateo.

I fisted my hair. *You're an idiot!* I'd let myself believe in fairy tales. I'd allowed this to happen.

Chloe.

I leapt off the bed, gripping onto one of the ornate four posts that adorned each corner as my legs gave way. I drew air deep into my lungs and waited for my limbs to steady. Whatever drug he'd given me to knock me out must've still been in my system, hence the shakiness in my thighs. After a few seconds, I felt strong enough to cross the room and try the door.

Locked.

Not at all unexpected. I'd run from Mateo once, even though he'd thought his compound impenetrable. Stupid man. Those mercenaries who'd broken in and almost managed to kidnap me and my daughter should have taught him that nowhere was bulletproof. But his arrogance and ego had always led the way and made his decisions for him.

I banged on the door. "Mateo!"

There was no answer, no footsteps parading down the wide, hardwood floor, no key being inserted in the lock. I banged again and again until my knuckles bruised. Pacing the room, I searched for anything I could use as a weapon or a means of escape, but Mateo's men had stripped the room of pretty much everything except for the bed. Even the attached bathroom was empty, apart from a roll of toilet paper and a bar of soap. I returned to the door, but when further banging brought no results, I went back to the bed and sat on the end, cross-legged. This was Mateo's idea of punishment—keeping me in the dark and away from my daughter. He'd done it before.

What would Johannes think when he returned to the hotel suite to find us all gone? Would he assume I'd left him, or would he search for me? I hoped he didn't look for me. He'd get drawn into the web of my life, the poison of it, and he didn't deserve that.

And I didn't deserve him.

But the joy of these last few weeks, of slowly unpeeling the layers of a dour, grumpy man and finding a kind, beautiful soul beneath, would stay with me for a lifetime. In my darkest moments—and there would be many—I'd retreat inside my mind and relive our time together, including the early days when he'd snarled and snapped and shut me down more times than I could count. Each one was a precious memory that would sustain me through the horrors my future held.

The lock rattled on the door, and I jumped up, my legs holding steady this time. Two armed guards walked in. One held a tray of food, and the other stood guard by the door. No sign of Mateo.

"Where is he?" I didn't need to state whom I meant by "he". They knew. And they ignored me.

The one with the tray set it on the bed without even looking at me. He moved away. I jumped in front of him. "I asked you a question. Where is he?"

His eyes cut to mine, then darted away. "All I've been told is to bring that to you."

"Bullshit," I snapped. "You're not leaving until you send your little friend over there to get him."

The guard heaved a sigh. "Stand aside."

"No." I folded my arms. If he wanted to get past me, I couldn't stop him, and he knew it. But I wanted to test the waters, to see how far I could push him.

"I don't want to hurt you."

"And you won't." I hazarded a guess that hurting me went way above his pay grade. If hurting me was on the agenda, Mateo would be the one to dole out such punishment, not this paid muscle.

He sighed again. "Please, stand aside."

"You can leave when Mateo arrives. So, like I said"—I

jerked my head backward—"he can go get him while you and I wait here."

His gaze moved behind me, and he jutted his chin. The door closed, and heavy footsteps moved away, growing faint within seconds. The guard returned his gaze to the floor, almost as if Mateo had ordered him not to look at me. Knowing Mateo, he probably had given him such an order.

It wasn't long before two sets of footsteps sounded in the hallway, getting closer and closer. I stayed where I was, my back to the door, eyes on the guard. The door opened.

"José, you can go."

Mateo. Finally.

I spun around, giving my husband—I *hated* thinking of him in those terms—a belligerent stare. José strode across the room and disappeared into the hallway, closing the door behind him, leaving just me and Mateo. I'd bet one of them had remained outside, though.

"Eloise. I've missed you." Mateo strolled past me and plucked a slice of toast off the tray. He bit into it, then pointed it at me. "You've caused a lot of trouble."

"Where's Chloe?" I demanded.

He took another bite, chewing slowly. "Such a slice of good luck that brought you back to me."

I fisted my hands by my sides. "I won't ask again, Mateo. Where. Is. My. Daughter?"

"*Our* daughter," he corrected. "Our daughter who you have kept from me for more than seven fucking months."

"You know why I took her. She isn't safe here."

"*She is safe*," he bellowed. "It's out there that she isn't safe."

"If she is so safe in here, behind these walls, then tell me why those men got close enough to touch her, to pick her up, to smell her hair." Nausea rolled in my stomach as the memories flooded back. "You did that to her, Mateo. You put her in danger, and as long as she's here with *you*, she'll always be in danger."

His eyes darkened, and he took a step toward me. "I see your time away has loosened your tongue, Eloise. I'll have to do something about that."

Threats. Empty threats. For all Mateo's faults, he'd never laid a hand on me. No, he had far more effective ways of exerting control over me. Psychological pain was his jam, and he'd spread it thickly, knowing that being apart from my daughter was torturous.

"I want to see Chloe."

"You will. When you've earned it."

What the hell does that mean? "Earned it how?"

He tapped his finger on his bottom lip, and his gaze traveled over my entire body. Head to foot and back again. My stomach rolled in revulsion, a new type of nausea sloshing around. I couldn't. I'd left him. I didn't love him anymore, if I ever had. I loved Johannes.

"No."

He arched a brow. "No? So you're telling me you don't want to see Chloe?"

"Of course I want to see her. She needs me."

"But your desire to see her isn't enough for you to agree to make love to your husband?"

"Mateo." Somehow, I kept my voice calm. "I left you to keep Chloe safe, but I also left you because I don't love you anymore. I married you too young, before I'd lived. Before I knew what I wanted."

"And what you want is Johannes Kingcaid?"

My lips parted. He knew. He knew everything. Oh God. *Ignore. Don't deny.*

"I don't love you, Mateo," I whispered.

"You married me. That means you belong to me. Forever."

I shook my head. "I don't belong to anyone. I'm not a possession."

His lip curled, and a dart of fear shot into my bloodstream. "Oh, my darling girl. Your innocence is what drew me to you all those years ago. I knew I could mold you into the perfect wife, the perfect mother. I did it once. I can do it again."

"No. It's too late."

"Too late." He nodded, pacing back and forth, his fingers drumming against his thigh. "You're right. It is too late. For some things. But not for us."

My mouth dried up. Something in his tone... Malice? Or triumph? I tried to swallow, but I couldn't. "What do you mean?"

"Unfortunately, not everyone has escaped your little adventure unarmed. Take that poor sap, Johannes, for example."

His lips lifted into a cruel smile, and something inside me cracked. No. Not that. Please God, not him. "What have you done?" I whispered.

"He should have known better than to touch what's mine. Kiss what's mine. *Fuck* what's mine."

"He didn't know, Mateo." I shook my head. "He didn't know I was married to you. It's my fault, not his. Please don't punish him for my mistakes. Punish me. I'm the one who deserves your wrath."

"Too late." He moved closer, his lips hovering a few millimeters from mine. "The desert around Las Vegas is so vast, isn't it? And there's Lake Mead, too. So many bodies hidden in there." He laughed. "At least he'll have company."

He smiled again, his eyes two soulless orbs set in a wicked face. My knees gave way. I stumbled and fell, jarring my spine as I hit the floor. "No." The word left my lips on a groan. "Please, no."

"You brought this on yourself, Eloise. And you'll have to live with the consequences of what you've done." He tossed the remains of the piece of toast at me. "Now eat your breakfast like a good girl, and don't give your guards any more trouble."

The door slammed, and the lock slid into its housing. I curled into a ball, pain enveloping me, seeping into every part of my body and soul.

Johannes. No. Not him. *Please, God, help me. Don't let this be true.*

Mateo was right. This was my fault. Mine. I'd lied to Johannes. I'd brought trouble to his door. I was gullible and naïve and selfish. My actions had put him in harm's way, and he'd paid the ultimate price. That would be my real punishment. Not being back here with Mateo in this gilded prison. Johannes's death would be my penance, his blood on my hands.

And I'd have to live with what I'd done for the rest of my life.

Chapter 29

Johannes

The answers are always there.
You just have to know where to look.

The police interview lasted thirty minutes. I guessed Nolen had exerted the enormous influence he had in this town to make them go easy on me, or maybe the evidence of self-defense was so overwhelming as to make it an open-and-shut case. Either way, I wasn't complaining. All my focus needed to be on finding Ella, and that started with locating her husband.

Wincing as I shifted my weight—fuck, everything hurt—I reached for my phone on the nightstand and dialed the private detective who'd uncovered Ella's real name. I'd asked him to dig a little deeper, and while I hadn't heard from him, in my experience, applying pressure often garnered faster results.

Once again, my theory proved accurate. He had an address in Oklahoma and more information on the husband. Turned out he was the worst kind of human. A drug dealer, a murderer, and now a kidnapper. And he didn't bother hiding it either, which led me to believe that he thought he was untouchable. He probably had the local and state police in his pocket and they left him alone to go about his business in return for huge wads of cash.

I hung up and navigated to Google Earth. Seconds later, an aerial view of a huge, walled-in compound appeared on the screen. Black dots surrounded the perimeter. Guards, I suspected. Getting Ella out of there with that amount of security would be virtually impossible. I couldn't exactly hire a bunch of mercenaries to storm the place, all guns blazing. For one, that was illegal, and unlike her piece-of-shit husband, I stayed on the right side of the law. And for another, Ella or Chloe might get hurt.

Fuck. There has to be a way.

I refused to admit defeat. I'd never give up trying to get her back.

A tap came at my door, and Ginny's face appeared, steeped in worry. I motioned to her.

"Come on in."

A sound broke from her throat as she crossed to my bed. A sob. "I'm sorry. I'm so sorry. Chloe was in my care and I... I..."

Comforting anyone, let alone an elderly lady I didn't know all that well wasn't a skill. But this woman mattered to Ella. Therefore, she mattered to me.

I patted her hand. "You couldn't have stopped them. It's not your fault."

She gestured to my face. "Are you okay?"

I dismissed her concern with a shake of my head. "I'll live. It's nothing."

"How will we find them?" Her chin wobbled.

"Oh I know where they are. Oklahoma." I was certain enough in my assumption to state it as a fact. "Did you know she was married?"

Ginny gasped. "No. Although from the day I met her, I knew she was running from something. But she was so closed-off about it that I never pressed. I figured when she was ready, she'd tell me."

"Same. Except I should have pushed harder. If I had, maybe her husband wouldn't have been able to get to her."

"So he took her against her will." A statement, not a question.

"Yes."

"Poor Ella," she whispered.

"Do you need anything? Nolen said the doctor had checked you over."

"I'm fine. A little shook up, that's all. What I need is for you to bring them home, where they belong."

"I will." Although I hadn't a clue how. "She ran from him for a reason. She wanted to be free."

"Can't the police do something? He can't just kidnap her. That's against the law."

Yeah, but men like Mateo Fernandez didn't abide by the law. I kept that thought to myself. There wasn't any point in scaring Ginny.

"Try not to worry." Easier said than done. I'd kept my voice calm while talking to Ginny, but my insides were fracturing, fear crawling into my veins and causing my heart to stutter. What if he hurt her? What if he hurt Chloe? What if I failed them even more than I'd failed them already?

"Do you want to go home?"

She nibbled her lip. "I should stay."

"There's nothing you can do here. Better to be surrounded by familiarity than holed up in a hotel room. I'll keep you informed on what's happening. I promise."

She nodded and squeezed my arm. "It would be nice to go home."

"I'll have the company jet take you back to LA, and I'll ensure there's a car waiting to drive you home."

"Oh, there's no need—"

"There's every need."

I sent Ginny off to pack. As I hung up from making the last of the arrangements, Nolen appeared.

"I have an address," I blurted before he was fully in the room. "She's in Oklahoma." Grabbing my phone, I showed him the image of the compound. "Her husband is a drug dealer, and a bigwig, from what my guy has uncovered. Getting Ella out won't be easy, and right now, I'm coming up empty as to how we even begin."

Nolen peered at the screen, his top teeth grazing his bottom lip. "Drug dealer. Fuck. That's some bad shit."

"Gee, thanks for your impressive insight."

Nolen chuckled. "There's the Johannes I know. Sarcastic fucker."

"I'm not in the mood, Nolen." I glowered at him. "You said you'd fucking help. So help."

"Easy." He squeezed my shoulder, like he had earlier. "I have a friend in the DEA. Let me call him and see if he knows this piece of crap, and what the agency might be able to do to help."

"Good."

I flung back the covers and tested my legs. They held, albeit a bit wobbly. The pain around my midsection though... Christ. If these were bruised ribs, according to the doc, then I was fucking glad they weren't broken.

"In the meantime, I'll head to your security office and help scour the CCTV. There has to be evidence of the three of them being taken from the hotel."

I felt sick at the thought of Ella. How scared she must be. If she came out of this with a single scratch, I would make it my business to see that fucker pay. I'd set fire to his compound and watch him burn. Fuck the law.

Nolen left to call his contact at the DEA. Avoiding mirrors—if Nolen thought my face was messed up, I didn't need to see it—I grabbed a sweater and pants from the closet, but as I pulled the sweater over my head, I paused.

What the hell?

The entire time I'd spoken with Nolen, the police, and Ginny, the vile result of my attack in London had been on display. I traced my fingertips over my scar. I had no recollection of undressing after I'd passed out by the phone, which meant Nolen must have undressed me before putting me in bed. But far more shocking was that I hadn't realized my neck was exposed. I *never* allowed anyone to see my scar.

Could be worry over Ella's whereabouts, but maybe it was more than that. Perhaps Ella had changed me in more ways than I'd first thought. She hadn't just opened my eyes to the possibility of falling in love again, but she'd also hurled a wrecking ball at the layers of protection I'd spent six years building up, and I'd been so entranced by her that I hadn't noticed them splintering.

Even more surprising, none of my visitors had stared. If they had, I'd have noticed, and their rubbernecking would have alerted me to the issue much earlier than now.

God, Ella.

I closed my eyes, allowing myself a few moments to absorb this enormous change in my life. Whether it was sustainable or if it was merely a result of the clogging fear for Ella's safety wasn't clear to me. Only time would tell if I reverted back to my old ways of hiding or forged forward into a new and scary world.

Something told me it would be the latter. All I needed was Ella by my side.

I put Ginny in a limo to the airport, and as soon as I'd seen her off, I headed for security. They were expecting me, and once the head of the team showed me how to operate the various cameras, I sat down and got to work. Nolen's staff was more than capable of managing without me, but I had to do something. I couldn't just sit on my hands and wait. I needed to feel useful or risked going crazy.

I lost track of time as I scoured the feed from hundreds of cameras scattered throughout the hotel, but so far I hadn't caught a glimpse of Ella or Ginny or Chloe. They were here somewhere, though. No one could avoid every single camera, even if they were looking out for them. And the lack of sightings led me to think that was exactly what Fernandez and his guards had done. But everyone made mistakes, and I had to believe that somewhere in this footage was the evidence I sought to prove he had taken her.

"Johannes." Nolen entered with a guy so tall that he

dwarfed me, and I topped out at six-four. "This is Brax. The DEA agent I mentioned."

"Hey." I reached for his outstretched hand. "Has Nolen updated you?"

"Yeah." He shook his head. "Mateo fucking Fernandez. Man's a nefarious asshole who thinks he's above the law. I've been trying to nail that fucker for years but haven't found one thing that'll stick enough for a judge to grant a search warrant. So he just keeps peddling his drugs and ruining lives, and there's not a damn thing I can do about it."

My heart sank. I fired a glance at Nolen, my message clear. *Thought this guy was supposed to help.*

"So Ella's screwed? Is that what you're saying?"

"No. I'm saying we need evidence that he's taken Mrs. Fernandez against her will. I have to have something concrete to take to the judge, no matter how small. I'll fight like hell for a warrant, but you've got to give me something to go on."

"Right." I returned my attention to the CCTV footage, scrolling through images from the service entrance of the hotel. I rubbed the heels of my hands into my eyes, my vision blurring from staring at the screen too long. Knocking back my pain meds, I refocused my efforts.

"Why don't you take a break?" Nolen suggested.

"*No*," I barked. "Every second counts. Imagine how fucking scared she is."

Nolen's hands came up to either side of his head. "It was just a suggestion. You've been through a trauma, too, Johannes. I'm only watching out for you."

"I don't need you watching out for me. I'm not a

goddamn child." I gave him my back. If all he was going to do was bitch and moan, he could fuck off.

I switched camera angles to finish checking this part of the hotel. The cameras were positioned to cover as much as possible, but every area had its dead spots, and I'd started to think that Ella had been spirited away using this method. If Fernandez had avoided law enforcement efforts to apprehend him, then the man was a clever bastard. He'd known exactly what to look for.

If this turned out to be fruitless, I'd—

"There!" I pressed Pause, the image freezing on a woman being held in the arms of a man, his face on full display. Her head was tipped back, her ebony tresses hanging low.

"That's him." Brax loomed over my shoulder, peering at the screen. "That's Fernandez."

I moved the footage a frame at a time, trying to get a different angle on Ella. Suddenly Fernandez turned, as if he'd heard his name or something had spooked him, giving us the perfect view of Ella's face. Her eyes were closed, and her mouth parted as if she was asleep.

Except she wasn't. He'd drugged her. I'd as good as smelled her fear when I'd confronted her with her marital state and she'd thought her husband had found her. She wouldn't go with him willingly. Not a fucking chance. And she certainly wouldn't feel comfortable enough to fall asleep in his arms.

"That enough for you?" I directed my question at Brax.

"Judge could say she's napping."

I growled. This guy was fast getting on my last fucking nerve. "Then *I'll* speak to the judge. If Ella was so happy with her husband, why has she spent all these months hiding out in LA under an assumed name, and with documents to back that up? It has to be enough." I banged the desk with my fist. "It has to."

"Easy." Nolen laid a hand on my shoulder. I shook him off.

"Give me the footage, and I'll see what I can do. No promises."

Fuck. That. If this guy didn't come up with the goods, then I'd find another way to get her out of there. He couldn't keep her there forever. I'd hire a team of people to watch his compound, night and day, follow the fucker wherever he went. However long it took for him to loosen the leash, I'd be there waiting to pounce.

I'd failed her, left her exposed.

I wouldn't make the same mistake again.

Chapter 30

Ella

Vengeance is an unforgiving bitch.

"Eat."

I turned my head, refusing to look at Mateo. He sickened me. He disgusted me. He was a monster, a vile creature. A sociopath. All he cared about was power and money and his possessions, and he thought of me and Chloe as the latter.

Chloe.

My heart ached for my baby. I didn't know how long I'd been out when Mateo had drugged me and snatched me from Nolen Kingcaid's hotel, but I'd counted two days and two nights since then, and not being able to hold Chloe, to comfort her and reassure her that everything would be okay, was a cavernous hole in my chest.

If I begged, he'd use it against me.

So I remained silent, refusing to eat, refusing to talk, refusing to give in to a single demand he made.

Fuck him. *Fuck. Him.*

"If you don't eat something, I'll force it down your throat."

I slowly shifted my gaze to him. What had I ever seen in this man? Except I knew the answer. An adroit con man had duped my seventeen-year-old self. Mateo was an expert in manipulation, and with my teenage hormones raging and the desire to rail against authority in full flow, I'd made the biggest mistake of my life.

Chloe was the only good thing to come out of my relationship with Mateo. As much as I hated him, I'd never regret her. She was my angel, my princess, my reason for living.

But Johannes had been my reason for living, too. Our relationship had been a slow burn, an inching toward the inevitable. My future.

And now he was gone. Killed under the orders—or maybe by the hand—of the man I'd brought into his life.

Mateo would pay. I'd see to it. Somehow, I would escape this prison, and I'd go to the police and tell them everything I knew about Mateo and his associates and his dirty money. Not the local police. He probably had them in his pocket. I'd go to the Feds. They'd listen to me.

One way or another, I'd see Mateo rot in hell for what he'd done. Vengeance was an unforgiving bitch, and I intended to give her free rein. To ruin this fucker. To make him wish he'd never laid eyes on me.

I picked up a dollop of mashed potato and tossed them at Mateo's pristine black shirt. "You fucking eat it."

His eyes flashed, both hands forming huge fists. I flinched, readying myself for a punch. He'd never laid a finger on me, but there was a first time for everything, and the venomous look in his eyes told me I was edging closer.

It didn't matter.

He could do what he wanted to me. I'd never surrender. I'd never again be the stupid, gullible, naïve girl he had coaxed away from her parents and corrupted with his enormous house and fancy cars and luxurious lifestyle.

You were right, Mom.

I'd given up my family for him, thinking he was the love of my life and that I knew better than my parents when it came to my happiness.

Such is the ignorance of youth.

Once all this was over, I'd pluck up the courage and reach out to them, try to make amends for cutting them so abruptly from my life, for withholding their only grandchild, and hope they had enough love in their hearts to forgive me.

"You want to do this the hard way, Eloise?" Mateo smiled at me, but it didn't reach his eyes. Fake. Just like his love for me. "Your choice."

He reached for a napkin and haplessly brushed globs of mashed potato off his ruined shirt. Standing, he picked up the tray and handed it to a waiting guard, then swept from my room without giving me a second glance.

I waited for the lock to turn, then forced myself to sit. I'd scoured every inch of this room for a weapon and come up empty, but I'd been thinking about this all wrong. I couldn't fight my way out of here. Mateo had too many guards for that plan to work. I had to be more cunning than that.

But how?

I ran my hands through my hair, snagging a nail on the hairpin that held my thick hair out of my eyes.

Yes! Why hadn't I thought of this earlier?

Removing it, I padded over to the door and dropped to my knees. I hadn't a clue how to pick a lock, but sitting here wallowing in my grief and burning with the need for revenge wasn't going to help me find Chloe and get the hell off this property.

Action. That was what was needed. The feeling that I was doing *something* to help myself rather than waiting for Mateo's next move.

If Mateo had a guard standing outside my room, I'd know in seconds whether this plan had a chance of working. He'd hear me playing with the lock, and he'd open the door. And if that happened, then I'd know not to waste any more of my time, and put my efforts into forming a new plan.

I inserted the pin in the lock and wiggled it about, more to make a noise than an attempt to break free. The door remained locked.

Still with the ego, Mateo.

He'd left me unguarded, resolute in his belief that I was helpless.

Screw you.

I played with the lock for a while, growing more frustrated as my efforts proved fruitless. Whenever I'd seen this on TV, it had always looked so easy.

It wasn't easy.

You're not giving up.

I took a deep breath, straightened the pin where it had bent inside the lock, and tried again. I must have been there for no longer than five minutes when I heard shouting and then the sounds of men running. I recoiled from the door, shoving the pin in my hair, but they ran right past my room.

What's going on?

I peered through the lock. Pointless. I couldn't see a thing. I pressed an ear to the door and listened.

A loud bang echoed through the house, followed by several cracking sounds, one after the other. I leapt back from the door, my heart hammering inside my chest.

Was that... was that... gunfire?

Oh, God. Chloe!

Chapter 31

Johannes

If she dies, I die.

One Hour Earlier...

The last forty-eight hours had been the longest of my entire existence.

Brax had finally secured a warrant on the basis of the video evidence of Ella being carried from my cousin's hotel and a written statement from me. He'd immediately assembled a team to storm Fernandez's compound, unable to hide his glee at finally getting a shot at the elusive drug baron.

He'd fought hard against bringing me along until Nolen took him to one side, and the next thing I knew, we were on a plane to Oklahoma. Once we'd landed, he'd bundled me into one of five vans, penned me in between two huge DEA agents in full riot gear, and told me that if I didn't obey every fucking order either he or any of his men gave, he'd shoot me.

I believed every word.

Not that the fear of getting shot would stop me from acting if Ella needed me.

The atmosphere in the van electrified as we inched closer to the compound. I felt Brax's eyes on me, and I lifted my chin and met his steely gaze.

"Remember what I said."

I gave him a curt nod, then returned my attention to the inky blackness outside. There wasn't even a hint of light from the moon, the clouds overhead far too thick.

Perfect conditions for the raid, according to Brax.

Thirty minutes later, the convoy of vehicles slowed to a stop, and Brax got on the radio, barking out rapid-fire instructions. From what I picked up, we were about a half mile out from the compound, and they'd travel the rest of the way on foot.

Only two individuals would be left behind in our vehicle. Me and one other agent. A babysitter, in case I went rogue. Smart of Brax, really, if infuriating. It *killed* me to sit here doing nothing, but I had to trust in these guys.

They had the training. I, unfortunately, did not.

I couldn't stop the constant fear of friendly fire, though. It happened more often than most of our armed forces cared to admit.

If Ella got hurt, I'd... I'd...

"Let's move."

The van doors opened and all but one of the agents

jumped out. The last one slammed the door behind him. They joined up with the agents from the other vehicles and disappeared into the obsidian night.

Seconds crawled by, turning into minutes that felt like hours. I must have checked my watch a thousand times, whereas the man sitting opposite me sprawled in his seat, his finger resting near the trigger of his assault rifle, eyes half-closed. Although I'd bet if anything happened, he'd go from zero to a hundred in the time it took me to blink.

For him, this was just his job, whereas for me, it was my life.

She was my life.

And it had taken her being snatched for me to realize how much I loved her.

My heart pounded, and my palms were slick with sweat despite the cool interior of the van. The waiting... God, the waiting was the worst.

What if it all went wrong?

What if Ella or Chloe got hurt?

It would be my fault. I'd brought the DEA here.

I scrubbed my hands over my face, and as I dropped them, I caught the eye of my minder. He gave a small smile and a nod as if to say, "Chill," but chilling wasn't possible. Not when I felt so powerless. I wouldn't *chill* until my arms were around Ella and I could satisfy myself that she was safe.

"Are you getting anything?" I asked. "Are they there yet?"

He shook his head. "They're going in dark."

"What does that mean?"

He tapped at the communication device attached to his right ear. "No comms until they make themselves known."

"How will we know?"

His smile grew. "Oh, we'll know."

I hadn't a clue what that meant, but I didn't like it. I didn't like any of this. I should have found another way, a less violent way. I shuddered, and my hands wouldn't stop trembling. I stuffed them beneath my thighs.

A loud bang echoed through the night, and I leapt out of my seat. "What was that?" A volley of gunfire followed, audible even from a half mile away. "Shit, shit. Is this it? What's happening?"

More gunfire. More explosions.

"God, what's going on?" I went for the door. He gripped my arm and almost threw me back into my seat.

"Sit. The fuck. Down."

The sound of an engine firing rent the air, and I caught sight of one of the other vans fired taking off toward the compound.

Was that for Ella and Chloe?

Please, please God. Let them come out alive and unharmed.

"If she's hurt... If your guys hurt her..."

"Relax, Mr. Kingcaid. We're professionals. It's what we do."

Relax? Is he crazy?

"If it was your girl in there, would you be able to relax?" I spat.

His mouth twisted, and he hitched a shoulder. "No."

"Then don't expect me to."

I lost track of time, the sound of gunfire peppering the

air. Then it stopped. I held my breath, waiting for it to start up again.

My minder spoke rapidly into his comms. "Echo Bravo, report."

Nothing.

Fuck.

"Echo Bravo, this is Zulu. Report."

A crackle sounded over the airwaves.

The DEA agent tried again. "Echo Bravo, this is Zulu. Come in."

Another crackle, then, "Zulu, this is Echo Bravo. Compound secured, targets apprehended."

Targets?

Did that mean Ella, or Fernandez?

"Are they okay?" My tongue felt too thick for my mouth. "Ella and Chloe, are they all right?"

He held up a finger. "The package?"

Package?

It was as if they were speaking a foreign language.

"We have them. Sending your way now."

"Is that them? Does he mean Ella and Chloe?"

"Yes."

"God."

I lurched toward the door again, only to find myself back in my seat.

Again.

"Let me out."

"Cool it. Let's wait until they get here. Last thing I need is you stumbling around in the dark and getting yourself shot or worse. Sit tight."

I glowered at him, my legs jiggling as I cocked my ears for the sound of a car engine.

There!

Faint, but getting louder.

My minder shifted his position and peered out the front window. I followed suit. Headlights. Getting closer. Closer.

I took advantage of his momentary distraction and threw myself out of the van, taking off at a blistering pace toward the oncoming vehicle.

"Ella!" I yelled into the night. "Ella!"

The van slewed to a stop and the side door opened. And then she was there and I had her in my arms, and I held her and kissed her hair and muttered words that made no sense, relief a raging torrent inside me.

Was she real? Or was this all a dream, and I'd wake up to find my life a living nightmare?

"Johannes. Oh God. Oh God. I thought you were dead." She pulled back and cupped my face, brushing her thumbs over my bruised cheeks. "He said you were dead. He killed you."

"I'm here." I ran my hands over her, checking for injuries. "Are you okay? Did he hurt you?"

"Look what he did to you." She skimmed over my cuts and bruises, then burst into tears. "I believed him when he said you were dead. I'm so sorry. This is all my fault."

"Ella."

I drew her to me, caressing her body, attempting to prove to myself that she was flesh and blood, and mine. She trembled. I held her close, squeezing her tight.

"I'm here. I'm alive. I'm going nowhere. It's a few cuts and scrapes. That's all."

I captured her lips with mine, drinking in the taste of her, the smell of her, the way her curves molded to my body. I knotted my fingers in her hair, anchoring myself in case my legs failed me and peppered her face with kisses.

"I'm the one who's sorry. So fucking sorry."

"What for?"

"For failing you."

"No. Oh, Johannes, no. All of this is my fault. I should have trusted you."

"I should have trusted you." I kissed her again. "Chloe?"

"She's fine. She's okay."

She took my hand and led me over to the vehicle. Inside, Chloe was fast asleep, curled up on one of the seats, both hands tucked underneath her head, her dark hair fanning out around her pretty face.

My heart constricted.

I'd never thought of myself as the paternal sort, but something about this kid tugged at me. Maybe it was just because she looked like Ella, or she'd been through so much and come out the other side unscathed. At least that was what I hoped. I guessed we wouldn't know that for some time, but with Ella's love, and my protection and unlimited funds to secure any help she might need, she'd thrive.

I'd make sure of it.

Brax clapped me on the shoulder. "Get in. We gotta roll."

"Airport?" I asked.

"Yeah."

I helped Ella into the van, where she sat beside Chloe, stroking her hair with the tenderness only a mother could offer. I sat on the bench opposite, exhaustion swamping me, but I couldn't take my eyes off them, almost as if I was scared that if I dozed off, even for a second, they wouldn't be here when I woke.

The van set off into the night, and I put in a call to Nolen. Despite the late hour, he answered.

"Tell me you've got them."

"They're here. They're safe."

Ella looked up and I mouthed, "Nolen." She nodded, then returned her attention to Chloe, not having broken stride on her rhythmic stroking of her daughter's hair.

"Thank God. Where are you now?"

"With Brax's team. We're headed back to the airport."

"Perfect. The jet's on standby, waiting for you."

"The company jet?"

"Yeah. I sent it as soon as you left for Oklahoma. There's security on board, too. Just in case."

My shoulders sagged in gratitude. One of the company's private jets would be far comfier for Ella and Chloe than the military plane I'd arrived on. I wanted to wrap them both in cotton and silk, and thanks to Nolen, I now could.

"Thank you, man. I owe you."

"Bullshit. Call me when you're settled back in LA."

"I will."

I ended the call and slid my phone into my pocket, returning my gaze to Ella. I'd never felt this kind of surge before, a need to protect, to nurture, to care for, but fuck me, it raced through my body, filling every crevice and dark corner.

I'd kill for Ella.

Die for her.

Burn the world to the ground if it kept her safe.

She'd changed me, irrevocably.

But the transformation wouldn't be complete until I'd confessed every secret, told her the truth about me, and listened to her truth, too.

Right now, though, all I wanted was to take them home and keep them there forever.

Chapter 32

Johannes

Laying ghosts to rest is
an enlightening experience.

Dusk fell as the sun sank lower over the horizon. Since we'd arrived home midmorning, Ella hadn't left Chloe's side for a second. On the flight back to LA, she'd told me that during her time in Oklahoma, she hadn't eaten, and since we got home, all she'd managed was to nibble on a sandwich.

Nor had she spoken much, other than to softly sing lullabies as she cradled her daughter in her arms. Whatever had happened to Chloe in the three days since she'd been taken from Vegas back to her home in Oklahoma, the poor little mite must not have slept much. My earlier hope that the experience hadn't damaged her ebbed a little, given how she clung to Ella and sucked on her thumb.

I hadn't spent a huge amount of time with Chloe, but I'd *never* seen her suck her thumb.

Ella caught sight of me hovering in the doorway. She smiled a little and held out her hand, beckoning me over. I crept into the room so as not to wake Chloe.

"How is she?" I whispered.

"Tired and confused, but she's safe. That's all I care about."

"And you?" I perched on the edge of the bed. "How are you doing?"

A fresh swathe of tears glistened in her eyes, but she held them back, blinking to disperse them. I wished she wouldn't. I wished she'd let it all out like she had at the moment of her release.

I wished she'd talk to me.

"I'm not sure what I feel, to be honest."

I tucked her hair behind her ear. "It'll come."

"That's what worries me." She ran her teeth over her bottom lip.

"You need to eat something."

She shook her head. "I can't. My stomach is in knots. Did you call Ginny?"

"Yeah."

She breathed out a sigh of relief. "Poor Ginny. She must regret the day she met me."

"I highly doubt that. She wanted to come straight over here, but I told her to leave it for a day or so. I hope that was the right thing to do."

"Yeah. It was. I'm not ready. Not yet. My mind is whirring. It won't stop."

"It will all seem better after a good night's sleep. I promise."

A sob broke from her throat, but she caught it, swallowing back the emotion. "I was so scared, Johannes. But I was mad, too. So angry. If I'd had a gun, I would have shot him."

You and me both.

"He's in custody. He can't hurt you any longer."

"But what if he gets out?" She spoke so quietly that I strained to hear her.

"He won't."

"You don't know him. He's a powerful man. He has friends in high places."

"You're safe with me. I promise. I won't let anything happen to you or to Chloe."

Her bottom lip wobbled. "I wish I'd told you everything."

I grimaced. "We've both made mistakes."

"Yeah." She sighed and held Chloe a little tighter. "I'm so tired."

I leaned over and kissed her forehead. "Get some sleep. I'll be right across the hall."

A part of me yearned for her to ask me to stay, and a piece of me died when she didn't. Trauma brought terrible consequences. I should know. It damaged relationships and broke people apart. It scared me what it might do to me if I lost Ella through this.

I crept from the room, closing the door behind me, and crossed the hallway to my bedroom. I lay on the bed for a while, eyes wide open, my mind racing. I wasn't sure at what point I'd drifted off, but I woke to the feel of Ella's arm snaking around my waist. I turned over and wrapped my arms around her, pulling her to me.

"I can't stay," she whispered. "I have to be with Chloe right now."

"I know." I kissed her hair, breathing deeply through my nose, memorizing the smell of her. "I'm here. Whenever you need me, I'm here."

She nestled into my neck. "I love you."

I squeezed my eyes shut, holding her even closer. "I love you," I murmured, seeking her lips with my own, the connection all too brief. What a time to share our true feelings, yet on some level, it was perfect.

Perfectly us. Perfectly flawed.

We lay together for a few more minutes, then Ella slipped from my arms and returned to Chloe.

But this time, I didn't mourn the loss. I embraced it. Celebrated the personal growth I'd experienced over the last few weeks since Ella had come into my life. As much as I needed her, Chloe needed her more.

K

"Bye!"

Ella waved off Chloe as she skipped down the path with Ginny to the car I'd provided. Ginny had offered to take Chloe for a few hours to give Ella and me the space to talk—with a security detail in tow, of course. I wasn't taking any fucking chances.

Over the last week, Chloe had gradually released the tight hold she had on her mother, returning to the cheerful, happy little girl she'd been in Vegas. Kids were so resilient. Adults far less so. Ella's viewpoint on the entire experience would take longer to process. But she would. I'd make sure of it.

She closed the door, sagging against it. "Boy, that was difficult."

"It'll do her good to get out of this house and back to some kind of normality."

"Armed guards following her everywhere is hardly normality."

"They're professionals. She won't even know they're there."

"I hope so."

I cupped my hand around the back of her neck and kissed the top of her head. "Trust me."

She tilted back her head, her eyes luminous and soulful, and brimful of love. For me. It took my breath away.

"I trust you. And I love you."

I smiled. "Don't think I'll ever tire of hearing you say that."

"Good. Because I plan to say it a lot. For a long time." She slid both arms around my waist and rested her head on my chest. "So, Kingcaid, we doing this or what?"

"I guess it's time."

She nodded. "Long overdue."

I led her into the living room and nestled her beside me on the couch. And then I told her everything about Sadie, about the robbery, about the terrible scars, both inside and out, that her betrayal and the attack had left me with. She listened without interruption, just giving me the occasional squeeze of encouragement and reassurance. By the time I'd finished, I felt like I'd been through some kind of exorcism and the dark cloud that had hovered overhead for the past six years dissipated.

"So that's why you wear these sweaters all the time?"

"Yes."

"And your therapist didn't help you find a way past hiding behind this clothing?"

"I never went to therapy."

Her eyebrows shot north. "Why not?"

I hitched a shoulder. "Didn't think it would help."

"And what about now?"

Squeezing her tight, I rested my chin on the top of her head. "With you by my side, I might just be in a place where I can consider it."

"Can I see it? The scar?"

A knot formed in my stomach. *I can do this.* If I could let strangers see the hideous, raised slash of a scar etched into my skin, as I had with the police in Vegas, then I could show the woman I loved.

I gripped the hem of my sweater and pulled it over my head, revealing a black T-shirt underneath. I closed my eyes.

"No." Ella brushed her thumbs over my eyelids. "Don't hide from me. Not from me."

I locked my gaze on her as she traced the bumpy, ugly thing with her fingertip. I waited for a wave of revulsion to hit me, but instead, a raft of goose bumps covered my arms, and my skin prickled in joy from her touch.

And then she kissed it. And kissed it again. And again, until every inch had felt the touch of her lips.

"Why do you hide it?"

I licked my lips. "To me, it's a sign of weakness, of failure." I shrugged. "I'm sure that sounds crazy to you, but it held me prisoner for so long. I trusted Sadie, and she sold me out. Strangely, it wasn't even almost dying that I found the hardest to deal with. It was living with the reality of my mistakes."

"Oh, Johannes." She tugged on her lip. "Did they ever catch her?"

I shook my head. "All that to get her hands on a million-dollar watch, a gold-plated cell phone, and a few thousand in cash." I laughed, the sound grating and bitter. "Now you see why I live so frugally. Look where flaunting riches got me."

She gazed at me for a few seconds, her eyes brimming with love. Shifting her body, she straddled me, tracing my scar with her lips for the second time. God, I could get used to this. With every kiss, she healed a broken piece of me. I gripped her hips, rocking my erection into her. *Christ.* I'd missed the feel of her heat, the curve of her hips against my palms. The sweet scent of her. Driven insane with lust, I pushed up her skirt.

"Ah, fuck. No." I tipped her off my lap. "I might be a selfish asshole, but I'm not that selfish. You've heard my story. Now I want to hear yours."

"Sex first?" She blinked at me, all coquettish and sultry. Christ, she'd be the death of me, and this time, I'd embrace it—crave it, even.

I groaned as she reached for my cock, capturing her wrist at the last moment. If I let her touch me, we'd spend the next several hours in bed, and before we knew it, Chloe would be home.

"No." I set her hand in her lap. "Talk to me."

She snapped off a loose cotton thread from her T-shirt and rolled it between her fingers, a sigh making its way up her throat. “My real name is Eloise Fernandez. My maiden name was Harper. My mother’s name is Eleanor, so I took ‘Ella’ from that and I took ‘Reyes’ from my maternal grandmother. I needed to disappear, but I yearned to hold on to my roots in some small way. Mateo never met my parents, nor was he interested in learning anything about them, so choosing that name felt safe enough.”

I frowned. “How come your parents never met him?”

She breathed out heavily. “They didn’t approve. When I met him, Mateo was thirty-two, and I was seventeen. They forbade me from having anything to do with him. So, of course, I rebelled.” She shrugged. “Teenagers, hormones, and being told I couldn’t do something was motivation to do the very thing my parents actively discouraged. I chose Mateo and lost my parents.

“What happened is all on me. As soon as I turned eighteen, I moved in with Mateo, and shortly after, we married. Mom and Dad reached out to me several times, begging me to come home, so I changed my phone number and gave the guards strict instructions that they were not to let my parents past the gates.”

She blinked a few times in succession and averted her gaze. “Last I heard, they got divorced, I think because of the stress of what happened with me. My mom remarried and moved to France. My dad lives in New York.”

She took a breath, and I waited until she’d collected herself, then encouraged her to continue. I’d purged my demons. Now it was her turn to purge hers. And then, maybe, we could both move on.

"At first, life with Mateo was... idyllic. I was eighteen, living like a queen in an enormous house with servants at my beck and call, a car on standby, all the designer clothes and jewelry I wanted. We vacationed on yachts and stayed in fancy hotels, and I thought I was the luckiest girl in the world. Not once did it occur to me to question how Mateo earned his money. I just enjoyed the spoils of other people's misery."

Emotions rippled across her face, and she tucked her chin into her chest. I ached to comfort her, but I refrained. There'd be plenty of time for me to soothe her pain and ease her guilt. Eighteen. Fuck, when I thought back to the kinds of things my brothers and I had gotten up to at that age, how we'd looked at life through a perfect lens, I wasn't in the least bit surprised that a far more mature Fernandez had duped the Ella she'd been back then.

"Just over six months before I left, there was a raid on the compound. Mateo had moved in on a rival gang's territory, and a lot of men were killed. Their plan was to kidnap me and Chloe until Mateo surrendered and returned what they saw as rightfully theirs." She closed her eyes, possibly reliving the terror of that moment. "Mateo returned just in time. He tried to brush it off as a business deal gone wrong, but by then, I was older and wiser. I began to poke around a little, ask questions, and it didn't take me long to work out how he made his millions."

"Drugs."

She nodded. "Drugs, and all the shit that goes along with being in that business. Right then I vowed to leave. Chloe wouldn't be safe as long as he dealt drugs, and she was my only concern, the only thing I cared about. It wasn't easy. I didn't have money of my own, and Mateo kept us so well guarded—for our protection, he said. But it was more than that. He thought of me and Chloe as possessions. It took me those six months to claw together enough funds to make a run for it. At first, I went to New Mexico, and Mateo almost caught us, so I ran again. And that's how I ended up in Los Angeles." She hitched a shoulder. "That's it. The whole sordid affair."

I pulled her to me then, comforting her in the only way I knew, with my hands and my lips and my words of love and adoration for everything she'd endured. In the end, it had brought her to me, but I wished we could have met without her having to suffer along the way.

"Are you going to reach out to your parents now that you're free of him?"

She ran her teeth over her bottom lip. "I've been thinking about it more and more over the last few weeks, but I don't know where to start. I'm scared they'll reject me."

"They're your parents. They love you unconditionally, whether or not they agree with your choices."

"Yeah." She sighed. "It's just so hard to make that first move. I don't even know their contact details." She sighed again. "I'm so desperate to see them again and have them meet Chloe, but my fear of rejection is holding me back."

An idea unfurled in my mind. It came with risks, and I wasn't sure whether I'd fuck things up rather than fix them, but I had to try.

"Oh God," she suddenly expelled, struggling to sit up from where I'd pressed her into the couch. "The award.

Fuck." She checked her watch. "It was three days ago. What happened?"

I gave her a crooked smile. "We won."

She squealed, leaping on me and covering me in kisses. Then she sat up, all the joy draining from her face. "You didn't go to the ceremony."

I angled my head to the side. "Taking care of you and Chloe was far more important than picking up some award. I sent Ryker and Stan instead."

Her jaw slackened. "Oh, Johannes. You've worked for that for so long. It was what you wanted. You should have been there to soak up all the glory."

I shook my head. "No. I thought I wanted it, but what I want more than any award or recognition or success is... you."

Her pupils flared, then dilated. "You have me, now and forever... on one condition."

Narrowing my eyes, I jutted up my chin. "Go on."

A smile danced on her lips. "Take me to bed and make me yours."

"You were mine a long time ago, Ella." I angled my head. "Or would you prefer 'Eloise'?"

She shook her head. "I'll always be your Ella."

Yeah. You will.

Chapter 33

Ella

There are surprises—and then there are SURPRISES.

Two Weeks Later...

The house felt so quiet without Johannes, but I guessed he couldn't stay away from work forever. He'd told me—no, ordered me—to take at least another week off, but I was antsy and more than ready to get back to the job I loved.

I'd broach the subject again tonight. Rattling around in this house with nothing to do reminded me of my life with Mateo when I'd been little more than a trophy wife.

Even the thought of it made me shudder.

The DEA agent, Brax, had called yesterday to let me

know that they'd filed multiple charges against Mateo and a fair number of his associates. Mateo's ego and arrogance had ultimately been his downfall, and I wasn't the least bit sorry.

I hoped he rotted in jail.

The sooner I could divorce him, the better. He'd fight me. It was in his nature to win, but however long it took, I'd keep going until I was truly free of him.

Chloe had returned to school yesterday—with a covert security team in attendance. She was unaware of her every move being watched, which was the only reason I'd agreed to such a heavy security presence.

Johannes had insisted that the school allow one of the guards to be located inside the building, and once he'd explained everything to the principal, she'd reluctantly agreed. It wouldn't be forever. But it would be for a while.

I peered through the living room window at the black sedan across the street that housed my own personal security. I'd refused to have them in the house, despite Johannes's disapproval. He'd given in... under duress. He did it because he loved me.

Who'd argue against that?

As much as I coveted independence after losing it to Mateo, I secretly loved the way Johannes had stepped in to take care of me and Chloe. It gave me the shivers, in a good way. As advanced as women had become, there must still be some part of us that adored a cloak of protection around our shoulders. And I wasn't ashamed to admit that.

I wandered into the kitchen and began to prep for tonight's dinner. Johannes had floated the idea of moving us to one of those gated communities, or a penthouse in a high-rise building crammed with security, but I'd declined. I'd had a gut full of that with Mateo. It would feel like a prison, and I refused to live in one of my own making because of Mateo.

Once the trial was out of the way, I hoped that we could live a more normal life without a security detail tracking us everywhere we went. And besides, Johannes had his own reasons for living where he did. I hated the idea that he'd be forced to change that just for me.

I put the chopped vegetables and spiced minced beef in the fridge and traipsed back into the living room. I flicked the TV on. Channel-surfed. Turned it off.

God, I'm so bored.

I grabbed my phone and sent Johannes a message.

Me: I'm going out before I lose my mind. Window shopping is better than being stuck here with nothing to do. Hint hint.

Three dots appeared.

Johannes: Well, you can, but then you'd miss the surprise I have for you.

Me: Surprise?

Johannes: Yeah, I'm on my way home.

I checked the time, frowning. Two thirty in the afternoon. Johannes always made time to come home for dinner, then he'd return to the club to oversee the opening, though the days of him spending sixteen hours at Level Nine or one of his other clubs were in the past. He'd promoted Stan to assistant manager reporting directly to Johannes, and handed over a lot of the day-to-day responsibilities, which left more time for us.

I wasn't complaining.

But two thirty was early, even by his standards.

Me: What are you up to?

Johannes: You'll see.

Excitement unfurled in my belly, and I paced as I waited for the sound of his car coming up the road. Twenty minutes later, I heard it, and I dashed to the front door to greet him.

He exited the driver's side, all long limbs and lithe, athletic body. Lust wound its way through my veins. I didn't have to pick Chloe up from school for another hour. Maybe we could—

My thoughts broke off when the passenger and rear doors opened and two other people got out.

I sucked in a breath, sputtering and struggling to find the right words.

My feet rooted to the spot, even as I yearned to run toward them.

It didn't matter. They ran to me.

Comforting arms surrounded me, lips kissed me, hands stroked my hair. Words were spoken, soft yet urgent, comforting, forgiving, happy words that unlocked a torrent of tears. I cried and cried as my parents squeezed me tighter, holding on as if they were afraid I'd disappear at any moment.

"Oh, Eloise, my baby," Mom sobbed in my hair. "We've missed you so much. So much."

I still couldn't find the words to tell them how much I'd missed them, too, how much I loved them. I searched for Johannes. He hadn't moved from his spot beside the car. His eyes held a hint of trepidation and worry, and the need to reassure him had me untangling myself from my parents' embrace.

"Give me a minute, Mom."

I rushed over to him and wrapped my arms around his neck. "I love you," I murmured, standing on tiptoes to kiss him. "I can't believe you did this, but I'll never forget it."

"You're not mad?" he whispered low enough so my parents couldn't overhear. "I worried I'd overstepped."

"I could never be mad at you for loving me so much that when I hurt, you hurt. It would have taken me so long to pluck up the courage to reach out, which would have meant more wasted time."

He pecked my lips. "Then go. Be with your parents. Reconnect. There's a lot to discuss."

"Chloe..."

"I'll pick her up from school, feed her, and take her to the park. When you're ready for me to bring her home, message me."

My heart bloomed with love for this man. I might have messed up on my first choice of life partner, but all that suffering had resulted in a reward far bigger than I deserved.

I had a beautiful daughter and this man right here. I was the luckiest woman in the world.

I led my parents into the house as Johannes climbed into the car and reversed onto the street. By the time I shut the door, all I saw were his taillights.

"Well," I said to Mom and Dad. "I guess we have a lot of catching up to do."

K

My parents and I talked for four hours. There was a lot of crying, of recriminations and regrets on both sides, but by the end, we laid several ghosts to rest and I had my Mom and Dad back.

For years, I'd blamed myself for their divorce, but when I plucked up the courage to tell them that, both of them vigorously shook their heads. Dad explained that they hadn't been happy together for a while, but they'd agreed to stay together until I turned eighteen before going their separate ways—as friends.

I could tell they were friends, too. They laughed and teased each other, and there was the odd affectionate touch, the kind that two people who knew each other well made. Their lives were full and happy, their estrangement from me the only blot on the landscape.

And thanks to Johannes, that painful sore had healed.

I messaged him letting him know it was okay to bring Chloe home. Introducing her to my parents, her grandparents, was a moment I'd never, ever forget. I took a mental picture, capturing every second, pushing aside pointless regrets of all the time they'd missed. We had our entire future ahead of us, filled with new memories and family time.

Mom helped me bathe and put Chloe to bed, and then she and Dad gathered their things to head off to the hotel Johannes had booked when he'd arranged to fly them over to reunite with me. He'd invited them to stay with us, but they'd declined, insisting that we should have our own space.

"You okay?"

Johannes slipped his hand inside mine and squeezed as the car ferrying my parents to their hotel disappeared down the street.

"More than okay." I reached up on tiptoes and kissed his cheek. "How long did you keep that a secret?"

"About a week. There were a few logistical issues to work through, and while your dad could have gotten here immediately, he refused to come without your mom, although it killed him knowing you were here with me and he'd have to wait to see you."

My heart squeezed. "They're still great friends."

"That's rare, but precious." He flicked my hair over my shoulder. "Like you."

I curved my hands around his neck, my thumb brushing his scar. After our heart-to-heart, he'd ditched the sweaters as well as the color black, and I couldn't be prouder of him. I pulled him to me, stealing a kiss.

"You hungry?" he asked.

I shook my head. "I prepped dinner, but that can wait until after."

He arched a brow. "After what?"

I grabbed his hand and took off up the stairs, giggling as we piled into our bedroom and fell on the bed. He hushed me, placing a hand over my mouth.

"You'll wake Chloe."

"Nah, she sleeps like the dead, and after all that excitement tonight, she'll probably go right through the night. Which means..." I rolled over until he was beneath me, and my thighs trapped his. "I can torture you for hours."

He grinned up at me, his smile a sight I'd never tire of. "I thought you'd be tired after all the excitement, too."

"Never too tired for you."

I bent over to kiss him, but instead of being on top, I found myself beneath him, my arms pinned beside my head. He kissed me, unhurried, his tongue toying with mine. Every time I tried to speed things up, he stopped, then started again. In the end, I gave up trying to take control. I closed my eyes and lost myself to the way he made me feel. My skin tingled, and an ache grew low in my belly, my clit dying for attention.

He removed my clothes, and his. I stared up at him, recalling those first times we'd slept together, where he'd insisted on keeping his clothes on. He'd come so far, and as egotistical as it might sound, I liked to think I'd had something to do with his recovery.

"You're stunning, you know that?"

He blinked at me as if surprised by the compliment. He touched his scar. "Even with this?"

I sat up so we were nose to nose and kissed every inch of the blemish that had imprisoned him for so many years.

"Because of this. You're strong and beautiful and kind."

"And broody, and dour, and sarcastic."

I laughed. "A complex man."

"Stop distracting me."

He lay me down and devoured me with his lips and his hands and his oh-so-talented tongue. By the time that tongue reached my pussy, I already teetered on the edge of an explosive climax. One flick and I fell into an abyss, my body taking over, heat spreading out from my core in waves and pulses that seemed never-ending.

I opened my eyes as Johannes loomed over me, his cock nudging my entrance. He pushed inside, slowly, an inch at a time, both of us groaning in pleasure. I stared down at where we were joined, and a swell of emotion came over me. I didn't know what made me say it. Maybe it was reconnecting with my parents again, or seeing how close Chloe and Johannes had grown, or possibly thinking I'd lost the man I loved only to find out he was very much alive.

"I want another baby. With you."

He stared at me for a moment, then shook his head and closed his eyes.

Oh, hell.

Talk about killing the mood. Maybe he didn't want kids. Or didn't want them yet.

Christ, I'm an idiot.

Swept up on a tide of joy, I'd chosen the worst possible time for a discussion such as this one. We should plan for kids in the cold light of day, not when his dick throbbed and wept with pre-cum, and I was all in post-orgasmic bliss.

"There's no rush. We don't have to if you don't—"

"The idea of putting a baby in you..."

His mouth captured mine in a ferocious, claiming kiss, and before I could take a breath, he thrust hard, expelling all the air from my lungs. I gasped and gripped his shoulders, hanging on as he took me with an urgency I hadn't felt from him before. His eyes were almost feral, stolen by lust. His hands rubbed and stroked and squeezed my breasts, my waist, my hips, and still he kept up a punishing rhythm, drawing me closer to another cataclysmic orgasm.

"Fuck," he panted. "Tell me you're close." He reached between us, strumming my clit. "Fuck, Ella. Come."

"I'm... I'm... ohhhh."

Every nerve ending lit up, setting my blood on fire. I was barely conscious of Johannes's drawn-out groan as he emptied himself inside me. He collapsed on top of me, his skin coated in a thin layer of sweat. I ran my hands through his hair, sweeping it off his forehead.

"I love you," I whispered.

Still connected, he rolled over, taking me with him. My hair hung like drapes, grazing his taut chest. He gathered it in his hands and arranged it over one shoulder.

"Not as much as I love you."

"Impossible."

He brushed his lips over mine. "Was I too rough? I didn't hurt you, did I?"

"God, no. That was... magical."

He chuckled. "I'll take that as a win."

"I'm sorry."

His smile turned into a frown. "For what?"

"For saying what I did when I did. It was wrong of me. We've never even talked about having kids, and for me to bring it up right when you... when we... well, you know what

I mean."

He gave me this look, a sort of frown coupled with confusion, then eased me to the side. My heart disconnected, floating inside my chest, adrift, as I would be without Johannes. And then he shuffled down the bed and kissed my stomach.

"Putting a baby in you will make me the happiest man in the world, and I'm already fucking ecstatic."

Relief rushed through me, my heart reattaching, beating strong and true. "Really?"

"God, Ella, yes. Did you think otherwise?"

"But we haven't talked about it. We haven't even been together that long. And a baby is... well, a lot. I honestly don't know what came over me."

He replaced his lips with his hand, his large palm almost covering my entire midriff.

"Time is meaningless. I love you. You love me. There are people who live together their whole lives and never achieve the kind of connection we have. A child would be a natural extension of our love."

He moved up the bed to lie beside me once more, threading our hands together.

"Before Sadie, before the attack, I dreamed of having a family one day, and for a brief moment in time, I'd thought she might be the one."

He laughed, a bitter sound that I didn't like. I kissed his shoulder in solidarity. If I ever got my hands on that bitch, I'd throttle her until her eyes popped out of her head.

Not that I ever would find her. If the police hadn't, then what chance would I have?

"Then when it happened, and I withdrew pretty much

from the world, I gave up on those dreams, throwing myself into the nightclub business instead. And now you..." He slipped his arms around me and pulled me even closer. "You've given me back those dreams. So yes, I do want kids. Lots of them. And I want them with you."

My chest prickled, happiness spreading through me. "I want that, too," I whispered. "I always wanted a brother or a sister for Chloe. I grew up an only child, and I never wanted that for her."

"I love her like my own. You know that, right? No matter how many kids come after her, she'll always be our first."

He looked so earnest, so worried, and my love for him tripled. "I know."

An idea I'd toyed with and then discarded roared back to the surface.

"I don't know if this will ever be possible, but I was thinking we could look into adoption. I mean, Mateo probably won't ever agree, but it's worth a shot, right? You're more of a father to her than he ever was."

"Oh, Ella." His eyes shone, and he brought my fingers to his lips, kissing the tips of each one. "I would be honored to adopt Chloe, but even if it can't happen, a missing piece of paper won't make a difference to me. Parents are the ones who raise children, not create them."

God. This man. My heart almost burst.

"I'm so glad I ran to LA and found myself at Level Nine. So blessed that you took a chance on me when you knew I was hiding something."

"If I look back now, something inside me changed that day. I wasn't aware of it, but my subconscious reached out and gave you that job when the businessman in me knew I should have sent you packing. It was as if an ancient instinct recognized you as my savior, my healer. My future."

"It was the luckiest day of my life."

"The luckiest day of both our lives."

Chapter 34

Ella

Time to give vengeance her head.

One Year Later…

I'd never been in a courtroom before, so I wasn't sure what to expect. It smelled… old somehow, a little musty, although the walls looked freshly painted and there wasn't a speck of dust anywhere in sight.

Keeping my eyes forward, I made my way to the witness stand, conscious of Mateo's dark stare burning a hole in the back of my head. My knees knocked, but I kept my spine erect and my shoulders back. Aaron, the district attorney in charge of this case, had briefed me well, although he'd warned me that the defense counsel would rip me apart trying to discredit me. I was prepared for that. I knew the truth, and Johannes believed in me. That was all I cared about.

I made my oath and swept my hands underneath my dress before taking a seat. I was the last witness in a three-week-long trial, the trump card whose evidence was supposed to put the final nail in Mateo's coffin. The pressure weighed heavily on me, but I was up to the task. I had to be. For my sake and for Chloe's.

I searched for Johannes, finding him sitting beside my parents and my mom's husband, and right behind the prosecuting counsel's desk. The sight of him, dressed in a navy blue suit and a pale blue shirt open at the neck calmed my racing heart. No more black sweaters and matching pants. He'd come a long way. We both had.

"I love you," he mouthed.

I dipped my chin in acknowledgment and wiped damp hands over my thighs. The assistant district attorney, a young, bright woman named Annette, approached me with a reassuring smile.

And so we began.

Two hours later, I stepped down from the witness stand, battered and bruised from some of the brutal questioning, but with my pride intact. I'd told the truth, and now it was up to the jury to decide what happened next. I couldn't do any more to influence the outcome. Somehow, I'd managed to avoid looking at Mateo once throughout the whole ordeal, but as I passed between the opposing tables, I caught his eye.

Hatred poured from his.

Victory flowed from mine.

Whether the jury found him innocent or guilty, I'd won.

We'd always have to be more careful than the ordinary man or woman on the street, but life came with all kinds of risks. All we could do was mitigate them to the best of our ability and live a full and happy life.

Johannes stood as I approached, and he caught my hand, leading me from the courtroom with my parents and stepfather following. I didn't look back, didn't need to. That part of my life was finally over.

"I'm so fucking proud of you," Johannes murmured as the door clanged shut behind us. I didn't get a chance to answer. Chloe tore from Ginny's hand and raced over to me. I'd struggled with what to tell her about today, but I also hadn't wanted to lie to her. She deserved to know the truth, however ugly it might be. I'd kept the details scant, and she'd listened carefully, then defiantly announced that Johannes was her dad, and he wasn't a bad man like that other one.

I swear my heart had almost stopped, my chest bursting with pride at my grown-up little girl.

So far, Mateo had refused to give up his parental rights, although the divorce was progressing. Maybe if he was sentenced to a long stretch inside, he might change his mind and allow Johannes to adopt Chloe. It didn't matter either way. We were a tight-knit family of three.

Soon to be four.

The baby kicked, almost as if it had heard me. I put an arm around Chloe and ran a hand over my extended belly. Three more months before we met this little one. I'd stopped taking my birth control pills the night Johannes and I had talked about having kids, but it had taken us another few months to fall pregnant. We'd had a lot of fun trying.

"Darling, are you okay?"

Mom's face pinched. It couldn't have been easy for her to hear about the attempted kidnapping of me and Chloe, or how I'd scrimped to scrape together enough funds to make a run for it, or how terrified I'd been when Mateo had caught up to me in Vegas and dragged me back to the compound. Those few days when he'd refused to let me see my daughter while allowing me to believe he'd had Johannes murdered had been among the worst of my life.

The only piece of information I'd kept to myself was how I'd gotten the fake I.D.'s that had allowed me to stay hidden for so long. I'd promised Diego when he offered to help me that I'd never rat him out. And I'd kept that promise.

"I am now." I released Chloe into Johannes's arms to hug my mom and her husband, Pascal, and then Dad, and Ginny, too.

"Are you coming back to the house?" Johannes asked.

He'd rented us a place just outside Oklahoma City for the duration of the trial, rather than stay in a hotel. Better for Chloe, and for us. Ginny was staying with us, too. She'd been such a godsend. A true friend. No, more than a friend. Family. She'd always have a special place in our lives. Without her taking me in, who knew where I'd have ended up? I shuddered at the thought.

Mom shook her head. "We'll come by tomorrow after Eloise has gotten some rest." Mom stroked my cheek. "You look a little pale."

"It's been a day." I gnawed on my bottom lip. "I hope the jury doesn't take too long to reach a verdict."

"Call us as soon as you hear." Dad hugged me again. "We'll be waiting for your call."

"I will."

We kept the atmosphere light for Chloe's sake, but as each hour passed, I grew more anxious. The longer they took, the more likely they'd return a "not guilty" verdict. That was always the way on those TV shows, so it had to have some basis in reality. I kept picking up my phone in case I hadn't heard it ring. Aaron had warned me not to expect a verdict today, but I'd hoped.

At six, Aaron called to dash those hopes. Apparently, the judge had sent the jury back to the hotel for the evening, so we wouldn't hear anything before tomorrow at the earliest.

Johannes bathed and put Chloe to bed while I channel-surfed without paying attention to a single thing, Ginny's quiet presence beside me a balm to the fear inside me. I lasted until nine o'clock when, eager for the day to be over and a new one to begin, I went to bed. Wrapped in Johannes's arms, I fell into a fitful sleep filled with nightmares of Mateo escaping justice and dragging me back to the compound.

The next morning, under Johannes's watchful eye, I forced down a bowl of oatmeal and a piece of fruit, but my stomach churned and rolled, the knot of anxiety pulling tighter and tighter. The baby kicked incessantly, no doubt picking up on my restlessness.

As a distraction, we took Chloe to the boathouse district. We walked along the river holding hands and eating ice cream and sugared donuts. We talked about the baby and made plans for the three of us to fly to Seattle to visit Johannes's parents the following month, before I got too big to travel. We did everything apart from talking about the only thing on both our minds.

Not that it mattered. Avoiding talking about it didn't change the fact that we were both drowning in nerves.

After lunch, we headed back to the car, and as we reached the parking lot, my phone rang. For a second, I froze, my eyes wide and locked on Johannes. I dove into my purse.

"It's Aaron." My voice shook.

"Well, answer it." Johannes's voice was steady, although subdued.

I pressed the green button. "Hello."

"Are you sitting down?"

My thighs trembled, and I reached for Johannes, clinging to his arm. "No."

"Then find somewhere to sit down."

This is bad news. I know it.

I caught Ginny's eye. She nodded and led Chloe a few feet away to give me some privacy. The last thing I wanted was to break down in front of my daughter and scare her.

I opened the passenger door to our rental and almost fell into the seat. "I'm sitting." Johannes crouched in front of me, his hands resting on my knees. He squeezed. I covered one of his with my free hand.

"Minimum of forty years before he'll be considered for parole."

"Oh God." I felt faint, hot, flushed. I tightened my grip on Johannes until my knuckles whitened. "Forty years," I whispered.

"Yeah," Aaron replied. "Thought you'd want to know right away. I'll call you later in the week."

He hung up, and I collapsed into Johannes's arms, tears spilling down my cheeks.

"It's over," I sobbed. "It's really over."

"It is. My brave, sweet, wonderful woman. I fucking love you."

He kissed me, his thumbs wiping away my tears as he'd wipe away all my tears, now and in the future. We'd both survived a terrible trauma, stumbling through the dark until our souls were ready to meet.

Nothing and no one would ever tear us apart.

A Begrudging Thank You from Johannes

I'm not one for sharing my inner thoughts, as I'm sure you can tell after reading my story, but when you're ganged up on by two strong women (namely Ella and Tracie) and ordered to write a thank you note, what's a man to do?

So, thank you for reading. I hope that you understand me a little better and have reformed your opinion of me as a douche. I mean, I was, at times, but I had my reasons. After what happened to me all those years ago, I believed I was damaged goods, unworthy of love, and trust was a major obstacle for me to overcome.

With Ella's support and love, I'm getting there.

Still not keen on the therapist idea though (shhh, don't tell her).

My story might have concluded, but there's still plenty more to come from the Kingcaid's so stick around.

Next up is *Mesmerized By You* where my cousin Nolen has his work cut out convincing his soul mate that he's worthy of her. Right now, she kinda thinks he's no better than the dirt on the bottom of her shoe. But if I know Nolen, he won't give up on the woman he loves. Sooner or later, he'll wear her down. I hope. He's a good guy who deserves happiness. But man, he's got a mountain to climb with Marlowe Beck.

If you can't wait for *Mesmerized By You* to release, then have you read the ROGUES series yet? You've already met Ryker Stone when Ella and I went to a business dinner with him. If you want to find out more about Ryker, then pick up your copy of *Entranced* today.

Or, if you'd like a free prequel to the ROGUES series, all you have to do is join Tracie's newsletter and your copy of Entwined will magically arrive on your device of choice. Go to her website at www.author traciedelaney.com and click on "Claim My Free Book" on the home page.

He promised to love me forever. He lied.

I met my soulmate when I was eight, and he was six.
On my twelfth birthday, he proposed.
At a party to celebrate my sweet sixteen,
he gave me a ring made of daisies.
When I left for college, aged eighteen, he cried.
And at twenty-four, he broke my heart,
shattering it into a million pieces.

But that isn't the end of our story.

A decade later, we're forced back together,
and once again, he holds my future in his hands.
Except this time, I'm older and wiser.
He pretends he's innocent, but I know the truth.
This time, I'm in control. He no longer mesmerizes me.
And Mr. Bigshot Billionaire is about to learn
that he can't have what he wants.
Me.

Acknowledgments

Writing a book is so much more than me sitting at my desk and bashing away on a keyboard. Each one of the people below play a crucial role in getting a book to market, and I am hugely grateful to them all.

To my amazing hubs who sends me texts when he knows I'm mid-flow so he doesn't interrupt my thought process. He's a diamond, and I'm so lucky that he chooses to put up with me!

To my amazing, kind, funny, and generous PA, Loulou. The graphics queen! Thank you for putting up with me and my "Didn't I tell you that already?" answering with a very patient, "No. But it's okay." I love you to the moon and back.

Incy, my critique partner. I still thank my lucky stars that we met. You never hold back, and I am enormously grateful for that. Mwah!

Lasairiona, my ass crack of dawn sprint partner and all round awesome chick. Thank you for your special brand of encouragement at six each morning (aka, get your ass in the chair and write, Delaney, or imma beat you!) We make one hell of a team. Also, Johannes said if you call him Jo-Jo or JBoy one more time, he's going to lose his shit. So please do. Let's grab some popcorn and watch the fireworks!

Bethany - thank you so much for your brilliant editing and wonderful suggestions. Also thank you for picking up all my past perfect tense issues. Gah, I hate them!

Jean - you are in my thoughts constantly. One day soon, I'm going to squish you!

Katie - Your man is here! Thank you for believing in him and encouraging me when I wavered (which was a LOT on this book). Look after him for me. He acts tough, but he has a soft center.

Jacqueline - FOUR CONTINUITY ERRORS! Are you kidding me? Gah! Okay, so there was only one typo but still. FOUR CONTINUITY ERRORS. I blame Johannes LOL. I was too busy trying to corral him where I needed him to go.

To my ARC readers. You guys are amazing! You're my final eyes and ears before my baby is released into the world and I appreciate each and every one of you for giving up your time to read.

And last but most certainly not least, to you, the readers. Thank you for being on this journey with me and taking a chance on a new series. I'm damned lucky to do this for a job, but without you, I wouldn't be able to. I hope you carry on and devour the rest of the Kingcaid series. There is plenty more to come.

If you have any time to spare, I'd be ever so grateful if you'd leave a short review on Amazon, Goodreads, or Bookbub. Reviews not only help readers discover new books, but they also help authors reach new readers. You'd be doing a massive favor for this wonderful bookish community we're all a part of.

Books by Tracie Delaney

BILLIONAIRE ROMANCE

The ROGUES Series

The Irresistibly Mine Series

The Kincaid Billionaire Series

PROTECTOR/MILITARY ROMANCE

The Intrepid Bodyguard Series

SPORTS ROMANCE

The Winning Ace Series

The Full Velocity Series

CONTEMPORARY ROMANCE

The Brook Brothers Series

BOXSETS

Winning Ace

Brook Brothers

Full Velocity

ROGUES Books 1-3

SPINOFFS/STANDALONES

Mismatch (A Winning Ace Spin Off Novel)

Break Point (A Winning Ace Novella)

Control (A Driven World/Full Velocity Novel)

My Gift To You

About the Author

Tracie Delaney is a Kindle Unlimited All Star author of more than twenty-five contemporary romance novels which she writes from her office in the freezing cold North West of England. The office used to be a garage, but she needed somewhere quiet to write and so she stole it from her poor, long-suffering husband who is still in mourning that he's been driven out to the shed!

An avid reader for as long as she can remember, Tracie was also a bit of a tomboy back in the day and used to climb trees with her trusty Enid Blyton's and read for hours, returning home when it was almost dark with a numb bottom and more than a few splinters!

Tracie's books have a common theme of women who show that true strength comes in all forms, and alpha males who put up a great fight (which they ultimately lose!)

At night she likes to curl up on the sofa with her two Westies, Murphy & Cooper, and binge-watch shows on Netflix. There may be wine involved.

Visit her website for contact information and more www.authortraciedelaney.com

Printed in Great Britain
by Amazon

38231419R00219